Martini Mondays

Palm Springs Poolside Book 1

J. L. Brannick

SMART MOUTH
PUBLISHING LLC

To Liz, who is everyone's best friend and free therapist. Thank you for forging our way into this writing journey, even if you won't let me read the good parts.

And to the drag queens in Palm Springs–you make Sunday brunch and bingo night so much better!

Chapter 1

"Fucking breast cancer," I whispered for maybe the thousandth time as I reread the text.

Ramone: Laurel, she's fading. I don't think she's going to make it thru the weekend. Can you come?

I quickly texted back.

Me: Yes, of course. Be there tonight.

Setting my phone down, I stared blindly out the small classroom window of the law school as the professor continued to lecture in his raspy, monotone voice. The news wasn't unexpected, but it still felt like a quick hard punch to my solar plexus.

After my first year in law school, I'd transferred schools and moved across the country to be closer to my Aunt Fern when she'd finally told me about her diagnosis. Metastatic breast cancer. I would have done anything for her, but I couldn't wish or pray her cancer away.

I hadn't known until after Fern's diagnosis there was such a thing as anticipatory grief. My mother died suddenly when I was eleven, and that intense, cutting pain had been clean and sharp. But with Fern's impending death, the pain of losing her seemed slow and insidious.

Grieving wasn't a linear journey I'd learned, and everyone seems to process it differently. I'd lost my mother, my uncle, and soon I would lose my beloved aunt. I was tired of losing and grieving.

I pulled my thoughts back to the present and started mentally compiling a to-do list for my trip to Palm Springs. Fern had moved there full-time after she received her diagnosis.

I rubbed my eyes absently, smearing my mascara, as I listened to my business associations professor drone on while he slowly paced around the classroom.

I'd started packing makeup wipes, along with a few other law student essentials, like ibuprofen, protein bars, and energy drinks in my bag. A friend sometimes carried a flask in his backpack. I didn't judge since I've had days when I would've considered it an essential too.

My phone vibrated, and I quickly checked the screen again.

"Ms. Payne. Please tell us what the Equitable Subordination doctrine entails from the reading assignment," Professor Blakely intoned at me, cutting into my thoughts.

The older professor had a preternatural way of knowing which students were unprepared or distracted. In my first year of law school, whenever I got called on, I'd been terrified. But the last three years of dealing with the ruthless, unremitting stress of law school had strengthened my tolerance level.

I looked at Blakely and straightened up. "The Equitable Subordination doctrine, also known as the Deep Rock doctrine, is from the landmark Supreme Court case *Taylor v. Standard Gas.*

The Supreme Court found, in part, that controlling shareholder claims would be subordinated to those of other creditors."

Blakely gave me a tiny nod. A head nod from him was the equivalent of getting a "well done" or "great job" from another professor. Getting an eye twitch from him was like getting slapped in the face.

"That's right, Ms. Payne. The Deep Rock doctrine has been interesting to see utilized in subsequent rulings . . ." Blakely walked past my desk as he continued lecturing.

After he passed, I checked my phone and continued going through my mental to-do list for my trip. This was my last class of the week. Thank you, God.

When class finally ended, I walked up to the podium and waited to speak with Blakely behind another student. When the student walked off, he turned his rheumy eyes to me. "Yes, Ms. Payne?"

"A family member of mine is ill, and I'll probably miss both classes next week. But I'll ask a classmate to record your lectures if you'll approve it."

Blakely's face softened a bit. "Ah, that's why you were checking your phone in class. Yes, that's no problem. Good luck to you."

I nodded thanks and walked out, unable to reply with the knot in my throat.

Early that evening, I watched the light filter through the Joshua trees as I drove through the Mojave Preserve toward Palm Springs. Wispy clouds hung low in the sky, painted orange and purple by the setting sun. I didn't stop this time to take photographs or listen to the desert, but just let my mind drift.

Fern was dying. She and my mother had been sisters and best friends, and Fern was my last connection to her. She was also a second mother to me.

The cancer had advanced, and the treatments seemed worse than the disease. I'd stayed with her as much as I could over my winter break. She was fading before my eyes, and there was nothing I could do to stop it.

A few hours later, I arrived at her house in Palm Springs. I pulled over to the left side of the driveway out of habit, so I wouldn't block her car parked in the garage.

I looked up at the vibrant yellow garage door in front of me, with the sunburst inlay that matched the front doors of the house. Fern wouldn't be taking her car out anymore, I suddenly realized. I sucked in a breath to steady myself.

She'd never drive her beautiful 1962 fully restored Neptune Blue Cadillac convertible again. I didn't know a lot about cars, but I thought Fern's convertible was a work of art.

Jackson, her late husband, gave her that car for their twenty-fifth wedding anniversary. It complemented Fern and her mid-century modern home in Palm Springs perfectly. I could picture Fern behind the wheel, with her beautiful gray-blond hair, her large dark brown sunglasses, and her signature blush-pink lipstick.

I remembered the first time I stayed with Fern after my mother died. Over that winter break, I flew alone from New York to Palm Springs to spend the holidays there.

Fern and Jackson picked me up from the airport in that convertible, with the top down and the heater blasting. Then we drove through Palm Springs together, enjoying the cool desert air.

Her low-slung, 1950s home glowed in the soft twilight. Tall palm trees and squat barrel cacti contrasted with the blooming bougainvillea that ran along the front yard. The cobalt blue sky almost hurt my eyes, and I could smell jasmine scenting the air.

The home hadn't always been Fern's primary residence, but when she was diagnosed with metastatic breast cancer, she decided to spend her last years here. Her best friend and his husband lived two doors down, and Fern also had other good friends in Palm Springs and Palm Desert nearby.

Fern liked to tell me the story of how she and Jackson met. "He lived in New York City at the time and had never been married before. But Jackson told me the first time he saw me, sitting behind my desk in my bright pink pillbox suit and jaunty neck scarf, he knew I was the one for him."

She'd smiled wistfully at me. "Jackson also gave me and Elise, your mother, a safe home and unconditional love for the first time in our lives. So how could I not fall in love with that suave older businessman?"

This would be the last time I'd come here to find Fern waiting for me. The light started to fade when I finally got out of my car and grabbed my bags from the back seat.

Chapter 2

The front door opened, and Ramone and Jonathan stepped out onto the front porch. They must have been watching for me. Jonathan took my bags, then hugged me, and Ramone took my hands in his.

"I'm so glad you're here, darling. Fern will be happy to see you." His eyes looked red and bloodshot.

Ramone had a slim build and thick salt and pepper hair, and he always hugged me or kissed my cheek whenever I saw him.

He loved Fern like a sister and treated me like his beloved niece. His mother immigrated from Argentina, and Ramone inherited her gregarious temperament, elegant style, and beautiful complexion.

Jonathan stood taller than Ramone. He was balding and a little heavier set, and had piercing blue eyes. He wasn't as effusive, but more pragmatic. If I wanted the unvarnished truth or an objective opinion, I went to Jonathan.

They'd purchased the butterfly-style, 1950s home a few doors down over twenty years ago when they'd moved from Los Angeles and opened a law firm together in Palm Springs. Besides Fern, they were what I loved most about visiting Palm Springs.

I adored them and soaked up their acceptance like a dry sponge. I couldn't remember a time when they hadn't been around.

"She's on pain meds, and she may be groggy," Ramone warned as we walked inside.

Jonathan nodded. "It's been a rough few days."

I took a deep breath in and out and tried not to let my emotions overwhelm me. "Is she in her room?"

Ramone shook his head. "She said she didn't want to be shut up in the house. She's on the back patio."

I headed toward the long wall of sliding windows that opened up to her private backyard area. The soft outdoor lighting on the cactus and desert plants gave off a low, muted glow. The warm evening air soothed me a little, and I could faintly smell Fern's perfume on the breeze.

She lay on a recliner, a blanket tucked around her. She looked small and frail, and an IV drip bag hung next to her, hooked up to her arm.

"How're you doing tonight?" I leaned over and kissed her cheek, then took her other hand and squeezed it.

"Oh, hello dear. I'm glad to see you. I'm sorry, though. I didn't want you to have to drive all the way here right before finals." Fern looked up at me with her milky, pain-filled eyes and gave my hand a weak squeeze back.

"Don't worry about me. It's my last semester, and I only have two finals. I've got it."

Fern sighed. "I so wanted to watch you graduate. I've been saving a wonderful dress I picked up in Italy a couple of years ago for the occasion."

"The black sheath dress? Or the blue Dior?" I asked, settling down in the recliner next to her.

Besides real estate, fashion and accessories were some of Fern's favorite topics. She'd shown me a few of the beautiful pieces she bought in Italy the last time she visited.

"The black dress would have been too hot for Las Vegas in late May." She smiled weakly.

"Then the blue one."

"Yes. I also had hopes of going out for a night on the town with the boys when I bought it," Fern said wistfully. She sometimes referred to Jonathan and Ramone as "the boys."

Sitting back, I smiled. "That would have been the perfect way to show it off."

"There's never enough time, is there?" Fern lamented.

"I hope you don't have any regrets. You lived more in a decade than most people do in a lifetime."

"I have, haven't I?" She smiled, then started coughing.

I stood up and grabbed the hospital-grade water bottle with the large straw on the side table next to her.

"Here you go. Take a drink." I placed the straw under Fern's mouth.

She leaned over and took a few small sips. Her coughing subsided, and she laid back on the recliner.

After a moment, she started talking again. "Laurel, one of my regrets is not discussing my affairs with you. Jonathan and Ramone know the particulars, but they've been pressing me to talk to you about it."

I leaned back in the recliner. "It just feels too final." I looked up at the tall, thin palm trees in the waning twilight. "I'm not ready for you to go. I've lost almost everyone I love, and I'm only twenty-six. My mother. Then Jackson. And now you." My voice grew soft.

Tears welled in her eyes. "I'm so sorry, honey. I don't want to go either. I thought we'd have more time. We haven't done most of the things I planned for us. You'll have to do it all without me." Fern looked so sad and tired. "Promise me you'll live your life and see the world. Enjoy being surprised."

I winced, then laughed a bit. I hated surprises. Everyone knew that. Fern knew it as well, but she delighted in springing little surprises on me.

When she traveled, she used to send me strange and wonderful little gifts from other countries. I loved getting those packages from her. It reminded me there was someone out there in the world who loved me.

But sometimes she sent me other things, like a package of condoms, and a certificate for a Brazilian wax when I was in college.

Then I thought about my senior prom. "Do you remember the date you sent me for my senior prom?" I asked.

"I certainly do," Fern chuckled softly. "I think his name was Lander. Or maybe Liam."

"It was Noah."

Fern smiled. "I was close then."

Fern somehow found out I didn't have a date for my senior prom dance in high school. So she'd recruited one of her friend's grandsons, probably by paying him, to take me to the dance. Fern had even sent a dress for me to wear.

I'd been mortified at first, but surprisingly it had been an enjoyable evening. I still corresponded with him a bit on social media.

"I still have a few surprises left up my sleeve."

I chuckled. "Aw, don't torment me like that. You know I hate surprises."

We talked a little longer until Fern started shifting in pain, and I asked Ramone to administer more pain medication through Fern's IV.

He'd become adept at it, and he was around the most, so he'd taken on the responsibility. Jonathan picked her up and took her into her bedroom. They kissed her goodnight, gave me hugs, then headed home for the evening.

I helped Fern get ready for bed. Thankfully, she'd been strong enough until recently to take care of herself, but she was too weak now.

So we changed her catheter, washed and moisturized her face, and helped brush her teeth the best I could.

Then I tucked Fern in and kissed her papery thin cheek. "I love you, Fern. Sleep well."

Fern lasted two more days. During that time, flowers and small gifts arrived several times a day. I read her the cards and letters, and Fern tried to comment about each person.

My roommates sent a beautiful spray of white lilies and a sweet note, telling her they wanted her to see and enjoy their flowers. Fern had smiled weakly.

It's a funny thing—when someone takes the time to be kind to a person you love and cherish, it indelibly endears them to you. My roommates were the best thing, besides being with Fern through her illness, that had come out of me transferring law schools from Brooklyn to Las Vegas and moving out west after my 1L year. It was a thin, silver lining.

The hospice nurse came the first morning and checked her pain medication and vitals.

"Fern's very weak, and I don't think she's going to last much longer," she told me outside Fern's door. While the nurse was there, I went for a run to give Fern some privacy.

I cried a little as I ran up to the Lykken trailhead. I didn't want to add to her burden, so I tried not to cry in front of her.

That afternoon before dinner, Martina, Fern's housecleaner and caregiver, came and straightened the house. She also did some laundry, then helped Fern bathe and washed her thin hair before Fern fell back asleep.

Martina gave me a tight hug after walking out of Fern's room. "I'm so sorry." Martina was about my age, and we'd become good friends over the past two years.

The next morning, Fern seemed to bounce back a bit. I helped her wrap her head in one of her beautiful scarves, then put on a touch of makeup. She decided we needed to take one more joy ride in her convertible. So we went out in the late morning.

Jonathan drove, and Fern sat in the front passenger seat with Ramone and me in the back.

Jonathan glanced at Fern. "Where would you like to go?"

"Down Palm Canyon Drive, I think."

So we first drove down Palm Canyon Drive, discussing some of the old and new businesses. Then Fern continued down memory lane as we drove by a few of her favorite homes and landmarks.

Fern pointed to an older motel. "This place used to have a little tiki bar."

The trip wasn't long, but it was memorable. We all knew it would be the last time we drove with Fern in her beautiful convertible. Ramone quietly sniffled next to me.

When we got home, Fern was tired but asked to be taken to the backyard again, where she drifted in and out of sleep on her recliner. The boys went home for the afternoon. I sat quietly next to Fern, trying to do some homework.

Early that evening, Jonathan and Ramone came over again, and we made a light dinner and virgin martinis. Fern still didn't eat but laid on the couch and grew quieter, drifting in and out as the evening went on. I knew I was losing her.

Finally, Jonathan carried her to bed.

Jonathan and I stepped out of her room while Ramone talked with her for a few minutes.

Ramone had tears in his eyes when he stepped out into the hallway.

He patted my cheek. "We'll be home when you need us."

Jonathan kissed my forehead, and they left. I went back into Fern's room and gently washed and moisturized her face again, then sat and massaged her hands. Ramone had administered more pain medication before they left.

Fern stirred a little. "I love you, Laurel," she whispered. "Jackson and I said if we'd ever had kids, we wanted them to be just like you." Her voice faded.

I gulped down my sob and gently put my arms around Fern's thin shoulders. "I love you too, sweet Fern. Mom and I were so lucky to have you." I held her to me for a few seconds.

Fern's frame was slight and emaciated, and the ravages of cancer and the treatments showed on her face and body. She looked at me as if trying to focus, but her eyes closed and her breathing slowed.

I sat silently by Fern's bedside that night, holding her hand and listening to her breathe. I finally laid down on my side next to her, and watched her chest as she breathed in and out. I dozed a little on and off during the night.

At two minutes after five the next morning, Fern quietly slipped away. I sat next to her for a little while, holding her hand, and felt it grow cold in mine. I finally let go and for some reason I didn't understand, I got up and tucked the blanket around her body. Then I walked down to Jonathan and Ramone's house to let them know she was gone.

Chapter 3

The next few days seemed to go by in a haze. I felt numb and distracted as we made the arrangements for Fern's cremation and celebration.

When Fern accepted she wouldn't be getting better, she'd planned her own end-of-life celebration instead of having a traditional funeral.

Ramone let me know the day after Fern's death. "She told me it would be for a few of her friends and colleagues, and she wanted it held at the iconic Inglenook Inn. Just a little dinner celebration."

I nodded. "That sounds like her."

"Fern also bought you the perfect black dress to wear. It's in a bag hanging in the back of her closet. She thought the dress would go well with your hair and delicate frame." Ramone eyed me critically. "She was right, as usual. You'll look very elegant and waif-like in it."

I sighed halfheartedly. "You realize the irony of wearing a black dress to a 'celebration', don't you?"

Jonathan patted my arm.

Ramone shrugged. "That's what she wanted, Lolly. We can do this for her."

"Yes, we can. You're right."

I went for a run the morning of the celebration. My high school counselor told me once I used running as therapy. I'd stared at her, wondering what her point had been.

Fern tried to get Victor, my father, to put me into therapy right after my mother died. I told him I didn't want to go, and for once he didn't force me. That was the only time I remember Victor and me agreeing about anything. In hindsight, Fern was probably right. I could have used therapy, but I hadn't wanted to talk to a stranger about my life.

I got home, then walked down to Jonathan and Ramone's house for breakfast. Jonathan and I sat at their kitchen bar, drinking coffee and watching Ramone make Belgian waffles. I loved their home almost as much as I loved Fern's.

Unlike Fern's newly remodeled kitchen, they'd restored their kitchen. They'd had the original cabinets stripped and then painted a cyan blue. Their countertops were white quartz with a subtle gold vein, and they'd updated the cabinet hardware to gold.

The sunny window above the kitchen sink sported bright lemon yellow curtains. Their kitchen had a wholesome 1950s June Cleaver feel to it.

I'd given them a large, handcrafted atomic wall clock a few years ago. I spent a mint on that clock, and had special ordered the colors to match their renovated kitchen. The clock had been worth every penny when I saw how much they loved it.

I sipped my coffee and sighed when I thought of Fern buying me a dress for her own funeral—or *celebration.*

Ramone patted my arm. "Oh, honey, she knew you'd just go out and get some off-the-rack thing from your favorite bargain discount store, and she would have been horrified. You'll love it. She also left you some fabulous shoes and jewelry to go with it."

"Yeah," I nodded reluctantly, "I probably will love it.

Later that morning I sat in her room, staring at the unopened bag hanging in the back of the closet. I missed my mom and Fern terribly, especially at a time like this. I rubbed at my sternum, trying to ease the dull ache there.

Another thing no one tells you is that grief can be physical sometimes. When I found out my mother had died, I remember feeling myself getting this tunnel vision. I couldn't see anything out of my peripheral vision, and I had to sit down because I'd felt so faint. Today, my heart felt heavy, and I had clammy hands and a knot in my throat.

Finally, I reached into the closet and pulled out the hanging bag. There was another bag below it with my name written on it. When I took the dress out, it didn't surprise me to see an expensive, well-cut, black designer midi dress that fell just above my knees.

I loved the dress. It had a soft swing skirt and an understated style. The signature blue shoes Fern picked out sported a nice block heel with two buckles. The shoes were a little more stylish than I'd have chosen for the occasion, but I had to admit they juxtaposed well with the dress.

When I opened the long, maroon velvet jewelry box, a letter lay on top. A faint whiff of Fern's beloved Chanel Gardénia perfume hit me.

I sat down on the bed, carefully opened the scented linen paper, and read Fern's letter.

My Dearest Laurel,

I just started my last letter to you, and I've already ruined my makeup. Aw well. You're one of my greatest joys. You, your mother, and Jackson have been the three loves of my life.

When you found out I had advanced breast cancer, you didn't have to move from Brooklyn, in the middle of law school no less, to be with me during my last years. But you did. You drove through that Mojave Desert so many times to be by my side for the surgeries, doctor appointments, and those terrible treatments. I'm eternally grateful for your dry humor and kind nature. You've brought me so much comfort and delight, especially during these last years.

I'm sorry your father has been such an abysmal disappointment. You know my view of him, so I won't belabor the point. Please don't let his cruelty, callousness, and failures color your life.

As you're aware, Ramone and Jonathan are the executors of my estate. They've been my attorneys and best friends for years. We have discussed my estate, and they will convey my wishes. I trust them implicitly, and if you ever need assistance or advice, they are a great resource.

Finally, I wish for you a beautiful life filled with happiness and love. When you find a partner, choose someone who takes care of you and your tender heart, makes you laugh, and loves you deeply. I pray that you have challenges, joy, and especially love—and all those wonderful human emotions in between that make up a well-lived life. I only wish I could have been there to see it all.

My Eternal Love, Fern

I sniffed the letter, and the smell of her perfume was both a comfort and an anguish. Tears dripped off my chin as I reread it.

Chapter 4

A magnificent flower arrangement and a beautiful, framed photo of Fern sat on a table at the Inglenook Inn where the celebration of life took place. Ramone, Jonathan, and I slowly circulated around the garden, talking with Fern's friends and colleagues.

I occasionally fingered the gold hoop earrings and braided gold chain Fern had given me to wear with the black dress.

At the beginning of the evening, Jonathan spoke a few words to welcome Fern's guests.

"Good evening, everyone. Ramone should be the one up here giving this brief speech, but he asked me to do it for him, so he wouldn't have to cry incoherently through the whole thing."

Several guests chuckled.

Jonathan looked around. "Fern loved people. She loved you all, and I think this evening shows how thoughtful and kind she was, because she asked us to keep the remarks brief and the martini bar well stocked."

That brought even more chuckles and a few murmurs about Fern's well-known love of a good martini.

"She also asked her niece, Laurel Payne, who was more a daughter to her, to say a few words." Jonathan turned to me.

Looking out at the crowd, I thought about Fern. I clenched my hands behind my back and fought against tearing up.

"Thank you for coming this evening." I cleared my throat a bit. "Fern is a person worth celebrating, and she wanted you to enjoy the evening and reminisce about your best memories of her. She was the kindest, most generous person I've ever known. And she was a consummate hostess."

A few people murmured in agreement.

"Most of us enjoyed at least one Martini Monday at her home, whether it was here, in New York City, or Italy, or wherever she was. So, if you have a drink, let's give her a toast."

I waited a moment for everyone to find a drink, then lifted my own.

"To our sweet, fabulous Fern." I glanced over at Ramone, and my voice got quieter. "May she be reunited with her beloved Jackson, and may she rest in peace and be free of pain." Raising my glass, I took a sip.

"To Fern," people around me echoed. I heard a few throats clearing and several soft sniffs.

Then Jonathan stepped forward and encouraged everyone to mingle and have an enjoyable evening. The crowd slowly dispersed into smaller groups.

A light buffet had been laid out, and there were several trays of champagne at the end of the buffet table. But the decadent martini bar set up in Fern's honor was the real hit of the night. Fern and

Jackson were known for their famous Martini Monday parties, and most guests had been invited at some point.

I studied the man behind the bar who deftly prepared drinks and avoided eye contact. He looked like he was in his early thirties and seemed tall and fit. His thick, slightly messy brown hair curled a little around his collar, and his features were striking.

"How did Fern know the bartender?" I asked Jonathan and Ramone. "He's an experienced bartender, but he doesn't seem friendly."

Jonathan looked over at the bar and chuckled. "That's Sebastian Mendoza. And he's not friendly. He was a good friend to Fern though. They've done a few real estate projects together and Fern adored him, even though he can be an asshole sometimes."

Ramone shook his head. "That was a fascinating conversation when Fern asked Sebastian if he'd be the bartender at her life celebration. He knew she was sick, but he didn't know she was dying."

"Sebastian took it fairly well," Jonathan added. "He told her it was a shitty way to break the news to him, but he'd be honored. He hasn't been a bartender for years. Sebastian owns a large property management company, along with several holdings around town, and he's a partner in a security firm."

Ramone watched Sebastian shake a cosmopolitan. "His offices are across the hall from ours at the Saguaro Complex."

"How come I've never met him before?"

Ramone shrugged. "He's not very social."

I thought I knew most of Fern's friends. "Where did they meet?"

"I think Fern first got to know him almost ten years ago when he was a bartender at Cecilia's," Jonathan said. "She'd ordered a martini, then sent it back. He came out to our table and asked her to explain exactly what he'd done wrong."

Ramone chuckled. "She got up and went behind the bar, then expertly prepared one herself while she talked him through it."

Jonathan shook his head. "She explained that even though there are few ingredients in a martini, it needed to be a perfect blend of 'temperature and dilution' I think is how she put it."

Smiling a little, I remembered Fern instructing me about whether to stir or shake a cocktail after I'd stirred a cosmopolitan once.

"Darling," Fern instructed, "you shake cocktails with juice or citrus in them. It livens up and releases all those wonderful flavors. And alcohol-based cocktails must be stirred. You don't want to over-oxidate them." It was a lesson I remembered.

Ramone took a sip of his drink. "I have to hand it to him. He listened, then he mixed another one under her tutelage and got it exactly right. They've been good friends ever since."

I noticed several women and a couple of men stop at the bar and try to strike up a conversation with him. He barely responded.

A couple who knew Jonathan and Ramone walked up to speak with them, and I excused myself and went over to the bar. Sebastian didn't look up at me or say anything, so I gave him my order.

"May I have a dry martini, please? With the right blend of temperature and dilution."

He paused for a split second, then began preparing my drink. Still without looking at me. I noticed a small scar running through his eyebrow. It seemed to enhance his excessively handsome face, but it also added to his standoffish demeanor.

Sebastian didn't say hello or mention he knew Fern. In fact, he didn't talk at all. He prepared my drink, deftly poured it into a chilled glass, then slid it over to me.

"Thank you. I'm Laurel Payne, Fern's niece."

"And I'm busy." He turned to another guest who'd just walked up and took her order. I stared at him for a second, then picked up my drink and left.

The couple talking with Jonathan and Ramone were just leaving as I walked back over.

"Did you meet Sebastian?" Jonathan asked.

"Not really. You're right, he is a bit of an ass."

He grinned, as if Sebastian hadn't let him down.

"Who's the couple talking with Fern's accountant over there?" I pointed.

"That's Aldo and Giverna Russo. Let me introduce you."

An hour later, I needed a break, so I walked around the lit pathway to the outdoor pool area. Sitting down on one of the pool chairs for a moment, I took in the pleasant evening air and fading sunset. Overflowing flowerpots surrounded the pool deck, and I smelled petunias and allium in the warm evening air.

The Inglenook Inn had a restaurant called Marvin's that was famous for live music, and it had hosted some of the most well-known Hollywood celebrities back in the day. I remembered having Sunday brunch there a few times when my mother and I came to visit Fern and Jackson.

I also remembered the front courtyard area had restrooms, so I walked over and used the facilities to freshen up.

When I came out, Sebastian stood a few yards away, leaning against the wall, checking his phone. Just then a pretty blonde woman in a sleeveless blue dress walked up to him.

Two of her friends walked by. "We'll wait for you inside, Mia," one of them said.

Sebastian looked up at Mia, and she stopped less than a foot away from him and grasped his arm. "Well hello, Sebastian. It's nice to see you here."

Sebastian stepped away, and she had to let go of his arm or get pulled by him.

"Mia," Sebastian said in a deep, flat voice.

"What are you doing here?" The woman looked around to see if anyone was with him.

I pulled out my phone and pretended to look at it so I could eavesdrop.

Mia gazed up at Sebastian and smiled. "Have a drink with me. I'm here with some friends, but they won't miss me."

"No."

She waited for him to say something else.

"No?" she finally repeated.

"No." Sebastian looked back down at his phone.

"Just 'no'? That's it?" She glared at him, disbelieving.

He glanced at her, irritation in his eyes. "Yes."

The woman put her hands on her hips. "Why are you being such a jerk?"

Sebastian slowly blinked. Then he looked back down at his phone.

Mia gasped a little. "Oh, my God. I can't believe I ever went home with you. You're such a prick."

She'd called him a jerk and a prick, but she still stood there as if expecting another answer from him. I should have left and given them some privacy, but it was like watching a train wreck and I couldn't look away.

Sebastian finally straightened off the wall. "I'm here for a friend's funeral, so it's not a good time to get hit on. Especially by someone who calls me a prick."

Mia gawked up at him. Then she put her index finger in his face and yelled, "You hit on me the first time we met. You're such a grumpy asshole."

Sebastian shrugged.

"I'm sorry for your loss and my bad timing," she said stiffly, then turned and started marching away. "You're still a prick though," she threw over her shoulder, holding up her middle finger.

Sebastian watched her go. I turned to stare at the woman stalking away and felt both embarrassment and reluctant admiration for her. Then I glanced back at Sebastian. Who was now glaring at me.

I'd given up pretending to look at my phone. It was obvious I'd watched the whole thing, but in my defense, it had been impossible not to. He looked me up and down with narrowed eyes.

Maybe I should have tried to say hello again, but the timing seemed off. So I just stared back at him with wide eyes for a few seconds, then turned on my heel and walked back to the celebration. When I was out of earshot, I started chuckling. I'd never heard anyone get called a grumpy asshole before. It felt good to laugh a little.

Later that evening, as the celebration wound down, I finally went over to the bar to thank Sebastian and officially say hello.

He'd been Fern's friend, and I felt obligated to be courteous. Again, he didn't look my way or acknowledge me when I walked up. I looked behind me to make sure no one was waiting for a drink this time.

I cleared my throat loudly and held out my hand when he finally glanced up at me.

"Hello. I'm Laurel, Fern's niece. Ramone said you were good friends with her, so I wanted to say thank you for hosting the martini bar. Jonathan and Ramone told me you did it as a favor to Fern."

Sebastian reluctantly straightened, then gazed at my outstretched hand for several seconds. He slowly wiped his hand off on a bar towel and shook my hand—once. Then he dropped it quickly.

I stepped back awkwardly. "Well, thank you again. And I didn't mean to overhear your conversation earlier with your, uh, friend."

Sebastian looked at me flatly. "You shouldn't fucking eavesdrop. And I'm not here for you."

I froze and stared up at him, then wiped any expression off my face. Mia had been right. He really was a prick.

"You and Mia were kind of hard to miss. And I'm not thanking you for your sake, Mr. Morena."

"It's Mendoza."

"Right," I replied without missing a beat. "I'm acknowledging and thanking you because Fern was a kind and gracious person who believed in good manners, even when someone doesn't deserve them."

Sebastian continued to stare at me as if he didn't like me. At all.

"Have a good evening," I ground out. Without waiting for a reply, I turned and walked off. And avoided the martini bar for the rest of the night.

Chapter 5

When I straightened up Fern's house and got ready to go back to Las Vegas, I walked into her bedroom and the emptiness hit me. Over the past two years, I'd spent countless hours curled up on the ivory velvet lounger tucked in the corner of her bedroom. While she sat propped up in bed, we discuss her health, my mom, and whatever else came to mind. I wondered why she never mentioned Sebastian.

Light filtered through the gauzy curtains, and the room still smelled faintly of her expensive moisturizer and perfume. A small collection of feminine trinkets sat on her dresser, and an exquisite landscape painting hung on the wall. There was a vintage photograph of Fern and Jackson on their wedding day perched on her nightstand.

Before Jackson married Fern, he'd purchased a couple of homes from an overextended builder in the area. One was this house in the Deepwell Estates. I'd heard Fern tell my mother that Palm

Springs became popular in the mid-1950s for people who worked in Hollywood and wanted a second home to get away.

"At that time, Hollywood contracts stated the stars had to live within a three-hour drive to the studios. Palm Springs was a perfect spot because of the mild winters, and its privacy. So you can only imagine what some of those stars got up to here." Fern's vague smile always made me wonder what she knew.

When my mom and I came to visit her, Fern would drive us through a few neighborhoods and point out various stars' homes, and tell us the local gossip and folklore.

She pointed out a house behind a tall hedge one day. "See that property on the corner there? That home is called The Lucy House. Lucille Ball and Desi Arnaz had it built. I heard he won the lot in a poker game."

"Who are they?" I'd asked.

Fern gasped in mock horror. "Lucille Ball was only one of the greatest women pioneers in the film industry. And Desi Arnaz was her fabulously multi-talented Cuban husband and business partner."

This led to an in-depth discussion about Lucille and her legacy, and about how she'd produced *Star Trek*. I stood in the doorway, lost in my thoughts, then turned and slowly walked out.

On my way out of town later that day, I met with Ramone and Jonathan at their office. Martina, Fern's caregiver, planned to stay at the house while it was empty so I texted to let her know I'd left.

"I feel torn about leaving right now," I admitted as I sat in Ramone's office.

Jonathan stood next to my chair. "You have to finish your semester. You're only four hours away if anything comes up, and Fern would be livid if you didn't graduate."

Ramone nodded. "Sebastian's company will continue taking care of her house. Everything else is running smoothly and has been for years."

Jonathan patted my shoulder. "When you come back after graduation, we'll sit down and have our official executor meeting and help you make some plans. Those were Fern's explicit instructions."

Ramone leaned back. "As for her house here, Sebastian's planning to set up a security system and a couple of outdoor cameras next week. You'll need to coordinate with him to get instructions and passcodes."

I winced, remembering my run-in with Sebastian. "Okay. Great." I knew Sebastian's office suite sat directly across the hall from Ramone and Jonathan's law offices.

"Are you still planning to come to Las Vegas for graduation?" I shifted in my seat, embarrassed for asking.

"Of course we're coming," Ramone said. "Fern booked a fabulous hotel suite several months ago, and she arranged for some light catering too."

Intense sadness hit me when I thought about Fern not being there. I'd only worked a little over the past two years so I could be free to visit Fern whenever my school schedule allowed. So I was flat broke and couldn't afford a celebration. In fact, I could barely afford groceries and gas. Fern hadn't known, and she'd assumed I had access to my college education fund.

When Victor, my father, found out I planned to transfer because of Fern's diagnosis, he'd called me in a rage.

"Laurel, why in God's name would you do something so stupid?" he'd sneered. "You're throwing away your only chance to make something of yourself. What an idiot. I'm not bailing you out when you graduate with a mountain of debt and no way to pay it back."

I tried to reason with him. "It's just for two years."

"If you're stupid enough to transfer to one of those sub-standard, dime-store, West Coast law schools, I'm not sending any more money to pay for your tuition. Let's see how far you get." Then he'd hung up.

He knew there were many excellent law schools in the West. But Victor seemed to feel I was choosing Fern over him, and it had been a major blow to our already fractured relationship.

I never told anyone, but Victor was the reason I'd gone to law school. I believed my mother felt trapped in her marriage to him, and he hadn't allowed Fern to take over my care when my mother died. He'd used the law to get his way, and I didn't want him to do that to me ever again.

"Tell Joey and Luke to come celebrate with us on Friday," Ramone said. "We'll make sure it's a tasteful, classy evening."

Jonathan grinned. "As tasteful as any party on the Las Vegas Strip can be. We'll meet you for dinner on Thursday evening when we get in." Jonathan looked down at his expensive watch. "You better get on the road so you're not driving in the dark. And, unfortunately, I have contracts to read and hours to bill."

Ramone nodded. "Drive safely and make sure you've gassed up and your phone is charged before you go over the desert." They hugged me and I walked out.

I smiled a little when I saw their sleek, professional law firm signage as I headed out the door. It read "Clark, Lewis, and Associates." Ramone's last name was Lewis, and Jonathan's last name was Clark. Everyone called their law firm Lewis and Clark.

When I looked up, I noticed a tall, dark-haired man in a black polo shirt with a company logo walking into the building. It was Sebastian Mendoza.

I raised my hand slightly. "Hello."

His eyes slid to me briefly then looked away, and he kept walking. Geez, what a jerk. I wasn't sure what his problem was, but I hoped I didn't have to interact with him much regarding Fern's house.

"Nice to see you too, Mr. Mayberry. Have a great day yourself," I said brightly as he walked by, pretending he'd actually answered me. I heard a grunt behind me, but I kept walking.

That afternoon, I took the Mojave Preserve route again. Occasionally, I pulled over to explore the desert and take photographs.

It wasn't a well-traveled route. Sometimes I just stood still in the desert surrounded by Joshua trees and brittlebush, listening to the near-complete silence, the smell of baked earth filling my nostrils.

My favorite route took me past Roy's Café and Motel on a small section of Route 66, and then through the Joshua tree groves in the Mojave National Preserve. After experiencing life in New York City and Brooklyn, the haunting quietness of the desert seemed like another world.

For my thirteenth birthday, Jackson had given me a ridiculously expensive digital camera. The camera was the last gift Jackson gave me before he died, and I cherished it.

My early photos were mediocre, but I eventually learned how to analyze perspective and composition and use shadows and light. I googled articles and YouTube videos, and later took a photography class in college. It gave me an outlet and helped me with my loneliness and depression after my mother died.

On the drive back to Las Vegas, around dusk that evening, I pulled off on Cima Road in the middle of the Joshua tree forest and took photos of the craggy trees in the twilight. As I stood in the desert, I grieved Fern's death, thought of my little brothers, and worried about my lack of plans for the future.

I was broke, and I didn't have any job prospects. Fern and her pending death had taken center stage in my life, and now I just felt empty.

When I got back to the townhome that evening, my roommates met me at the door.

Luke hugged me. "I'm sorry we couldn't come."

He was in the National Guard, and he had obligations that weekend. He reminded me of a rugged version of Chris Evans, and he worked out religiously.

Josephine also gave me a tight hug. "How'd everything go?"

She went by Joey, and she was taller than me and had better curves. Joey's dark blond hair curled like large corkscrews.

I teared up again for what seemed like the millionth time. "Thanks, guys. It was hard, but I was expecting it. She died peacefully in her sleep."

We talked over a bottle of cheap wine and leftover seafood enchiladas Joey brought home from the Mexican restaurant where she worked. I told them about Fern's last days, and her celebration. Then we complained about upcoming finals and homework assignments.

"Thank you for the flowers." I squeezed both their hands. "You made Fern laugh with your note."

I'd met Joey during the mandatory guided tour of the law school a week before the semester started two years ago. We'd ended up in the same tour group and had struck up a conversation.

Toward the end of the tour, Joey mentioned that she and Luke were staying in a temporary apartment in North Las Vegas when the condo they'd planned to rent had been unexpectedly sold. They were both 1L students and had grown up in Las Vegas together.

The North Las Vegas neighborhood they were staying in wasn't a good one. We agreed to meet for dinner that night since I didn't know anyone else in Las Vegas, and Luke came along.

So I proposed they ditch the temporary apartment and move in with me, and they'd jumped at the offer, and we became friends and roommates since then.

Joey yawned so hard, her jaw cracked. "I'm done. Let's go to bed."

I nodded. "Yeah, me too."

We stumbled off to bed. My last thought before I drifted off to sleep was of Sebastian's surprised grunt when I'd called him Mr. Mayberry.

Chapter 6

A week before graduation, I took a quick weekend trip to Palm Springs to check on Fern's house and talk with Jonathan and Ramone. That morning, I'd handed in my last assignment, and I only had one more final to go.

When I pulled up to Fern's house early Friday evening, I noticed a newer gray truck parked in my usual spot. I parked next to it and got out. A ladder stood in the middle of the porch, and the front door stood cracked open a bit.

"Hello? Martina, are you here?" I called out.

No one answered, so I walked through the house searching for the owner of the gray truck.

I finally went out to the backyard and looked around, calling out a few times. "Martina? Ramone? Anyone here?"

"You don't need to shout." I heard a low, irritated voice answer right behind me.

I let out a scream and whirled around. Sebastian Mendoza stood there with his hands on his hips.

As he glared down at me, I vaguely registered that he looked good. His muscular legs and tight, firm butt were even better in well-washed jeans than dress pants, and his forearms and biceps popped with his hands on his hips. The bastard.

"Holy shit." Sucking in a breath, I stepped back. "You scared the crap out of me. Why didn't you answer before you were standing right behind me?"

He shrugged.

"What are you doing?" I tried again.

"Working," he answered shortly.

"Okaaay. What kind of work?" I drawled out.

"Installing cameras."

I waited for him to expand. "Whoa there, don't talk so fast. I can't keep up." I shook my head. "Do you know where Martina is?" It was almost six, and I hoped Martina and I could get dinner together. The house seemed too empty without Fern there.

"No."

I finally lost my patience. "Okay then, Mr. McDonald. It was really great talking with you again. Please lock up when you leave, and have a lovely evening."

I turned to walk back inside, but he latched onto my arm and stared down at me. "Where do you want the cameras installed?"

I looked at him blankly for a few seconds.

"The security cameras?" he repeated impatiently.

"I don't know. Didn't you talk to Ramone?"

"It's your house now. How many and where?" He let go of me and folded his arms across his chest.

"It's not my house. It's Fern's house." I swallowed. "You need to ask Ramone or Jonathan."

I looked around slowly at the backyard. "It's Fern's house," I repeated softly, then turned and walked back inside. He didn't stop me this time.

I went to the kitchen and opened the fridge, not seeing what was inside. Then I pulled out my phone and texted Martina to see if she wanted to meet at Rubio's and split a shrimp burrito for dinner. She texted back with a thumbs-up emoji, and I left the house.

Later that evening, I walked down to Ramone and Jonathan's place. We discussed a few issues and then had drinks out on their back patio.

"I ran into Sebastian Mendoza again at Fern's house when I got in," I told them. "I know you said he can be short sometimes, but it seems like he really doesn't like me. Do you have any idea why?"

Ramone looked puzzled but not worried. "Has he said anything rude or offensive to you?"

I shook my head. "Not really. He doesn't say much of anything. Or if he *has* to talk to me, it's one or two words."

Jonathan didn't bother looking up from preparing his drink. "I wouldn't think twice about it. He can be taciturn, and he's fairly abrupt."

I nodded. "Okay, I won't worry then." That was easier said than done.

An hour later, I walked back to Fern's house and went to bed after saying goodnight to Martina. I lay there, staring up at the ceiling, until I finally drifted off to sleep.

The next morning, the scent of brewing coffee drew me to the kitchen.

Martina stood yawning in front of the coffee maker. "Good morning, I just made coffee. You want some?"

My hair felt like a bird's nest after my restless night. "God bless you. I slept maybe an hour total. I should have just gotten up and studied instead of staring at the ceiling."

She winced in sympathy. "I've had a lot of nights like that lately."

Martina was in the middle of a divorce. While we drank coffee, I asked how it was going.

"Not well. And that's all I want to say about that. How's law school going?"

I shrugged. "It's almost over. And that's all I want to say about that."

She laughed like I hoped she would.

I went for a swim a little while later, and after twenty laps or so I called it good.

When I came back into the house, Sebastian stood leaning against the kitchen counter with his arms crossed, talking to Martina. He glanced up when he heard the door open and stopped talking. His eyes quickly scanned my body.

I hadn't bothered with a coverup, and my towel was wadded up in my hand. I wore a simple black bikini, but I still felt almost naked in front of him.

I raised my chin. "Hello." Then I turned to Martina. "I forgot to tell you, Ramone invited us to dinner tonight. He's making seafood risotto."

Martina lit up. "That sounds delicious. I love when Ramone cooks. It's like getting a five-star meal without all the fancy restaurant bullshit."

Then she glanced at Sebastian and realized I hadn't invited him. I sighed a little in resignation.

Sebastian probably heard my sigh, but oh well. "I'm sure they'd be... happy to have you come too. I can text Ramone."

"Don't bother." He turned back to Martina. "Think about what we discussed. I'll talk to you later." He stood and started walking out. I waited until he'd almost reached the entryway.

"Goodbye, Mr. Moriarty. It was great seeing you again too," I said to his back. I saw him pause, shake his head, then walk out.

Martina looked at me quizzically. "You know his last name is Mendoza, right?"

I waived my hand. "Mendoza, Mayberry, Manson. Whatever."

She laughed and shook her head.

Ramone's seafood risotto and Italian parsley salad were delicious. We also brought key lime pie as our contribution to dinner. The only problem was, Sebastian came after all.

When I saw his truck in their driveway, I stopped short. "What's *he* doing here?"

Martina smirked. "I asked Ramone to invite him personally, and Sebastian knows Ramone's a superb cook." She pulled my arm, and we started walking again.

I really didn't want to spend a whole evening with Sebastian.

Martina saw my face and laughed. "What? He's not that bad."

"That's easy for you to say. He doesn't treat you like you have leprosy or something."

"Sebastian doesn't like many people. Probably most people. Okay, he likes maybe three people—on a good day."

I rolled my eyes. "I'm pretty sure I'm not one of those three people."

She shrugged. "He's even an ass to them, so I wouldn't lose any sleep over it."

I'd changed into a periwinkle jumper and leather sandals, and even styled my hair and spent a few minutes on makeup before we left. Ramone liked to tease me if he thought I hadn't made a reasonable effort.

I straightened my shoulders. "Right. I've been through worse. I can handle Mr. Grumpy Asshole McGrumpster."

Martina laughed. "I dare you to say that to his face."

"No, thank you. I'll only be saying it behind his back."

She nodded. "That's probably smart."

"We're here," I called out when we walked in.

"In the kitchen," Ramone called back.

Sebastian and Jonathan sat at the bar while Ramone prepped the salad. The kitchen smelled like sautéed garlic and butter, and my mouth started watering.

"Hello, ladies." Jonathan held up his hand.

Sebastian glanced at us. "Hey." I was surprised we got that much out of him. It was probably because Martina stood next to me.

"Perfect timing. And you both look fabulous." Ramone glanced down at my jumper. "Fern must have given that to you. It's very chic."

I raised my eyebrow. "You're so adept at giving backhanded compliments."

He grinned. "Why, thank you."

"I got it myself a few years ago." My eyes slid away. "But Fern might have picked it out."

He pointed his wooden spatula at me. "Ha! I knew it."

I rolled my eyes. "What can we do to help?"

"Nothing. It's ready. Sebastian brought the wine."

We helped Ramone carry food to the beautifully set dining table, then sat down to eat.

Somehow, I ended up sitting next to Sebastian. The table was big enough, but his arm kept brushing against mine. He didn't seem to care.

Finally, I put my fork down. "Would you mind sliding your chair over a little? I'm left-handed and we keep bumping elbows."

"No." He kept eating.

After a minute, I turned to him again. "No, you don't mind sliding your chair over? Or no, you aren't going to?" I finally asked.

"You're fine." He kept eating.

I huffed and slid my chair over. Then I saw his lip twitch. The bastard.

"If I accidentally bump your elbow and spill wine all over you, don't blame me, okay?" I batted my eyelashes.

Sebastian raised his eyebrow, but continued eating.

Ramone and Jonathan watched us raptly from across the table, and Martina smirked but kept shoveling food in her mouth.

Jonathan pointed his fork at me. "Are you still working in the legal clinic at the law school?"

"Yes, but I'll be finishing up next week. I'm going to miss those little juvenile delinquents."

I'd been working as a law student attorney in the juvenile court clinic at the law school, and I'd told the boys about some of my more interesting clients.

Ramone leaned forward. "My favorite case was the kid who stole the golf cart and spray-painted it florescent orange."

Martina smirked. "It sounds like he plays too much *Grand Theft Auto.*"

"Is he the one who cut the top off so it would be a convertible?" Jonathan asked.

"Yeah, and he got charged with a felony because the golf cart was so expensive. That kid is sweet, but his impulse control is nonexistent."

"Do you want to practice juvenile law?" Ramone asked.

Sebastian paused and glanced at me, almost like he was curious about my answer. I tried to ignore him.

"Maybe. It feels like I'm doing something meaningful, and I get along pretty well with the kids." I pointed at Martina. "It's like you working in elder care and hospice. You helped Fern so much, especially toward the end."

She nodded. "I get it. You feel like all the time you spend at work isn't meaningless."

"Yes, that's exactly right." My shoulders slumped. "But I don't think I can afford to be a public defender, at least not right away. I might have to do private practice first."

Ramone and Jonathan glanced at each other, and Sebastian studied me. I looked down at my plate, embarrassed about saying so much in front of him.

After dinner, we took the key lime pie out to the back patio and enjoyed the mild evening temperatures while we polished it off. Sebastian didn't say much.

I finally patted my stomach. "Ramone, that was delicious. Thank you. Let me help clean up."

Jonathan raised his hand. "I've got it. Ramone cooks and I do the dishes."

Sebastian stood up. "I'm taking off. Thanks, it was great."

"Yes, thank you. That *was* delicious," Martina added.

We all stood up and carried our dishes inside, then said our goodbyes. It had been a nice evening, even with Sebastian there.

I was glad I'd come for the weekend, and I felt a little less lonely that night when I climbed into bed.

On Sunday morning I cleaned up and said goodbye to Martina, then drove back to Las Vegas.

Chapter 7

Over the last two years, as Fern's health steadily deteriorated, working in the law school clinic had been a saving grace for me. Most the teenagers I worked with in the juvenile court were friendly, decent kids.

And when I met their parents, sometimes I understood why they had mental health problems or other serious issues. I could relate with them, and I realized my dysfunctional, almost nonexistent relationship with Victor could have been worse.

When we had time between hearings at court, I'd often ask them about themselves. I learned a lot about miscellaneous teenage things, like the latest young adult books, types of music, and several strange TikTok trends.

I also enjoyed working with my second attorney mentor. The law school ran a mentorship program where they paired a law student with a local attorney.

The first attorney I shadowed was the go-to attorney for escorts in Las Vegas charged with prostitution-related charges. I didn't know why I'd initially been paired with him. Vince Van Buren usually wore silk suits, expensive cuff links, and hand-tooled, Italian leather shoes with red soles. He also liked to brag about how much money he made.

"Laurel, honey, I usually make more by noon on the first Tuesday of each month than most attorneys make the *entire* month," Vince told me one day. "And I give my clients a ten percent discount if they pay in cash instead of running it through my office."

He'd winked at me. "Fewer taxes that way."

Vince knew that area of law well, but his fees were steep. I felt a little sick when he told me what he charged, even with his ten percent "cash" discount. I decided after a few weeks to find another mentor.

Eventually, they paired me with a blunt, no-nonsense juvenile court public defender named Pamela Shen. Pamela was the antithesis of Vince, and her clients and colleagues seemed to like her competent, no-bullshit demeanor.

My last court hearings with Pamela were on Tuesday afternoon. Late Tuesday morning before graduation, I finished my last final. I thought the exam had gone reasonably well, and I was relieved to expel all the information I'd crammed into my head over the last few days.

As I walked out of the law school and headed to the courthouse, I realized this would be my last time as a student there. A deep sense of relief and unexpected nostalgia hit me.

When I walked into the courthouse, my favorite bailiff, Deputy Millet, was on duty. He had an impressive Sam Elliott mustache, and he usually had at least one bad pun or joke ready about my last name every time I saw him. I wondered what he had in store today.

"Hello, Ms. Payne. How're your finals going? Have they been *painful* this semester?" Deputy Millet asked.

I smiled. "I got done with my last one this morning. And that pun was bad, Millet. Just so bad."

"That hurts, Payne. I'm going to have to take a *pain*killer."

The other bailiff laughed and chimed in. "I've got a few 'pain' puns for you. If you joined the military, you'd become a Major Payne. And if someone murdered you, they'd be known as a Payne killer."

Shaking my head, I pointed at Deputy Millet. "He's already used those. Someone help, I'm being 'punned' to death."

Pamela walked up to the metal detector. She wore a boxy brown polyester suit and her usual black orthopedic shoes. She usually wore ill-fitting, outdated suits, polyester blouses, and comfortable shoes. I liked Pamela, and besides her wardrobe, I wanted to be like her when I became an attorney.

"Are they wracking their brains for more Payne jokes?" she asked.

"Yep. I thought after almost nine months, they would run out by now. But no such luck." I waited for her, and we walked toward the courtroom together.

Deputy Millet yelled down the hall at us. "I thought of one more. What did your mom want to name you after twenty-four hours of labor? Ima Pain."

"Weak!" Pamela yelled back without turning around.

Pamela and I said goodbye later that afternoon after our last hearing together. She gave me a no-nonsense hug and a pat on the back, then picked up her oversized bag and headed back to her office. I'd invited her to my small graduation celebration, and Pamela planned to come and bring her husband.

I checked my phone as I walked out of the courthouse. Ramone had sent me a text two days ago, telling me I needed to call Sebastian about the security system at Fern's house. He also forwarded me Sebastian's contact information.

I'd waited until after my last final to worry about it, and I finally pulled up his number and drafted a text.

Me: This is Laurel Payne. Ramone told me to contact you regarding the security system at Fern's. Please send codes and manual links. I can figure it out.

I revised the text twice before getting annoyed at myself and hitting send. Then I headed to the grocery store. I hoped my roommates weren't sick of pasta because it was cheap and filling.

Suddenly at loose ends, I didn't have any homework, tests, or assignments due for the first time in a very long time. And Fern wasn't there anymore to talk. So I went home, cleaned the townhome, and made dinner.

By the time I looked at my phone again two hours later, Sebastian had texted me back.

Sebastian: Call me to set time to meet

After basically ignoring me or putting up with his short, curt responses over the past month, *now* he wanted to talk to me. I noticed it was after five; I'd text him tomorrow. Or the next day. I didn't plan to call him, ever. I pushed aside the uncomfortable thought that I was trying to annoy him.

Two days later, I texted Sebastian back.

Me: You can just send the codes and manual links

He didn't return my text until late that evening, and it was brief and clipped.

Grumpy Asshole: Monday morning at eight. Be there.

He didn't ask if that time worked for me, and he didn't even acknowledge my request for the manual links and login information. Okay, then. My half-baked plan to get under his skin seemed to have worked. I'd also changed his name to *Grumpy Asshole* in my phone to make myself feel better. It kind of worked.

Chapter 8

"Hi Lolly!" I heard two high-pitched voices say over my phone speaker the next morning while I made coffee.

"Hey, Boo. Hi, Lennie." I smiled as I listened to them run around their kitchen back in New York, yelling my name and talking to me at the same time. William and Leonard were my five-year-old twin brothers. They were born during my sophomore year in college, and I loved them instantly.

Back then I was going to school in Brooklyn, so I went to see them whenever I could. I'd started calling Willie "Boo" because he'd loved playing peek-a-boo so much.

Chloe, my step-mother, liked to tell people the twins were her little "oopsie babies," so I doubted Victor and Chloe ever planned to have children.

Chloe sighed long and loud over the phone. "They miss you, Laurel." Her voice sounded a little accusatory.

"I miss them too."

My relationship with Chloe had been strained and formal before the twins were born, but it was a little better now.

Willie and Lennie both started talking to me again, telling me about their toys, their friends, and the cut on Lennie's forehead he'd gotten when he jumped off the top bunk. I understood about half of what they said, but I got the gist of it.

"Ouch. Lennie, you need to have your mom text me some photos of it so I can see your cut," I commiserated with him.

"Yeah, I will. It was gross. It bled *a lot*. And Willie started crying."

"I did not!" Willie shouted. "Well, you cried too. And you got blood on Mom's pajamas. And Dad was mad. He even called you a 'little shit'!"

Chloe sighed. I hated it when the twins told me Victor called them names and yelled at them. I knew what it felt like, and I didn't want that for them.

"William, don't say shit," Chloe admonished.

"Why not? Dad says shit. And damn, and hell, and fu–"

Chloe cut him off. "William, enough. Your father shouldn't say shit, or any of those words."

"Hey, did you guys get the package I sent yet?" I asked, trying to change the subject.

"Nooo," Lennie said.

"What did you send?" Willie yelled. He was a yeller and didn't understand the concept of an "inside voice" yet.

Chloe groaned. "Please tell me it's not more screaming monkeys or water pistols."

I smiled. "No, I promise. These are completely quiet and don't require any assembly or clean up."

Chloe was silent for a minute. "Why do I still have a bad feeling?"

"Chloe, I promise. It's nothing bad."

"We're okay with something bad," Willie chimed in.

I had to laugh. "I bet you are."

I talked to them for a few more minutes until they'd had enough and ran into their bedroom to get dressed for school.

"Bye, Lolly!"

"Make sure your clothes match," Chloe yelled after them. "I swear those two try to put on the most mismatched outfits just to embarrass me. When are you coming back to New York?"

"I don't know yet. I just got done with my last final a few days ago, and after graduation tomorrow I need to go back to Palm Springs and take care of a few things."

Chloe paused. "I'm sorry your father isn't coming to see you graduate. He's still angry about you transferring. It's annoying to have to listen to him rant about it."

"It's okay. I knew he wouldn't come. We haven't talked in months."

Chloe paused. "Well, I can't take the boys out of school, but how do you feel about us coming to see you when the school year ends? Maybe for a week or so?"

I was so surprised I didn't answer for a minute. "Who exactly would be coming?"

"Oh. Just the boys and me."

"I'd love that," I answered, relieved Victor wouldn't be with them. "But are you okay to meet me in Palm Springs? I planned to go back there for a month before the house sells."

"I've never been to Palm Springs. I think we'd enjoy it."

"That sounds wonderful. I have to warn you though, it's going to be hot that time of year—like center of the sun hot. But you guys are more than welcome to stay with me at Fern's house."

"It would likely be after the boys get out of school in a few weeks. We'd love to stay there, if you're comfortable with that. You've mentioned her pool is nice."

Chloe had called me a couple of days after Fern's death to offer her condolences, and she'd sent flowers along with a pleasant note, adding Victor's name to it. I doubted Victor knew she'd sent anything.

I hadn't heard from Victor since winter break, when I'd flown to New York for a week to spend time with the twins. I'd stayed in Brooklyn with a good friend from college, and went to the house on weekdays when I knew Victor would be at work.

I'd texted him to let him know I was coming. He never responded, and I hadn't heard from him since.

Two days after talking with Chloe and the boys, I received a string of photos and texts from her. Lennie's stitches and black eye were indeed impressive, and I especially loved the video of the boys running around in their new matching cowboy hats.

A few weeks ago, I'd seen the cowboy hats while I was at the mall at Caesar's Palace trying to replace my broken-down running shoes. The cowboy hats were expensive, but I knew the boys would love them. So I held off on new running shoes, and a few groceries, because every five-year-old boy should have a cowboy hat.

I also thought Victor would loathe them. I decided it was a win-win.

Chloe sent a meme of herself slapping her forehead and mentioned in her texts that the boys tried to sleep with their hats on that night. But Victor did *not* like the hats and wouldn't let them. I decided the cowboy hats had been worth every penny.

The day before graduation, I ran over to the university bookstore to pick up my cap and gown for the graduation ceremony. When the clerk pulled up my name, he looked at me and smiled.

"Congratulations on graduating cum laude. That's impressive, especially for law school." He pointed at the gold cords sitting on top of my graduation robe in the plastic wrapping. The store clerk was good-looking in a bad-boy-next-door kind of way, and had a tattoo sleeve up his right arm.

I looked at him blankly for a moment, a little distracted by his smile. "Sorry, what did you say?"

He eyed me critically. "Congratulations on graduating cum laude? With honors? You knew, didn't you?" He pointed to the gold cord again.

I stared at him a moment longer, then started tearing up a little. I didn't say anything for a few seconds, and pulled a breath in and out through my nose.

H smiled a little. "You didn't know, I take it. Well, I'm happy I could tell you then."

I was a little embarrassed about tearing up, and shook my head. "No, I didn't." I handed him my credit card, and he looked down at my name.

"Well, Laurel Payne, I wish you weren't graduating this year, so I could see you around the bookstore more often. Or even outside the bookstore."

Blushing a little, I smiled because I wasn't dead and he oozed flirty charm. I looked at his name tag. "Thanks, Dylan."

Dylan grinned as he rang me up. "Really, congratulations. That represents a lot of damn hard work. I hope your family is proud."

I thanked him again and waved goodbye, then automatically reached for my phone to call Fern with the good news. I stopped short when I realized I couldn't call her. And I wouldn't be calling Victor.

My buoyant mood deflated as I walked across the commons, and my chest ached with how much I missed Fern. But I shook myself and texted my roommates to give them the short version of finding out I'd be graduating cum laude from hot-guy Dylan in the bookstore.

Ramone and Jonathan had to work on Thursday longer than they expected, so we met early Friday for breakfast at the Hard Rock Café before the graduation ceremony. It was close to the law school, and Luke came with me.

Joey had gone out to celebrate with some of her classmates after finishing their last final. She hadn't gotten back until after three in the morning, and she groaned miserably into her pillow when I knocked on her bedroom door.

She sounded horrible, so I left Gatorade and a bottle of ibuprofen on her nightstand, with sticky notes that read "DRINK ME" and "EAT ME" on them.

Jonathan and Ramone had already ordered everyone mimosas to celebrate by the time we walked in.

Luke shook their hands. "Thanks for letting me tag along. Joey's a little hung over, so it's just me." We scooted into the booth.

"We know law school can be brutal, but it's not a weekend. Is this typical for her?" Jonathan asked.

"No. She rarely drinks. She says she can't afford to get sick." Luke answered.

"She's better than us, and we're pretty lightweight." I pointed to Luke. "She had to take out student loans for law school, so she's not going to jeopardize her career and her ability to pay them back."

Luke looked at me quizzically when I mentioned Joey's student loans without mentioning my own. His schooling was paid for through the National Guard, but he knew I'd taken out loans for at least half of law school because he'd heard me commiserating with Joey about it. I gave him a slight shake of my head.

Jonathan watched us. "Well, I hope she's feeling better so she can join us tonight."

Our server came to the table just then to take our order.

Chapter 9

The graduation ceremony later that morning was brief, and most of the speakers kept their remarks short. No one was sad about that. But I was affected when I watched several of my classmates walk across the stage to get their diplomas. For most of us, law school had been a long, intense journey.

We'd suffered and bonded through grueling study sessions, sleep deprivation, and grade curves. And now we were moving on. It had been a month of endings for me.

After the ceremony, I took some photos with several friends and said goodbye to a few professors and staff. Then I found Luke and the boys in the foyer. I basked in Jonathan and Ramone's surprise and delight over me graduating with honors.

Ramone fingered my gold cords. "Laurel, we're so proud of you. We didn't know you'd be graduating with honors. How come you didn't tell us? Did Fern know?"

"I didn't even know *myself* until I picked up my cap and gown two days ago."

"How could you not know? Darling, you did check your grades periodically, didn't you?" Ramone asked.

"Yes, thank you very much. But I didn't know what the GPA cutoff would be, and I didn't think I was even eligible as a transfer student."

I hadn't obsessed about my grades the last two years and hadn't interviewed with any firms. I didn't know where I'd be living when I graduated, or if Fern would have been alive then. The thought of my unemployment made my stomach tighten, but I pushed it aside.

Jonathan turned to me. "Have you heard from your father today at all?"

"No, and I'm not surprised." I shrugged, but my shoulders felt tight.

Ramone hugged me. "I'm sorry, Laurel. I can't imagine missing my daughter's law school graduation because she moved away for a couple of years to help a sick family member."

Luke turned and hugged me as well, and I squeezed him back. "Thanks for being here today. It means a lot."

"Are you coming back to Las Vegas this summer?" he asked.

"Yes. I'll need to clean out my room when I figure out where I'll be living. Is your friend still planning to move in?"

"Yeah."

When I transferred to UNLV, Fern told me she had some real estate connections in Las Vegas, and she'd find me a suitable place to live. I didn't know that meant she planned to buy a little townhouse near the law school. By the time I found out, she'd already purchased it and was having the townhouse updated.

I'd been upset at first and didn't feel like I could accept Fern's generosity, until Jonathan told me she simply looked at it as a real estate investment. Fern planned to hold it for a few years and earn appreciation, then sell it for a profit. So when Joey and Luke became my roommates and rented the other two rooms, I'd been relieved and grateful we could cover costs and expenses.

"I have to go. I have Guard this weekend. Can you get a ride home?" Luke asked.

"Yes. I'm going to miss the hell out of you guys. You and Joey saved me when I first transferred here. Please come visit me in Palm Springs this summer."

"Palm Springs is gonna be hot as Satan's balls this summer." He tugged on my tassel. "I hear it's hotter than Las Vegas most of the time. Maybe we'll come see you in October over fall break. We could go camping in Joshua Tree."

"Oh, thank God," Ramone said. "She'll have someone else to go with her. She's always trying to drag us out there. My idea of a good day camping is finding a nice out-of-town spa with a mud bath."

Jonathan shook his head. "There's no such thing as a good day camping." He turned to Luke. "We're sorry you'll miss her graduation party tonight. Good luck next year, and don't be a stranger."

"I don't know where I'll be in October, but let's plan to get together," I told Luke.

He hugged me one more time, kissed my cheek, and took off. I watched him go, feeling depressed that I probably wouldn't see him again for almost six months.

Ramone squeezed my arm in silent understanding. "Let's plan on meeting next week to discuss Fern's estate when you get back to Palm Springs."

I turned to him. "Monday morning is out. Sebastian Mendoza is coming to Fern's house bright and early to review the new security system with me." I grimaced. "I can't wait."

Jonathan grinned. "Monday mornings are usually pretty busy at the office anyway." He pulled out his phone to check his work calendar. "I didn't know Mendoza made house calls anymore. He usually sends one of his crew."

"That's true." Ramone looked down at his own phone calendar. "Martina told me he gets too impatient and rude, and I think he's been propositioned a few times."

I thought about Mia, the woman at Fern's life celebration, and laughed. "That probably doesn't go over well."

Ramone smiled. "No, I hear it doesn't."

Jonathan studied his calendar. "Let's meet on Monday afternoon at three. Does that work?"

I nodded, still thinking about Sebastian. I could see him offending his clients with his abrupt demeanor, and they'd probably annoy him right back. I thought he had the personality of a rabid, feral badger. It was too bad he didn't look like one.

My graduation celebration that evening at the hotel suite was a small, relaxed party with good food and a handful of my favorite people. The champagne and hors d'oeuvres, and the spectacular view of the Las Vegas skyline, lent to the festive, low-key mood. Fern knew me well, I reflected.

Joey had valiantly rallied from her raging hangover, and she drove over with me. But she turned a little green when Ramone offered her a full flute of champagne.

"No, thank you," she croaked.

I shook my head at him. "Ramone, you're just being mean. Joey, there's ice water at the bar. I also have some ibuprofen in my purse."

"I'll have water. I already took a couple of painkillers—I just hope they kick in soon."

"You may not feel well, but you look fabulous," Ramone told her. He turned to me with mock surprise. "And so do you, darling." I had on the black dress Fern had given me for her life celebration.

Later that evening, Ramone and I gazed out at the sparkling lights in the Las Vegas skyline.

I turned to him. "I wanted to wear this dress since Fern couldn't be here to celebrate my graduation in person. Now I know she's here in spirit."

He smiled sadly. "Of course, she would have reminded you that wearing black this time of year in Las Vegas is not de rigueur."

He was right, and it made me smile a little and miss Fern even more.

When Joey and I got home late that evening, Joey sighed as she sat on the couch and took her shoes off.

"Am I being selfish to wish you had another year of law school left?"

"Yes, you are." I shuddered. "Don't wish that evil on me."

"Damn it, I'm going to miss you. You're the preppy East Coast sister from another mister I didn't know I always wanted."

"Aww, thanks. I love you too. And if you ever fall on your ass, I'll laugh first, but then help you get back up."

She chuckled then sighed. "Who's going to make me a shitty martini every Monday?"

"Shitty martinis? So rude." I unbuckled my shoes, then flopped down on the couch next to her and grabbed her hand.

She smirked. "Hey, I said what I said. Dirty martinis are just... ick."

"I'm counting on you to carry on Martini Mondays here, even if you throw them on Wednesday night and serve Diet Coke instead. It's tradition. As long as you put your drinks in fancy martini glasses, you're good to go."

"We'll still have them. Our geriatric neighbors would revolt if we didn't."

That was probably true. We'd invited our next-door neighbor, Ida, one Monday evening almost two years ago. We wanted to thank her for watering our scraggly little flowerpots outside our front door and bringing in our packages sometimes.

Ida loved Martini Monday so much, she invited herself the next week and told a few of her friends in the neighborhood about it. And they'd invited themselves. It had snowballed from there.

I yawned loud and long. "It's so late. I need to go to bed."

She sighed. "Yeah, I have to work two shifts tomorrow."

We both hauled ourselves up off the couch and hugged each other goodnight.

Joey squeezed my arm. "If I don't see you tomorrow, make sure you find me before you leave on Sunday so I can say goodbye."

Then I headed off to bed. Because I had to get on the road tomorrow so I could meet grumpy-asshole-Sebastian bright and early on Monday morning.

Chapter 10

I pulled into Fern's driveway in my little sedan that was packed with clothes and personal items. Tomorrow morning, Sebastian Mendoza would be at my doorstep bright and early, but in the twilight, the house looked quiet and a little forlorn.

The bougainvillea still bloomed, and the porch lights glowed in the dark. Martina must have left them on for me. I loved the house, but I dreaded going inside without Fern or Martina there.

The house still smelled faintly of lemon cleaner, and it felt so still and quiet. I reflexively started calling out to Fern, but quelled the impulse. Getting busy, I brought the rest of my things inside.

That night, I slept poorly and had strange dreams about my mother, Fern, and Jackson taking me to brunch at their favorite Italian restaurant in New York City. Then they walked me to the subway station and told me I needed to go home and check on my little brothers.

I couldn't figure out how old I was in my dream, where "home" was, or if my brothers were even alive yet. I woke up sweaty and despondent and lay still for a few minutes. Then I rolled out of bed and went for a run since I was already sweaty.

The early morning temperature was a balmy eighty degrees when I started out. It'd taken me a while to adjust to the hot dry temperatures when I first moved to Las Vegas, but the winter months more than made up for it.

I continued to sweat as I passed a few other people out running or walking their dogs, trying to take advantage of the cooler morning. One consolation was the late May evenings, which were usually perfect for dining and sitting outside.

By the time I got home, I'd shaken off some of the melancholy and felt a little better. I made a big pot of coffee, took a shower, and got ready for the day.

After eating a quick breakfast, I went outside and cleaned up the yard a bit. The backyard area was surrounded by a tall block wall and Ficus hedges.

It was completely private and peaceful, and my favorite part of Fern's house. As I finished up, I heard the front doorbell ring.

Hurrying through the house, I opened the front door just as Sebastian leaned over to ring the doorbell again. He had on a nice short-sleeved white shirt with his company logo, and olive pants that fit him well.

I stared up at him. "I was in the backyard. Come in."

Sebastian stepped into the foyer, then closed the door behind him. I stood there, looking up at him with the dustpan in my hand.

As the seconds passed, I became annoyed at his lack of greeting, and waited him out. I'd grown up with Victor and his passive-aggressive silent treatments. I could stand here all day if I needed to.

He finally looked at the dustpan in my hand. "The yard crew is coming this week. You don't have to do that."

"I wanted to."

We continued silently staring at each other. Sebastian broke eye contact and glanced down at my legs, then back up at me. His dark brown eyes bored into mine. It was such a shame he was so good-looking.

I finally sighed, breaking the tension. "I'm just spit balling here, but based on our last texts, I assume you want to discuss the new house alarm and cameras. But unfortunately, you'll have to talk to show me how they work. Or, once again, you can still just give me the codes and manuals."

"I have no problem talking, Ms. Payne."

"Call me Laurel. My mother was Ms. Payne."

"You called me Mr. Morena, then Mr. Mayberry." He shrugged. "I didn't want to assume."

I suddenly felt a little guilty. "Right. I do remember your last name, but you were being rude, and I wanted to annoy you. Let me go throw this away, and you can show me the security."

"Huh." Sebastian blinked slowly, but didn't say anything else. If I planned to wait for an apology from him, I'd probably be standing here all day.

I threw the leaves and fronds away, and when I came back Sebastian stood in Fern's kitchen looking around.

I leaned back against the counter. "It's strange being here without Fern, isn't it? Would you like coffee?"

Sebastian nodded. "It is strange. And yes." He sat down on a barstool.

I poured him a cup and held up the half-and-half container in silent question. He shook his head. I poured myself another cup and added a splash of cream.

I watched Sebastian over the rim. "How did you know Fern? And Martina?"

Sebastian eyed me for so long, I wondered if he might not answer. "Martina's my cousin. I met Fern at Cecilia's, and eventually introduced them."

I put down my coffee cup in surprise. "No way! I never would've guessed you're related to Martina. She's so friendly and nice." I winced, realizing how rude that sounded. Although it was kind of the truth.

I tried to change the subject. "It was great she could stay here over the past month."

"Her husband's a mean, lazy fucker. He was mad she had a nice place to stay." Sebastian fell silent again, and I was a bit surprised he'd spoken several full sentences to me.

He put his coffee mug down as if realizing the same thing. "I have other shit to do today. I hope it doesn't take you too long to figure the system out."

And just like that, the grumpy asshole was back.

I rolled my eyes. "Okay, Grumpy Butt. I'm all ears."

"I prefer Mr. Mulberry."

I shook my head. "It was Mayberry."

His lip twitched. "That too."

"Too bad, you've graduated to Grumpy, like in the *Seven Dwarfs*. I think I'll call you G for short."

He shook his head, and I smiled.

Rolling my shoulders, I pointed at the security keypad. "Okay, let's do this. What do you need to show me?"

We went over the system and the outdoor cameras, and he walked through how to adjust the settings.

"I think you got it," Sebastian admitted grudgingly after I'd added the apps to my cell phone and pulled up the cameras.

"Gee. Thanks, G." I laughed at my own bad joke. I'd heard a lot of mediocre jokes from Deputy Millet over the past year, and it felt good dishing them out.

Sebastian stared at me blankly. I shrugged.

We also discussed the yard and pool maintenance schedules and pest control visits. All while Sebastian spoke in short, clipped sentences.

"Pool guys are Monday and Thursday."

I nodded while I took a few notes on my phone.

He put his hands on his hips. "Pest control will text you."

"Okay."

"Yard crew comes every Wednesday."

When Sebastian finished his instructions and was getting ready to leave, I couldn't resist one more jab. "I've got some constructive criticism, G. You shouldn't talk so much, and you need to stop interrupting people. I couldn't get a word in edge-wise."

Sebastian shook his head and started for the door.

I yelled after him, "I'm having Martini Monday tonight. Fern would've wanted you to come. Feel free to bring a date or plus one. Although I doubt it'll be Mia." I grinned at his back.

Sebastian stopped at the front door. I wasn't sure, but I thought he might've banged his head against it.

"What time?" he asked tersely.

"Seven."

He nodded and opened it.

"Goodbye G! You have a nice day too!" I said loudly right before he shut the door.

Later that afternoon, I walked into Ramone and Jonathan's law office. It was blistering hot outside, and the cold air conditioning felt delicious on my skin.

"Hi, Grace. It's good to see you."

"Hey, Laurel." Grace, their longtime paralegal and good friend, greeted me when I walked in. She didn't look up as she typed, probably sending an IM to let them know I'd arrived.

Every time I heard Grace talk, it reminded me of Roz, the nasally receptionist from *Monsters, Inc.* Grace even sported cat-eye reading glasses that hung on a fancy chain around her neck.

"How's your golf game nowadays? Are you still getting out regularly?" I asked her.

Grace lit up. She lived for two things—golf and her wife, Sheila. "I lowered my handicap by two strokes, and even qualified for the Super Senior Women's State Am this year."

I patted her arm. "That's so exciting. I bet Sheila's happy for you."

Grace beamed. "I let them both know you're here. You can wait in the conference room since this is an official visit."

"Thanks." I walked back and planted myself in their smartly furnished conference room.

Jonathan came in a few minutes later. "Ramone's coming. The client he's talking to conveniently forgets that Ramone is gay, not her therapist, and happily married."

"Ah. Awkward. I'm sure he handles it with his usual charm."

"Yes, but he'd rather not hear her whine for hours on end. He's reminded her, in writing, that therapists charge less per hour than he does."

Ramone bustled in with a file and his laptop. "Hey, sweetie. Nice dress."

"All right," Jonathan said. "Let's get this official meeting started. Then we can unofficially decompress later tonight over shitty martinis." Jonathan didn't like martinis.

Ramone sat down and leaned back. "I have Fern's file and notes here. How much do you know about her estate?"

"Not a lot. I was in high school when Jackson died. She always planned to gift the bulk of it to women's shelters in New York and here in California."

"What holdings and assets are you aware of?" Jonathan asked.

I shrugged, wondering why there were bringing this up. "Her home in Palm Springs, and the small property in Italy." I paused. "And her townhome in Las Vegas. I don't know about anything else. She did say she planned to keep the townhome while Luke and Joey finish law school, no matter what happened. I hope that's still the case." I looked at Jonathan, seeking confirmation. "They're getting another roommate, so they'll continue to pay the full rent and expenses." I shifted in my seat, suddenly worried.

Ramone and Jonathan exchanged glances, and Ramone leaned forward. "She changed her will and trust about five years ago.

She took out a very sizable life insurance policy and named the women's shelters as beneficiaries."

"Ramone and I were hoping she mentioned this to you," Jonathan added. "Fern was our client, and we couldn't tell you unless she gave us permission, or we would've said something. The women's shelters will be well taken care of, but the bulk of her estate is going to you."

I heard him but I didn't compute what he said.

"I'm sorry?" I asked.

"Most of her estate is going to you," Jonathan repeated.

I rocked back and forth in the chair and thought for a moment, looking down at the table without seeing it.

"Okay, okay." I struggled to process what this meant to me. "So, Joey and Luke should be able to stay in the townhome for a little while then. That's a relief."

I looked at Jonathan again for confirmation. He was less emotional and more pragmatic than Ramone. He just sat patiently, waiting for me to process the news.

I stared at them. "And the Palm Springs home won't have to be put up for sale in the fall."

Ramone studied me. "What are your thoughts about the house?" he asked quietly.

My eyes filled with tears then, as the magnitude of what they'd told me sunk in.

"I think..." My voice was thick, and I cleared my throat. "I'll keep it and live in it for a while if that's okay." Then I wouldn't be homeless in a couple of months.

Ramone squeezed my hand. "Oh, sweetheart, you're breaking my heart. We'd love for you to keep it, even though it's not up to us. Come here, you need a hug."

Jonathan sighed and rubbed his eyes. "Ramone, you promised to stay professional during this meeting."

"I lied," Ramone answered unrepentantly, giving me another big hug. "And you knew I wouldn't be able to, so don't act so surprised and disappointed."

Over an hour later, I walked out of their office, absently waving goodbye to Grace. I still didn't know exactly what Fern's estate entailed. But I was emotionally drained and cried out, so we set another meeting in a couple of weeks after I'd settled in.

They gave me instructions to take a copy of the living will to Fern's bank and get the account switched over so I could access it to pay the monthly bills and have a little money to live on. They didn't know how much I needed it. Apparently, I was already listed as the beneficiary on her account.

Standing outside their law firm door for a moment, I stared blankly at the floor. Someone with a deep voice cleared his throat in front of me. I looked up and saw Sebastian staring down at me. He had the most beautiful chocolate brown eyes, I thought absently.

"Hello," I croaked.

He looked at my face for a moment, then motioned to it. "You've got something–" he started to say, pointing under my nose.

I could feel a watery substance dripping a little from my nose. My eyes were also probably puffy and red. But I couldn't bring myself to care. "I know. I can feel it. But..." I gazed past his shoulder, wondering why Fern hadn't prepared me. And I wanted her here so I could yell at her right then.

Sebastian let out a sigh powerful enough to part my hair. "Stay." He turned and went inside his office.

I absently watched him through the glass door. Leaning over the tall counter, he grabbed something, then walked back out with a handful of tissues and handed me the wad. "Now you don't have to use the back of your hand."

Then he tucked a strand of my hair behind my ear. I stared up at him like he'd just struck me. Stepping back, he folded his arms. "Your hair was going to get in it."

I gave a watery snort and wiped at my nose and eyes. "You're funny, G. That sentence had more than three words, I'm impressed."

"You okay?" he asked reluctantly.

"Yes. No. I will be, eventually. I just had a meeting with Ramone and Jonathan about Fern's estate." I gulped. "I keep getting gobsmacked by that woman."

He sighed again. "Don't we all, Snotty."

I tilted my head. "Are you calling me one of the Seven Dwarfs' names? Because if you are, it's Sneezy, not Snotty."

He shrugged. "Sneezy, Snotty. Same thing."

I squinted at him. "It's not the same thing, Grumpy. Get it right. Thanks for the tissues." I didn't sound very thankful. "I'll see you and your plus one tonight."

He *still* didn't say "goodbye," or "see you later." He just turned and started walking away. Good Lord, the man needed a firm lesson in basic decorum and manners. His poor parents must have given up on his grumpy ass.

Rolling my eyes at his back, I muttered loudly, "Thank you for the invitation, Laurel. See you tonight, Laurel."

I thought I heard a soft chuckle as I turned and walked out.

Chapter 11

My latest conversation with Sebastian rolled through my mind as I wandered through my favorite grocery store, distracted and without a grocery list. I idly wondered who he would bring tonight, and whether he'd even come.

Our old housekeeper warned me that going to the grocery store without a list was a bad idea. I also hadn't eaten lunch yet, so it was the perfect trifecta for a grocery shopping disaster—I was hungry, distracted, and had no list.

As I wandered through the bakery section, I pondered on Fern leaving me her Palm Springs home and her other real estate. I also wondered where I should take the bar exam. Now that I'd graduated, I needed a bar license and a job to actually practice law.

My choices had suddenly opened up. My plan had been to finish law school, be there for Fern until she passed away, then go back to New York after I graduated.

Only the thought made me queasy. I loved so many things about New York, but I didn't want to go back while Victor still lived there.

After circling the bakery area twice, I decided to contemplate my life, the bar exam, and my career another day. I went through a few aisles, then finally hit the liquor section.

Getting my phone out, I started searching for different martini recipes. I saw classic recipes, fruity recipes, and even a couple of vegetable variations—hard pass on those.

And then I came across the one I wanted to try. A Snickertini—a martini that tasted like my favorite candy bar. The recipe called for caramel vodka, Irish cream, Baileys, mini Snickers, whipped cream, and a few other high-calorie ingredients. I quickly scanned the recipe again, then went back through the store.

Martina brought one of her other cousins, Matías, and his wife, Camila, to Martini Monday. I found out Matías owned the pool maintenance and installation company Fern used.

"Where'd you end up moving to?" Ramone asked Martina while he pulled little quiches and mushroom caps out of the oven.

I assembled the martini ingredients and listened to the conversation. Martina had separated from her husband a while ago and was living temporarily in Fern's house while I'd finished law school.

Martina sat down on a barstool. "I'm staying with Sebastian in his spare bedroom right now. He says it's fine, but he's not the roommate type."

"Doesn't he live in that two-bedroom he remodeled over by the east end of the Tahquitz golf course?" Jonathan asked.

"Yeah. It's a nice place. But it only has two bedrooms, and he uses his spare bedroom as a home office."

Matías chuckled. "I think Sebastian is more worried about losing his naked hot tub time. His hot tub is sweet, and his backyard is completely private. Camila and I should know. We used it a few weeks ago when Sebastian went out of town."

Camila blushed and pushed his shoulder. "Matías, nobody wants to hear it! Jeez."

He grinned and wiggled his eyebrows. "What? It wasn't the first time, either."

Camila turned bright red and glared at him.

"I hope you used a condom." Sebastian stood in the doorway with his arms crossed.

"Eww. Me too," Martina said. "I've been in that hot tub, and the pool. Multiple times."

Camila put her hands up to her face. "Would you all just stop?"

Ramone turned to Sebastian. "We need to have Martini Monday at your house next week. I want to see this hot tub."

"Fuck no."

"Wow, that must be some hot tub," I muttered.

Sebastian walked over and looked down at me. "You need to keep your front door locked."

Then he glanced down at the martini ingredients I'd lined up. "What's all this?"

I handed him the printed Snickertini recipe. I'd already drizzled chocolate sauce in the martini glasses and put them in the freezer for a few minutes to set.

He grunted as he read through the recipe. Then he watched me pick up another ingredient. Finally, he nudged me away with his hip, taking the bottle of Baileys out of my hand, and setting it down on the counter.

"They'll be too sweet." He took over assembling the martinis.

I shrugged and moved over. "Okay, G. Have at it."

The kitchen went quiet, and when I looked up, several pairs of eyes were on us.

"What?" I asked.

Ramone shook his head. "Nothing." Everyone started talking all at once.

When the Snickertinis were done, we took our drinks and food out to the back patio. It was still hot outside, so we set up a couple of misters. The tall palm trees rustled in the breeze, and a few crickets chirped around the yard.

Ramone raised his glass and made a toast. "Everyone, I propose a toast to Fern. This is our first Martini Monday without her. She was a truly fabulous woman, and she's sorely missed."

"To Fern," everyone toasted as they clinked their glasses around the table and drank. We were silent for a few moments.

Jonathan finally held up his glass. "This is delicious. Which means it doesn't taste like a martini at all. More like a liquid candy bar."

Martina smacked her lips together. "I can feel my insulin levels spiking. But it's yummy."

Camila elbowed Matías. "You need to learn how to make this."

"If it gets me another trip to Sebastian's hot tub, then absolutely."

Camila groaned, and everyone started laughing.

Jonathan took pity on Camila and changed the subject. "Sebastian, how do you like having Martina as a roommate?"

"It's fine." Sebastian reached over and took a mini quiche off my plate.

"Hey, get your own." I swatted at his hand.

He ignored me and popped the quiche into his mouth.

Martina pointed at Sebastian. "He's a good roommate. Unless you want someone who'll talk to you once in a while."

Sebastian looked at her. "We talk."

"Yeah, if you count two-word sentences and grunts," she retorted.

I barked out a laugh. "Oh, my God! I thought it was just me."

Sebastian shook his head and grabbed a mushroom cap off my plate.

I slapped at his hand again, and pointed at Martina. "Why don't you come back and stay here with me until you figure out your divorce and where you want to live?"

Martina stared at me, her drink suspended halfway to her lips.

"Well?" I continued. "There are two separate wings in this house. It's big by Palm Springs' standards. I also promise I'll talk to you, and it'll be more than two words at a time."

She carefully set her glass down. "Are you serious?"

"Yeah. Or I wouldn't have brought it up. It's so quiet here without Fern. I don't know where I'm going to practice law, but I should be here for at least six months."

I took another sip and moaned a little at the rich, chocolaty flavor. Sebastian stared at me.

"What? It's so good. Nice job, G." I patted his arm, then looked back to Martina. "I have to warn you, though. My stepmother and two little brothers are coming in a few weeks to visit me. The twins are awesome, but loud. And sassy. You should get along great."

Martina started nodding. "That would be wonderful. I'll pay rent and help with the utilities and groceries. I'll also keep cleaning the house."

"We'll clean together." I held up my glass across the table, and Martina clinked hers against it with a big smile.

Ramone cleared his throat. "On that thought. Lolly, what do you think about signing up for the California State bar exam? You can do late registration until the first day of June."

Jonathan sighed. "Why don't you 'fess up and tell her you already signed her up? I'm sure Fern was in on it too. I saw the email confirmation two months ago."

Ramone glared at him. "All right! It's true." He turned to me. "Fern and I already signed you up to take the California bar. It was her idea. Mostly."

Jonathan shook his head. "That's just great, throw her dead aunt under the bus."

"Well, it was! You know how Fern got when she had one of her brilliant ideas. No one could say no to the woman, not that I ever really wanted to."

Ramone turned back to me. "I already signed you up for the bar prep course too."

I stared at them, speechless. While my mouth hung open, Sebastian reached over and took a grape off my plate. I was having trouble processing, about both the bar exam and what was going on with Sebastian.

Matías looked over at Sebastian. "I guess now isn't a good time to talk with Laurel about the fixer-upper in Demuth Park."

Sebastian shook his head. "Probably not. We'll fill her in later."

I stared at Sebastian. "What are you talking about?"

He studied me. "Fern and I bought another fixer-upper together a while back. It's almost time to remodel it."

I rubbed my forehead. "Why am *I* a part of it?"

"Because you now legally own Fern's estate," Ramone told me patiently.

I pointed at him. "Which I didn't know about until today. Why do I always feel like I'm playing catch-up when Fern's involved?"

Jonathan leaned back and smiled. "Because you are."

I glared at Jonathan. "I appreciate your honesty." I didn't appreciate it at all.

Reaching over, I nabbed a strawberry off Sebastian's plate. He smiled slowly as he watched me bite into it.

Chapter 12

Martina moved in the next evening after she got off work. Sebastian helped her, and I realized I'd probably be seeing a lot more of him. But his long stare, and the butterflies in my stomach, worried me.

When I first met Martina, Fern told me she worried about her, and called Martina's husband a "reprobate and a scoundrel." Fern had good instincts, so I worried about Martina too.

The first two weeks Martina stayed at the house, I noticed she didn't bring much with her, she carefully cleaned the whole kitchen whenever she used it, and she always turned the volume way down when she watched TV or listened to music. I didn't know how to make her feel more comfortable, so I just let her figure things out.

We usually saw each other at breakfast, then in the evenings we sometimes had dinner together and watched a movie or swam. We also hosted a Martini Monday, and sometimes invited Jonathan, Ramone, and Sebastian to dinner.

The dinners with Sebastian were a little awkward at first. He seemed to watch me, but he still didn't talk much. I couldn't tell if he felt obligated to check on Martina, or if he enjoyed hanging out with us.

"Where's the rest of your stuff?" I finally asked Martina a couple of weeks after she moved in.

"Some of it's still over at Sebastian's house, and I have some long-term things in his storage unit."

"Why don't you bring the rest over? It would probably be nice for you to settle in, and we get along just fine. And stop scrubbing down the kitchen every time you use it. You make me feel like an underachiever."

She grinned, then hugged me. "Yeah, it's been great. You're right, I should settle in. Do you want to ride with me over to Sebastian's house to get my things? We could stop and pick up some shrimp tacos at La Perla's on the way back."

"Sounds good. I've been looking through bar exam material today, and I need some comfort food. I'm going to clean up a little first." I pointed to my old t-shirt and shorts.

Sebastian's house was located in a cul-de-sac east of the Tahquitz golf course, not far from Fern's house. Martina mentioned the property had been a wreck when he first bought it.

The house was now painted a light gray with charcoal trim, and his front door sported a bright tangerine color with horizontal glass panels. His front yard landscaping had raked lava rock and tall saguaro and barrel cacti. The overall effect was clean, with sharp crisp lines. It reminded me of him.

Martina parked in the driveway, and we went inside to grab the rest of her things.

As we walked through his living room, I quickly glanced around. He had a nice couch, two navy blue armchairs, and a large newer TV on his wall. There weren't many decorations, but a *Popular Mechanics* magazine and a couple of books sat on his coffee table near the remote.

Martina went into the spare bedroom, and I followed her. There was a bed tucked in the corner, and a couple of black-and-white framed maps hung on the wall. The room was a little messy where she'd left some of her belongings, but Sebastian's desk was clutter-free.

Martina pointed towards the kitchen. "I'm going to grab a few garbage bags. I forgot to bring boxes."

I walked over to the prints on the wall to get a closer look, then glanced around the room. I was looking through the books on the bookshelf, when I heard a loud knock on the front door, then a few seconds later a man shouting.

At first, I wondered if it was one of Sebastian's neighbors, then I heard what the man was saying to Martina.

"You fucking bitch, Marty. Do you think you can just walk away and blame me for everything? And I'm going to let your fat ass go?" I thought his voice sounded a little slurred.

I pulled my phone out of my back pocket and turned on the video as I ran down Sebastian's hallway. Martina stood in front of the man, trying to block him from coming into the house. He grabbed her upper arms and squeezed.

He appeared to be in his late twenties, and had on casual work clothes. The man was blandly handsome, but his face was mean and angry. I was pretty sure it was Kenny, Martina's estranged husband.

He stood about six inches taller than Martina and weighed at least fifty pounds more than her. Kenny pushed his way into the foyer, then shook Martina hard, and shoved her back.

"I called the police, asshole," I lied loudly as I stalked toward him with my phone up. I hadn't had time to call the police, but he didn't know that. I *hated* bullies.

Adrenaline coursed through me, but I willed my hands and voice not to shake. "They're on the way right now. I'm also recording you. Martina, step back behind me."

Martina stood there, shaken and crying a little, with her hands in front of her as if trying to ward him off.

"Martina," I said again. I reached forward and grabbed her hand, then gently pulled her behind me and away from the man. "You must be the ex-husband. They forgot to mention what a *pinche pendejo* you are."

The man's face got even redder, and he took a threatening step toward us. "Who the fuck are you?"

I shuffled back, taking Martina with me. "This is not your house, and you're trespassing right now."

I scrambled to remember what Pamela and my criminal law professor had said about giving notice to a trespasser, and the elements needed for a protective order. Or maybe a restraining order? Oh, hell, I couldn't remember. But I doubted this guy knew the difference.

"You need to leave. And do not call, text, or contact Martina in any way from now on, unless it's through your attorney. Or she's going to file a protective order against you."

He reared back. "The fuck I will!"

"If you need to contact her, you go through your attorneys. If you need to drop anything off for her—attorneys. I think you get the picture. Right, Martina?" I gently squeezed her hand.

Martina nodded. "Yes." Her voice got louder. "And I'm sure your lawyer charges more than mine, even though he's a moron. I hope you have to use him. A lot."

"I'm not going through our fucking lawyers," he said, taking a menacing step toward her.

"Don't even think about it unless you want to add assault charges," I snapped. "And she has a lot of family and friends who are not afraid of some jackass like you."

"Do you think I care about her stupid fucking family?"

"Do you think Sebastian won't kick your ass when he finds out you assaulted Martina *in his house*?" I shot back. "Leave. Now."

He stood there, breathing heavily, looking at us with naked hatred in his eyes. But I could see fear creeping in.

I held my phone higher. "The police should be here in about thirty seconds. You probably don't want to still be inside when they get here, Kenny."

Kenny looked at Martina and pointed his finger toward her face. "This is not done, you little bitch," he spat.

"Gah, make up your mind! First you call her a fat ass and then you call her a little bitch," I mocked, trying to deflect him from getting in Martina's face again. "She's hot, sweet, funny, and *way* too good for you. And everyone knows it."

Martina was beautiful and kind. And a little crazy. I had no idea how she'd ended up with someone like this guy, and I wouldn't let him run her down. "You also shouldn't be calling *anyone* fat with that beer belly." I pointed down at his slightly protruding belly with my free hand.

He turned on me. "This is none of your business, you fucking cunt. If I ever see you again without a camera in my face, you're going to be sorry."

I rolled my eyes. "Martina, has he always been this dumb? He keeps threatening us on live video. You just can't make this stuff up."

"You two better watch yourselves," he said softly.

Kenny gave us both another hateful stare, but he probably couldn't think of another insult because he stormed out the front door and slammed it behind him.

I ran to the door and opened it in time to see him stomp toward Martina's car. He had his keys out, ready to do damage.

"You can add criminal mischief and burglary to your charges if you damage her car." I conspicuously held my phone up and followed him outside.

He seemed to lose all control and started yelling obscenities, then turned and stalked toward me.

"Give me your fucking phone, you stupid fucking bitch!" he screeched in a high-pitched voice.

I backed up a few steps. "See that security camera up there?" I pointed to the discreet camera I'd noticed when we walked in. "You touch my phone, and you'll also be charged with interruption of a communication device. It's a felony."

He finally stopped, then turned and stomped to his car. When he peeled away, I blew out a breath and stopped recording. I was shaking a little and felt sick to my stomach.

Martina stood just outside the front door, bent over with her hands on her knees, crying and laughing at the same time. I approached her slowly, not sure what to do.

"Don't have a mental breakdown on me, Marty."

She stopped crying and started scowling. "I hate that nickname. He's the only one who calls me that." She wiped her eyes and took a deep breath, then let it out.

"Yeah, Martina is better," I agreed. "No offense, but I don't like him. At all."

She stared down the road where he'd peeled out. "I don't like him either. This could have gone a lot worse, and I think we need straight tequila shots to go with our shrimp tacos after that."

"Did you have to call him? I think we handled the situation just fine," I grumbled as she parked in Fern's driveway next to Sebastian's gray truck. We grabbed the food sacks and got out.

He'd pulled up right before us, and he got out and scanned us carefully.

His eyes were furrowed and angry. "You guys okay?"

Martina nodded. "Yeah, we're fine. Thanks to my smartass bodyguard." She pointed to me. "Laurel got the whole thing on video. And she called Kenny fat, a *pinche pendejo*, a dumbass, and maybe an asshole."

Sebastian raised his eyebrows and slowly turned to me. "Remind me never to make you angry."

"Too late, Grumpy."

He grinned, and I blinked. He had a killer smile and beautiful white teeth.

"She also told him he has to go through the lawyers from now on to contact me. Then Kenny called her the C word." We started unloading our dinner onto the kitchen counter. "Laurel, send me the video. I'll go get my computer, and we can watch it while we eat."

I stopped short. "Hmm, we don't need to watch it. You already told him what happened." Martina ignored me and went to get her computer.

Sebastian grabbed some plates from the cupboard. "Text me a copy as well."

"I really don't want to."

"I really don't care," he answered, walking over to me.

"No."

Sebastian set the plates down and silently held his hand out, palm up. I stared at it.

"Give me your phone, *cielo*," Sebastian said softly.

The endearment and his smile must have paralyzed my brain. I slowly pulled out my phone and handed it to him. He took it and punched in my code.

"Hey! How'd you know my code?"

He didn't look at me. "You say it out loud sometimes when you unlock your phone."

"I do not. Do I?"

"Yeah, you do," Martina answered from the hallway, her computer in hand.

Sebastian pulled the video up and forwarded it to Martina and himself.

I pointed at Martina. "You can share this with your attorney and maybe the police, but no one else, okay?" Then I thought about it. "Maybe Ramone and Jonathan too. But that's it."

Martina rolled her eyes. "Ramone *is* my attorney. Now shush, I've got it pulled up."

Sebastian handed me back my phone. "You need to change your code, and not say it out loud anymore."

I nodded and reluctantly shuffled over, my food forgotten, to watch the video.

When I heard myself call Kenny a *pinche pendejo* on the screen, I winced. "He was being a complete dick."

"Shhh," Sebastian said, not taking his eyes off the screen. He grabbed me absentmindedly around the waist and pulled me to the side to move me out of the way.

My phone had mostly captured the red-faced, irate Kenny, and only my voice could be heard. Thank God. It was still pretty bad though.

We finally got to the end of the video, and I turned to them. "The communication device charge wouldn't really be a felony, but I'm pretty sure Kenny doesn't know that."

Neither one of them spoke. Then Martina looked over at Sebastian and started laughing. He shook his head and grinned back at her.

Martina finally sobered up. "That jackass was going to key my car."

Sebastian put his hand on Martina's shoulder. "I think this gives you serious leverage."

"You have no idea what an asshole he's turned into over the past year." Martina's eyes started filling with tears.

I pointed a finger at her. "Don't start crying, Marty. If you cry, I'll cry too."

Martina glared at me, but she'd stopped crying. "I *really* hate that nickname."

"What? Is it too soon?"

Sebastian laughed and pulled me into him. "Nice work, *mi cielo*," he said quietly in my ear.

Martina stared at us, and I stared back at her, my mouth hanging open. I was seriously freaked out.

"Okay, let's eat!" I practically shouted. I didn't know exactly what was happening, and I liked Sebastian's casual hug and endearment way too much.

Chapter 13

Sebastian spent most evenings with us over the next few days. I felt jumpy and out of sorts with him around, but I was getting used to his taciturn personality.

On Wednesday, I already had an appointment with Jonathan and Ramone, but we got sidetracked with the "Kenny" altercation. Ramone had reviewed the video and wanted to discuss the incident with us.

Ramone specialized in family law and estate planning, and Jonathan worked primarily in real estate law. But he occasionally got dragged into Ramone's cases.

Someone must have mentioned the video to Grace. "Can I come in and watch it, too? Ramone said I had to ask you."

"Oh, for the love of—I don't want everyone to see what happened."

"That's a yes, then? Ramone wants Jonathan to watch it too. And he asked one of Sebastian's business partners, who used to be a police officer, to give his input."

My shoulders slumped in defeat. "I'm supposed to be here figuring out Fern's estate, not watching that video."

Graced waved her hand dismissively. "Fern had her estate running like a well-oiled machine before she passed, and it'll be fine for a little while longer. You can go into the conference room, and I'll round everyone up." She hurried out the door to Sebastian's office across the hall.

I trudged to the conference room where Martina sat at the table, looking at her phone.

She glanced up. "You don't look happy. What's wrong?"

"Almost everyone I know, and even a few people I don't know, are going to be looking at that video."

Martina smiled. "I know. It's a relief to have other people see what Kenny's actually like."

I nodded and let it drop. She was right—if this helped with her divorce, it was worth a little embarrassment.

A few minutes later, Ramone bustled in with Jonathan behind him. "Laurel, it looks like you and Martina had an interesting day yesterday."

"Just tell me what's in the video so I can go back to work," Jonathan grumbled behind him.

Ramone smiled. "You'll thank me later. I wonder if we have any snacks in the break room."

Grace walked back in with a bag of Skinny Pop popcorn, and Sebastian and another man came in behind her.

I sank into a chair at the conference table and put my head in my hands. "Popcorn? Really? It's like you guys are going to a matinee."

"What? It was in the break room. There's Coke, Coke Zero, and water, if anyone wants a drink."

Ramone raised his hand, and Grace took a few drink orders.

Jonathan made introductions. "This is Damien, one of Sebastian's partners with MAD Security and Investigations. They do work for us sometimes. Damien, this is Laurel."

Damien grinned, and a dimple popped in his cheek. He was about the same height as Sebastian, and he had dark blond hair and gray-blue eyes. And he was almost as good-looking as Sebastian.

"Hi, Laurel. I hear you're Fern's niece. I'm sorry, she was a great lady." He walked around the table and shook my hand.

"Thank you. I miss her."

"We miss her too. Sebastian tells me you're carrying on her Martini Monday tradition. I'd love to come sometime." He hadn't let go of my hand yet, and he reached out and clasped my arm. "You have her smile and beautiful blue eyes." He flashed his dimple again.

"Thank you. You have lovely eyes too?" I wasn't sure why I'd said it like a question.

Sebastian grunted and stepped behind me, grabbed my waist, and slowly pulled me backward until Damien had to let go of me.

Damien grinned even wider. "It's like that, huh?" he asked Sebastian cryptically.

Sebastian didn't hesitate. "Yeah. Hands off, you flirty fucker."

My heart sped up, and I looked over my shoulder at Sebastian. "Hi, Grumpy. Like what? Because until a couple of days ago, you barely spoke to me."

"So?"

I shook my head, exasperated. Martina grinned, and Damien laughed out loud.

Grace came back just then, huffing like she'd been running, with her arms full of drinks and treats.

I looked at the snacks and shook my head. "Are those Twizzlers? And Milk Duds?"

"Yes. What'd I miss?" She looked around eagerly.

"I'll fill you in later." Damien winked at Grace. Lord, he *was* a flirty fucker.

Jonathan redirected the conversation. "Let's get started. I actually have work to do today. Laurel, can you walk us through what happened?"

I sat. "The video speaks for itself, and it's not very long. Although it feels like it is. I suggest watching it first, then if you have questions we can go from there."

I clutched my hands together and sighed. "Before you all watch it, I'd like to say, in my defense, that Kenny is a complete asshole, and he was already manhandling Martina when I got there."

I shifted uncomfortably with all of them staring at me. "I just hope I didn't make the situation worse."

Jonathan glanced at Ramone. "Now I *do* want to see this video. Grace, will you start it?"

Everyone moved their seats to face the TV monitor hanging on the wall. Grace popped her Diet Coke can, then started the video.

At first, only the foyer floor at Sebastian's house was visible. Then the camera swept up and showed what happened. While we watched Kenny manhandle Martina, I heard Damien call Kenny a "motherfucking asshole" under his breath. When the video ended, everyone was quiet for a moment, and I squirmed in my seat.

Damien looked at Sebastian. "You fucker," he said under his breath. "If you screw it up, all dibs are off."

Sebastian gave him a slow, gloating smile. I shook my head, feeling like a chewed up dog toy they'd soon forget.

Damien finally turned to Ramone and Martina. "Okay, here's my take as an ex-police officer."

For the next few minutes, they discussed having us make a formal complaint to the Palm Springs Police Department, and having Martina take out a protective order against Kenny.

When they finished talking, Damien grinned at me. "You did a good thing by getting Kenny on video behaving like this. There's no way his attorney will want a judge to see it."

I couldn't help it. I blushed, then mentally blamed it on his damn dimple. Grace ask if they could watch the video again, and at that point I was ready to go.

"I've seen it enough times. I'm heading home. Martina, let me know when you want to go to the station."

Martina nodded. "I'll text you later."

Sebastian stood too. "I'll walk you out."

"You don't need to."

"I know."

He took my arm and led me out. "I'll be over later, and I'm bringing dinner. Tell Martina. You two are going to be tired after giving your statements."

"Don't feel like you have to repay us for dinner—"

"I don't." He studied me for a few seconds. "See you later, *cielo.*"

He turned and walked back into the office building.

When Martina and I finally left the police station late that afternoon, I felt wrung out. We'd given our report to Officer Robertson, who appeared to be in his mid-forties and had a large mole on his eyelid. He'd taken our statements, watched the video, and promised to file a report on the incident.

"You both need to be careful. This guy has some anger issues." He motioned to Kenny on the computer screen. "You embarrassed him. Start paying attention to your surroundings. I also suggest getting a small personal security alarm, and maybe some pepper spray as well."

When we got home, we locked all the doors. Officer Robertson had freaked us out a little. I pulled out my computer, and we were in the middle of looking at personal safety devices when Sebastian rang the doorbell.

I opened the door wide and stepped aside. "Thanks for bringing dinner. You didn't have to do that."

Sebastian looked me up and down. I had on a casual little sun dress in deference to the weather. I suddenly felt under-dressed.

"Make sure you re-lock that." He tilted his head toward the front door.

I flipped the lock, and we walked to the kitchen.

Martina glanced up from the computer. "We've been looking at these keychain security alarms. The police officer recommended we both get one. Any advice?"

Sebastian put the bags on the kitchen bar and walked over to look at our favorite options. "How about you both don't leave the house for a while?"

Martina shook her head. "I have work, and Laurel has her step-mother and brothers coming to visit. Staying home isn't practical."

Sebastian sighed. "Then a strobe light-siren combo and pepper spray. And don't be alone if you can help it."

"I'm also ordering a stun gun," Martina muttered.

He unloaded the white takeout cartons from the bags, and I grabbed some plates. He also got out wine glasses, pulled a bottle of white wine from a paper bag, then poured two glasses and slid them across the bar to us.

"Oh God, how did you know I needed this?" Martina asked, picking up her glass.

I looked at Sebastian. "Thank you. That was... very nice of you." My voice sounded surprised. He smirked.

I pointed to my wine glass. "Aren't you having any?"

"Fuck, no. Can't stand the stuff." Sebastian pulled out a bottle of beer from a six-pack and stuck the rest in the fridge.

We started dishing up the Thai food he'd brought.

Martina sniffed then groaned. "Holy shit, I'm *sooo* hungry."

"Me too. This smells amazing." I dished up some jasmine rice and topped it with green curry.

"Cheers." Martina raised her glass and clinked it against mine. "To new roommates, to new... whatever you two are, and a new beginning when I get rid of Kenny the asshole."

"To getting rid of Kenny the asshole," Sebastian agreed and clinked her glass with his bottle.

I tilted my head at her. "Whatever we are?" I thought her comment was odd. "G, what are we, anyway? Friends, and soon-to-be home rehab partners?"

Sebastian looked at me over the neck of his beer bottle. "You can call it that if it makes you feel better." He took a drink.

His comment confused me so much, my fork hung in midair halfway to my mouth. Were we more than friends? Less than friends?

"We're not friends?" I tried to sound casual, but I wanted to make sure I'd heard him right.

"No. We're not friends," He said firmly. He didn't look up as he filled his plate. He also sounded a little angry.

Hurt speared through my chest. I put down my fork slowly and blinked at Sebastian, trying to keep my face neutral. "Huh. Good to know, I guess."

Martina asked him a question, and they talked about a work issue for a few minutes.

I'd been stupid to think he'd started to consider me a friend. Then I remembered the first time I met him at Fern's celebration, and the times after that he'd been cold and indifferent.

But hadn't he warmed up since then? He even seemed to flirt with me sometimes. I'd thought so, anyway. But maybe he only talked to me or came by the house because he felt obligated to Martina. And maybe to Fern.

Victor had taught me a hard lesson. It took two people to make a relationship or friendship work, no matter how badly one or the other person may want it.

Martina cut into the silence, interrupting my thoughts. "Thanks for dinner. After the day we've had, this is heaven."

"You're welcome." He forked some chicken pad thai into his mouth.

I fiddled with my glass. "Yes, thank you. You didn't have to, but we appreciate it." My voice was a little stiff, so I quit talking and started eating.

I'd lost my appetite but didn't want either of them to guess how upset I was. When I finished eating, I rinsed and loaded my plate into the dishwasher and cleaned up the kitchen a bit.

Then I excused myself. "I need to go call my stepmother and iron out a few details about her trip. And talk to my little brothers." I nervously wiped my hands on the front of my dress. "Sebastian, thanks again for dinner." I smiled weakly.

Walking over, I hugged Martina—because I needed a hug right then. "Goodnight, if I don't see you before I go to bed." I walked out of the kitchen.

I shut my bedroom door and pulled out my cell phone to call Willie and Lennie. If my heart hurt a little, that was on me for not managing my expectations better.

My life was already filled with loss, indifference, and rejection. I could handle this now. It was just a little hurt in the larger scheme of things.

Chapter 14

I felt a little hollow inside. Since our last dinner together, I successfully avoided Sebastian, but I knew Martina wondered what had changed. Having my twin brothers come visit was a welcome distraction.

"Hi Lolly! Guess what?" Willie jumped up and down excitedly from the curb of the pickup area at the Palm Springs International Airport. Lennie stood next to him, grinning. Chloe stood beside them with her hands full of luggage, and her normally perfect, ash blond hair thrown up in a messy bun.

She looked tired and wilted, and I could understand why. As much as I loved and adored the twins, even the thought of traveling eight hours on a plane with them exhausted me.

The boys looked a lot alike, except Lennie stood a couple of inches shorter, and he had angelic curly light brown hair. Willie had the same hair color, but it was straight as a pin, and he had a cowlick that couldn't be tamed.

Their flight got in around eight that evening and the sun had already set. But the temperature still hovered around a hundred degrees. I pulled my car over in the passenger pickup lane and hopped out to give them hugs and help with their luggage.

I loved the Palm Springs airport, and I had so many wonderful memories associated with it. The airport retained a subtle, nostalgic feel that seemed to welcome visitors with its breezeways and courtyards.

"Hello, my little troublemakers!" I bent over and scooped them up in a big hug.

"Guess what?" Willie asked again in his usual loud voice right next to my ear.

"Do you really have something to tell me, Boo, or are you just going to say 'chicken butt'?" I set the boys down when my back started groaning.

"Well, I was. But this is better. A guy on the plane? He puked. A lot, and it was gross." Willie wrinkled his nose but had a big smile on his face.

Lennie nodded vigorously. "Yeah, he threw up so much he filled his barf bag, and Willie gave him ours. And he gotted some barf on Willie's hand."

"It was so gross. And I smelled like barf 'til Mom wiped it off."

I looked over at Chloe, who stood there on the curb in a half-daze, and decided I needed to get them all out of the heat.

"Okay, here's the deal. This story is way too good to rush. You need to save it up for when we get in the car, so you can tell me everything." I held up a finger. "And my roommate, Martina? She's going to want to hear it too, even if she says she doesn't. So go grab the bags from your mom."

They ran over to get their bags, and I wrestled the luggage into my small trunk. It was a tight squeeze, but with a little maneuvering and a hard slam of the trunk, I got it all in. I'd researched and ordered two car seats online for the twins when Chloe confirmed they bought plane tickets and were really coming.

My credit card had taken a hit. I couldn't believe how expensive decent car seats were. But when Chloe and I got them buckled up, and I sat in the driver's seat looking back at their smiling little faces in my rearview mirror, it was so worth it.

Chloe plopped into the front passenger seat, and I cranked the air conditioning up. The boys started telling their barfing story again right away.

When they wound down, Chloe sighed next to me. "You were not joking about the heat, were you?"

"Nope, not even a little. And it's not that hot yet. It cools down a little in the late evening and early morning right now though, and swimming is great. Have you guys eaten?"

"No," Willie yelled.

"Yes," Chloe corrected him. "We ate during the layover in Phoenix."

Lennie chimed in. "I'm still hungry."

I glanced in the rearview mirror. "I have a couple of frozen pizzas, or chicken nuggets, and we can go swimming if you're not too tired. Or we can go tomorrow. But no barfing in the pool. One barf incident a day is enough."

I turned to Chloe. "I'd ask you how the plane ride was, but I think I have a good idea."

Chloe shuddered. "It was horrible. On a scale of one to ten, it was a negative twenty-five."

"Well, I thought it was great," Willie piped up.

I smiled at him in the rearview mirror. "I bet you did, Boo, I just bet you did."

We got to Fern's house and unloaded their luggage. After they went to the bathroom and cleaned up a little, we decided on a frozen pizza. While it baked, the boys regaled Martina with their throw-up story, then she asked them how they liked New York.

Lennie shrugged. "It's okay. I want a dog, but my dad says no."

Willie expounded. "He usually says 'hell no' and one time he said 'fu—'"

Chloe interrupted. "Okay, Willie. They just need to know your father said no."

"Well, he did. And he yelled at Lennie and made him cry."

Lennie nodded and picked up his pizza. Chloe looked embarrassed. I'd hoped my father would be kinder to the boys than he'd been to me, but it didn't sound like much had changed.

We skipped swimming that night. Chloe looked wrung out, and the boys were even showing signs of slowing down. I remembered they it was almost midnight for them.

I turned to Chloe. "Why don't you go to bed, and I'll get these two tucked in?"

Chloe groaned and stretched a little. "Oh my God, that sounds so nice. I don't remember the last time I felt this tired. Thank you." She squeezed my hand and turned to the boys. "Give me hugs."

Lennie ran over and hugged her. Willie went a little more slowly and gave her an unenthusiastic side hug.

I smirked. "That was a sad, pathetic little hug. Try again."

Willie threw his arms around Chloe's neck and squeezed hard. "'Night, Mom. Let's go swimming tomorrow, 'kay?"

"Absolutely. Love you, William. Love you too, Lennard." She got up, picked up her wine glass, and shuffled to her room.

"I'm going to call it a night too." Martina looked at the boys. "Let's go get ice cream tomorrow night, okay?" They both nodded enthusiastically.

The boys ate a few more bites of pizza and talked about their first year of school, their friends, and their favorite toys. I noticed they didn't mention Victor once.

When they were done, I took them to the spare office bedroom with the pullout bed turned down.

"Okay, my little stink bombs." I walked over to the desk and picked up a children's book off the top of a stack. "I've been saving these books for you, and I'm going to read one a night while you're here. It's a series of books. Jackson started giving them to me for Christmas when I was about your age."

Lennie whined. "Why can't you just tell us a made-up story like you usually do?"

I smiled at him, happy he liked my stories. "I swear you'll like these. And I'll also tell you a made-up story afterward if you go get cleaned up and ready for bed." I started digging through their little suitcases. "I bet you guys still have barf cooties from that guy on the plane."

Willie giggled. "We don't have barf cooties!"

I looked him up and down. "Better safe than sorry."

After they got ready for bed, I tucked them in on each side of me and grabbed the old children's book off the nightstand. The cover showed a cartoon picture of a stout, black-and-white dog who appeared to be farting.

"This story is about a sweet little dog who has the same problem you two have. He farts big, stinky, loud farts. All the time."

The boys started laughing and protesting.

"I don't! Willie does, but I don't."

They both blamed the other for having the stinkiest farts and then we settled in and started reading. The boys giggled through the entire book and loved it so much, they asked me to read it again. I remembered laughing so hard my stomach hurt when Jackson read it to me the first time almost twenty years ago. Some memories were meant to be shared.

The next afternoon, I put up a couple of sunshades across the pool, and the boys swam until they were exhausted and sunburned. We'd gotten a late start that morning, lounging around making chocolate chip banana pancakes shaped like smiley faces, and a dog's butt, according to Willie. He was probably inspired by last night's book.

There weren't any pool toys at the house, but the boys enjoyed Fern's oversized, luxurious floating lounger with the multiple drink holders. We told Lennie, who preferred to swim naked, that he had to put his swimsuit back on about five times.

Finally, Chloe gave up. "Okay, Lennard, when your little white bottom gets sunburned because you won't keep your clothes on, don't come crying to me."

"It won't. Lolly will put sunscreen on it, won't you?" Lennie gave me big puppy eyes.

I gave him the stink eye back, but motioned him over. "You know I love you when I'm willing to put sunscreen on your bare little butt, Len." I briskly sprayed sunscreen on him. "But you have to do your front part. I don't love you *that* much."

Lennie was the streaker in the family. When I'd told Luke and Joey about Lennie's habit of shedding his clothes at odd times, Luke insisted every family had at least one nudist.

"It's true. I swear there's usually one kid, or uncle or cousin somewhere, who's a natural-born nudist," he'd insisted.

Joey raised her eyebrow. "So, who is it in your family?"

"Who do you think? Me," Luke said seriously. I hoped the twins could meet them one day.

I swam with the boys for an hour or so, then got out and sat next to Chloe on the recliners, watching them play in the shallow end. Chloe looked like a catalog model in her oversized floppy hat, expensive-looking white suit, and a gauzy matching coverup. I wore a faded gray baseball cap and a simple bikini.

"How was your graduation?" Chloe asked. "I'm sorry we couldn't be there. The boys were finishing end-of-year testing, although why they test kindergarteners nowadays I'll never know."

"It was nice. And thank you for the beautiful bracelet."

She smiled. "You're welcome. When are you coming back to New York?"

I fiddled with my earlobe and looked over at the boys. "I'm not planning to move back to New York. Besides the twins, I don't have anyone else there. And I'm signed up here in California to take the bar exam in late July. Ramone and Jonathan also offered me a position as an associate at their firm."

Chloe stared at me through her designer sunglasses with her mouth open. "You're not coming back to New York? What am I going to tell the boys?"

I didn't know why I felt guilty. Until the twins were born, Chloe and I didn't a relationship. When Victor married Chloe, and we all lived together in New York for a few years, I felt like a ghost sometimes. Chloe had never been cruel to me, but she hadn't really been a stepmother, or even my friend.

I rolled my shoulder. "I'll come and see them a few times a year. And I hope they come visit me."

"Where are you going to live?" Chloe asked, sitting up in the recliner.

"Here in Palm Springs. She left me this house." Victor and I hadn't spoken in months, and they didn't know yet that Fern left me her home. Or the bulk of her estate.

"I don't understand. I thought the house needed to be sold. Didn't Fern leave her estate to some homeless shelters or something?" Chloe waved her hand.

"Women's shelters. And she made a few changes to her trust since then. Ramone and Jonathan are her executors. She left me this house, and I'm keeping it and living here. At least for a while."

I didn't want Victor finding out that Fern had left me her estate. Whenever something or someone made me happy or brought me joy, it seemed like he tried to destroy it. I didn't trust Victor—not with my emotional or my physical well-being.

He would find out about the house eventually if the boys were allowed to keep visiting me. But I didn't want him to know about the rest of it unless I had a good reason.

"The boys and you are always welcome to visit me. I hope they do, just like I did with Aunt Fern."

Chloe didn't say anything, which was strange for her.

I continued. "I'm happier here, and I have friends."

I thought about Sebastian and felt hurt all over again, but I brushed it aside. We sat in silence for a few moments, watching the boys splash each other under the sunshade.

Chloe finally sighed and sat back. "It's a beautiful house and a wonderful neighborhood. I can see why you love Palm Springs." She looked over at me. "But we probably won't visit again during the summer. Next summer, let's plan a trip to the mountains. Or maybe Alaska. Just not somewhere that puts the Sahara Desert to shame."

Chapter 15

A few days later, I chased a naked Lennie down the hall to the open front door. We'd eaten an early dinner, and then Chloe made them bathe.

They were still wound up from their trip to the Palm Springs airplane museum, and Lennie was zooming around with his toy F/A-18 Super Hornet model jet when the doorbell rang. Martina beat Lennie to the door, but he wasn't far behind.

I laughed as I ran after him and took hold of his shoulders. "Len, you're buck naked. You can't answer the door without clothes on."

Sebastian stood there with a sack in his hand, looking down at Lennie. Martina stepped to the side so Sebastian got a good look at us.

"Oh." I stopped short and quit laughing. "Uh, hello. This is Lennie, my little brother. Lennie, this is Sebastian. Lennie doesn't like wearing clothes around the house. Or anywhere."

Sebastian raised an eyebrow, then looked down at Lennie again and nodded seriously. "I know how you feel. Sometimes I walk around my house naked too. You should probably wear clothes around the ladies though. Most of the time."

Martina tried to smother her laugh, and I stared at Sebastian. Had he just made a joke?

"Come in." Martina opened the door wide.

"See, Lolly? He doesn't like clothes either." Lennie smiled triumphantly. I imagined Sebastian without clothes and started getting a little warm.

Chloe bustled into the foyer. "Leonard James Payne, what have I told you about running around the house naked? Go get your pajamas on, or no story tonight." Chloe pointed her finger toward the bathroom.

"Okaaay," he whined. "Bye, Sloth Man." He ran off, his airplane held high in the air.

"It's Sebastian, not Sloth Man!" I yelled down the hall then turned back and made introductions. "Chloe, this is Sebastian. He's Martina's cousin and Fern's friend."

Sebastian narrowed his eyes, but I sure as hell wasn't introducing him as my friend after our last conversation.

Chloe held out her hand. "I'm Chloe, the twins' mother."

"Hello." Sebastian shook her hand.

Chloe sighed. "That kid is going to end up in jail for indecent exposure if he keeps this up."

We walked into the kitchen, and I waved my hand. "Lennie will be fine. He's just pushing a few boundaries and trying to get a rise out of us."

Sebastian smirked. "Or he just likes being naked. Nothing wrong with that."

Martina laughed and took the bag from Sebastian. "Those two are the funniest kids. Willie doesn't talk, he yells everything. And Lennie just wants to be naked. What's up with you?"

"I need to double-check the security system I put in the other day. I also brought some *paletas* from La Mariposa."

Martina's eyes lit up. "You're definitely my favorite cousin, but don't tell Matías. You, ladies, are in for an amazing frozen treat. What flavors did you get?"

"Coconut, lime, and strawberry."

"Looollly, we're ready for our story," Willie yelled from down the hall.

"Good choices." Martina dug through the bag. "We'll save some for the boys tomorrow since they just bathed and brushed their teeth. And we might save you one, Laurel."

I started backing out of the foyer. "I'll eat mine with the boys tomorrow." I glanced at Sebastian. "Thanks for the *paletas*. Have a good evening."

He studied me but didn't say anything. I turned and walked out as Willie hollered again.

Two days later, I reluctantly called Sebastian.

He picked up on the first ring. "Hey."

"Hello, Sebastian? This is Laurel Payne. Martina's roommate and Fern's niece."

"I know who you are, and I have your name in my phone." He sounded annoyed.

"Uh, can you recommend a plumber?" I finally asked him. "Willie tried to be helpful and put his shot glass in the sink disposal. I didn't realize it was there, and it broke and got stuck."

"Who the fuck is Willie?" he asked.

Why did he sound mad? "William, my five-year-old brother? You met his twin the other night."

"The one who doesn't like clothes."

"Yeah. I didn't want to bother you. But I called Ramone and Jonathan to see if they could help, and Jonathan told me to call you. He said when it comes to household repairs, he and Ramone are like two toddlers performing brain surgery."

Sebastian grunted. "That's pretty accurate."

"I'm calling to see if you can recommend a plumber."

"You don't need a plumber. I'll take care of it, but I can't come until early this evening."

I grimaced, then was glad Sebastian couldn't see my face. "You don't need to come over. If you can just recommend a plumber, or have one of your maintenance crew swing by, that would be great. And send me the bill. If Martina were here, we'd probably try to fix it after watching a YouTube video or two." I was rambling, and I couldn't seem to stop myself. "But with the boys around, I'm afraid they'd want to help and get hurt."

"No. I'll be there around six. And don't try it. You'd probably cut yourself."

Even though I'd worried about that exact thing, I was offended. It was okay for *me* to question my skills, but not him.

"If you can't recommend anyone, or don't have a maintenance person, I can just wait for Martina to get home. Never mind, we'll do it."

Sebastian growled. "I said I can get to it this evening. I'm texting Martina right now and telling her I'll be there."

I was silent for a moment. "Okay, thank you. We appreciate it." I didn't sound very appreciative. "We're taking the boys to the aquatic center in Palm Desert today. If we're not back, just come in and do what you need to do. And send me the bill when you get done."

"Just don't fucking touch it." Then Sebastian hung up. Well. That was rude, even if he *was* coming over to fix my disposal.

Martina had made dinner in the slow cooker, and the house smelled delicious when we got home in the late afternoon. The boys took a bath, and we'd wrangled them into their pajamas. They'd just eaten and were in their room playing when the doorbell rang.

Martina answered it, and Sebastian walked into the kitchen behind her with his toolbox. "Do you want to stay for dinner? I made slow-cooked black bean enchiladas if you're hungry," Martina asked him.

"If you have enough. Smells good. Let me get this taken care of first."

I awkwardly raised my hand. "Hello. Thanks for coming."

He gave me a long look, then he put his toolbox on the floor next to the sink and walked out to the garage. He came back with the shop vac.

Chloe was still in the shower, and Martina leaned against the counter and just watched us with a funny smile.

I cleared my throat. "Thank you again for coming. You didn't need to do that. But thank you."

"It's not a big deal." Sebastian squatted down under the sink and reached in to unplug the disposal. "I've been wondering though. Why did a little kid have a shot glass?"

I reached up to scratch my earlobe. "Willie's not a great eater. I was trying to get him to drink some milk, and he said he'd only drink as much milk as would fit in the glass."

"Huh. Smart kid."

"You have no idea. He'd make a brilliant attorney since he tries to negotiate everything." I needed to stop talking.

He took a pair of pliers and a small flashlight out of his toolbox, then leaned over the sink and dug some larger pieces of glass out of the disposal. Martina grabbed a paper towel, and Sebastian put the pieces on it. When he'd gotten as many shards as he could, he took the shop vac hose and stuck it down the sink, then turned on the switch.

The noise drew the boys from the other room. Lennie came out without a shirt, but at least he had his pajama bottoms on this time. Willie ran over to Sebastian's side and started jumping up and down next to his toolbox.

"What're you doin'?" he asked loudly.

Sebastian looked down at Willie. "I'm getting the broken glass out of the sink."

I pointed at Sebastian. "Willie, this is Sebastian. He's Martina's cousin."

Lennie came over and stood next to Willie. "Hi, Batman."

"His name is Sebastian. Not sloth man or Batman," I corrected.

Sebastian glanced at Lennie then smirked at me. "It sounds like you're not the only one who struggles with names."

I tried to look innocent. "Huh."

"I put the glass in there." Willie bounced up and down next to me. "I didn't mean to. I told Lolly I was sorry. She didn't even yell at me."

"You cried," Lennie volunteered.

"Did not! I only cried a little. I thought she was gonna be mad. And make us stay in our room all night." Willie looked like he was going to cry again.

"Boo, it's okay. Stuff happens sometimes. He's going to get the glass out and fix the sink. He's really good with his hands, and he knows what he's doing."

Sebastian looked over at me and grinned. "She's right. I am really good with my hands, and I know what I'm doing."

Martina smothered a laugh, and I felt my face heat up again.

Sebastian turned to the twins. "You can watch if you want."

Willie nodded. "'Kay."

Lennie pointed at Sebastian's chest. "You can take your shirt off. Lolly said if I keep my pants on, I can take off my shirt sometimes. I bet she'd let you too."

Sebastian pinched his lips together, probably to keep from laughing. "I'm good for now. But I appreciate the offer." I blushed and wanted to slap my forehead.

He bent down low to adjust the bottom of the disposal with a slender tool he'd gotten out of his toolbox. I noticed how his thigh muscles bunched when he squatted down. Then I looked away so I wouldn't get caught staring.

The boys stuck their heads under the sink too. Willie chattered away, and they offered Sebastian different tools from his toolbox. The job probably took three times as long, but Sebastian was patient and answered their questions.

Chloe walked in as they were finishing up. "Come on, you two. Let him work. Hello, Sebastian. Thanks for the *paletas* the other night. I tried the coconut one, and it was delicious."

"No problem. The boys were helping me. Let's turn it on and see if we fixed it." He stood up and turned on the water, then flipped on the disposal. It sounded smooth and quiet.

I clapped my hands together. "You guys did it! See Willie? If stuff gets broken, it's no big deal. We just use our brains and figure it out. You're way more important than any stuff."

Lennie looked at me. "Dad called me a 'little shit' when I broke the TV clicker."

Willie nodded and started tearing up again. "And guess what? He screamed and pushed Lennie down and made him hit a chair. Then Lennie started crying."

I was so mad, I stood there for a few seconds with my hands fisted and tried to get myself under control. I knelt down and pulled them in for a hug.

"Well, he's wrong. You guys are way more important than stuff. You're kids, for crying out loud." My voice started to rise, and I tried to get my anger under control. "No one should make you feel bad, or yell at you, or push you around for hell—*hello* sake!"

Willie nodded his head against my shoulder. "Yeah, 'cause he's bigger than us."

Chloe cleared her throat nervously. "Okay. If you two want to watch your show before you go to sleep, we have to start now. Have you brushed your teeth yet?"

She took them by the shoulders and started steering them toward the bathroom. Willie broke free and ran over and hugged me again. Then he gave Sebastian's leg a quick hug. "Thanks for fixing the disposing thing."

He ran down the hall to the bathroom, and I crouched there for a second. I couldn't even find humor in Lennie screwing up Sebastian's name again.

When I got up, I started pacing the kitchen. "That bastard. I hate him. He yells and swears at them—for being kids. And he shoved Lennie. If he's done it once, he's done it a hundred times."

"True," Martina agreed. "What are you going to do?"

I sighed and put my hands on top of my head. "I don't know. But I have to do something."

"What does Chloe say about it?" Martina asked.

"Nothing. But I need to talk with her." I looked up and started.

I'd forgotten Sebastian was there. He leaned against the counter with his arms and ankles crossed, studying me.

Martina finally reached up and took plates out of the cupboard. "Well, let's eat. I'm starving."

On Lennie and Wille's last night in Palm Springs, I read them the final book in the farting dog series. Then I told them a story about two young mutant lizard fighters with names similar to theirs.

They'd seen a few lizards out in the yard and were fascinated with them. Then Chloe and I tucked the boys into bed and headed out to the back patio.

I groaned. "I'm so tired. I didn't know it was possible to be this tired and still be awake."

We sat in the recliners, looking up at the stars and drinking sangria left over from dinner. They'd be flying back to New York in the morning, and we decided to celebrate our last night with Italian food. The boys got pizza, and we made eggplant parmesan.

Chloe smiled dryly. "Welcome to my world. It's usually not this crazy, but I get tired by the end of the night. It's amazing how well I sleep after chasing them around all day."

I turned to face Chloe. "Does Victor ever help with the boys?"

She sighed. "No. He's usually at work anyway." Chloe was silent for several moments. "I'm worried that as they get older, his lack of involvement will hurt them."

"Honestly? It probably already has." I took a sip of sangria then screwed up my courage. "And his yelling, nitpicking, and cruel comments. Him hurting Lennie? That's not okay."

She fidgeted with her wine glass. "I know. I just don't know what to do, or what would be best for us. I don't know if it would be better or worse to stay."

She turned to look at me. "Laurel, I've never told you how sorry I am I wasn't a better stepmother to you when Victor and I first got married. You just looked so much like your mother." Chloe paused and looked up at the sky. "I was also probably jealous of you."

"What? Why?"

"Because I was self-centered and shallow. You were this quiet, strong, tragic young woman. And already beautiful at thirteen." Chloe chuckled weakly. "See? I told you I was shallow. When I moved in, you and Rosa had a system down. And she obviously preferred you." Chloe sounded a little bitter, even now.

I mentally sighed. Chloe admitting she could be petty and shallow was probably a big step for her. But it didn't change the past. I'd heard a term once that seemed to describe her—a conversational narcissist. I didn't think Chloe was an actual narcissist, but she had a habit of steering most conversations and situations back to her.

Rosa had been our housekeeper when I was younger. After my mother died, she tried to help me until I was old enough to fend for myself.

I thought about telling Chloe how lonely I'd been back then, and how I would've loved to have her friendship. But that time had passed, and I wanted to have a good relationship with her now. Mostly because of my little brothers.

"It's all right," I finally said. "We're friends now. Fern and Jackson were there for me, and I had Rosa and some good friends in school. I turned out okay."

Then I gave Chloe a little unvarnished truth. "But Lennie and Willie? They deserve to be loved, and not ignored, or yelled at, or pushed around and made to feel unwanted. And they shouldn't have to grow up in a house where they're afraid of their own father. You need to protect them. You're all they have."

Chloe nodded jerkily and looked up at the sky again. She didn't say anything else until she got up a few minutes later to go to bed. I could see tears glistening in her eyes. She turned to me before walking inside. "You're wrong about the boys only having me, you know. They also have you. Good night."

Chapter 16

I didn't know exactly how I ended up eating dinner with Sebastian and Martina that night.

Willie and Lennie had gone back to New York over a month ago, and the house seemed so quiet and empty without them. Before they left, I'd packed the farting dog books in their luggage and gave them each a Western-themed Lego set as going-away presents. One set even had little cactus Legos in it.

We still talked every few days, and Chloe seemed friendlier since their trip. But other than phone calls with the twins, seeing Martina at the house, and the Martini Mondays, I barely talked to anyone.

Holing myself up in either Fern's office, a coffee shop, or the public library, I feverishly studied for the bar exam. I had just under three weeks to go, and I planned to pass that hellish exam the first time, or die trying.

Late that afternoon, I sat at the kitchen table, rubbing my tired eyes, when Martina walked into the kitchen and tossed her keys and phone on the counter.

"Hey. How's the studying going?"

"It's going. I'm ready for a break though. I stopped retaining information about an hour ago."

"I'm starving, and it's Taco Tuesday. La Bonita is also having a two-for-one mango margarita special."

I stood up and rotated my spine and shoulders. "Sounds fabulous." I shook my head. "Ramone is rubbing off on me. Now everything is 'fabulous.' Let me get cleaned up a little and let's go."

"Okay. Sebastian's going to meet us there. He'll get us a table."

Stopping short, I stared at her. "I didn't know you were meeting anyone. I can just grab something here."

"No. I already told him we're both coming. Go put on something besides running shorts and a tank top—I'm going to wear my little red sundress." She waved at me. "Go make yourself presentable. We'll leave in twenty minutes."

I didn't want to make a fuss after I'd already agreed to go, but my nerves kicked in when I thought about eating dinner with Sebastian. Over the past month, I'd seen him at the house a few times, and he'd come to Martini Monday at Ramone and Jonathan's house.

But I'd been skittish around him and careful not to be too familiar. I finally admitted to myself that I'd started liking him before he made it clear he didn't want to be friends. So it was my fault for getting hurt.

We walked into La Bonita a half hour later. I'd changed into a short white skirt and a stretchy purple top. I briefly wondered briefly why I'd made an effort, then looked at Martina in her flirty red sundress.

Nerves rolled through me as we walked toward the table. Sebastian sat watching me, and I straightened my shoulders and decided I could do this. If Martina wanted to hang out with both of us, I could handle it. I just had to develop a thicker skin.

It was too bad he was such a handsome bastard, I thought for the thousandth time. His hair looked a little longer, and it curled slightly around his neck. His black shirt also showed off his sculpted arms and biceps.

When we got closer to the table, Sebastian pinned me with his dark brown eyes. Then his gaze slid down to my legs and stayed there for several seconds. I felt the urge to tug my skirt down, but I resisted. Two mango margaritas and chips and salsa sat on the table.

Sebastian slid out of the booth and stood. "Hey, *prima*." Then he turned to me. "How's the studying coming?"

Martina and I slid into each side of the booth, and Sebastian startled me when he slid in next to me, caging me in. Shifting, I tried to give myself a little more room.

Clearing my throat a bit, I scooted forward. "Good, I think. My brain hurts though, and I'm sick of tort law."

Heat ran through me as his thigh settled next to mine. Then he slid a margarita toward me.

"Tort sounds like a dessert." Martina scooped up some of the chunky salsa with a warm chip and stuffed it in her mouth.

"I wish." I turned to Sebastian. "Thanks for the margaritas."

"I told them Martina was meeting me here, and they asked if she wanted the usual." A smile crinkled the corners of his eyes.

Martina took a big sip and sighed happily. "Have you ordered yet?" She picked up a menu.

"Not yet. Francesca should be coming by again soon."

"Francesca Romero?" Martina asked.

Sebastian nodded.

Martina's eyes squinted. "I thought she moved."

He shrugged.

She grinned. "Has she hit you up for some more hot tub time yet?"

Sebastian shifted a little and pointed a finger at Martina. "No. And don't bring it up, *pequeña mierda*."

A couple of minutes later, a pretty server with long brown hair and expertly applied makeup walked up to our table. Her tight tank top read "La Bonita!" in hot pink sparkly letters across her ample chest. She wore a little black miniskirt and rhinestone flip-flops.

Cocking her hip, she pushed her chest out. "Hi, Martina. Sebastian said you'd be joining him." She gave Martina a big smile, then turned to me and her lips turned down. "He didn't mention anyone else though."

Then her eye twitched when she took in Sebastian sitting next to me, his thigh pressed to mine. I wanted to tell her it wasn't what it looked like.

Martina picked up another chip. "Hi, Francesca. This is Laurel. I thought you quit and were planning to move back to Modesto. What happened?"

Francesca answered while she stared at Sebastian and me. "Oh, you know. Plans change. Sebastian, how've you been?"

Sebastian ignored her and studied the menu.

She tried again. "What's new with you?"

"Nothing." He didn't look up.

When he didn't say anything else, she kept talking. "I haven't seen you in a while. What're you doing later tonight? Do you still have that sweet hot tub?"

"I have plans," Sebastian answered shortly. He leaned back and put his arm on the booth behind me, then picked up a strand of my hair and started fingering it. "We'll have three fish taco platters and a Modelo for me."

My stomach did a long slow roll as I felt him gently tug my hair strands.

Francesca stared down at his hand playing with my hair. "Fine." She spun around and walked away. She hadn't stuck around long enough to pick the menus up after Sebastian had ordered.

Martina laughed softly behind her menu. "That's what you get when you 'hit it and quit it' around town too much. She's not very nice, so I'm glad she didn't stick."

I looked at her. "What does that mean, 'hit it and quit'–oh. One of your 'hot tub hookups,' huh?"

I shifted forward in the seat, trying to dislodge his fingers from my hair. I understood now why he'd sat next to me and played with my hair in front of Francesca, and a knot formed in my chest.

Sebastian shook his head. "You're both *pequeña mierdas*."

Martina gathered up the menus and put them at the end of the table. "If we're little shits, then you're a big one. I'm just glad you ordered the same thing for all of us. There's less chance she'll spit in all our taco platters."

This was the second woman I'd seen Sebastian brutally turn down, and I decided I'd gotten off lightly. For the rest of the meal,

I tried to ignore him, and asked Martina about her work week and her plans over the next three weeks while I'd be out of town. I was taking the two-day bar exam in Los Angeles and planned to drive to Las Vegas to see my roommates when I got done.

"When are you taking off?" Martina asked me as we ate our tacos. She turned to Sebastian. "Grace and Sheila offered to let her use their little mountain cabin in Idyllwild for a couple of weeks to study for the exam."

The quaint mountain town was about an hour away from Palm Springs, and I needed to get out of the heat for a while.

Sebastian gave me several long looks, but didn't say much while we ate.

Martina finished off her margarita, then slid out of the booth. "I'm going to the bathroom." She took off before I could volunteer to go with her.

I pushed bits of rice around on my plate and kept quiet while I waited for her to come back.

Sebastian stared at me. "What's up your ass?" he finally asked.

My head jerked up. "What do you mean? And nothing's up my ass. Quit being crude." I set my fork down.

"You used to tease me and give me shit. Now you're quiet around me, or you ignore me. Are you pissed about something? What's going on?"

I licked my lips nervously. I didn't know why he was asking me this. What did he want me to say?

Clearing my throat, I looked over at him. "I'm not sure what you're talking about—or asking. Since we met, you've made it pretty clear you want to be left alone." I was getting upset and doing exactly what I promised myself I wouldn't do.

His eyes narrowed. "I thought we were past that. Now tell me what's going on."

I looked at him quizzically. "I thought we were too. But then you made it very clear—again—that you didn't want to be friends. I don't want to annoy or irritate you by continuing to try." I took a deep breath.

Francesca came back just then with the check. "You can pay here or up front."

"I'll pay here." I started digging in my purse.

Sebastian deftly pulled out his wallet and threw some cash on top of the check. "That should cover it."

He didn't even look at Francesca, but watched me as I finally pulled my wallet out.

Francesca rolled her eyes, took the money and check, and strode off. Her flip-flops made an angry clomping noise as she walked away.

"Let me pay."

Sebastian shook his head.

"At least let me pay for mine and Martina's portion then." I pulled out three twenties and tried to hand them over.

"No."

"Please?" I held out the money.

"I've got it." He gently pushed my hand back into my lap. "Now, are you going to answer me?"

"No."

Sebastian raised his eyebrow. "No?"

"That's what I said."

He sighed, then turned toward me and took a strand of my hair again. "Our wires aren't just crossed, they're completely fucked up. Some of that's on me."

I shifted restlessly in my seat and faced forward. Being this close to him did strange things to my body.

"I know you need to focus on your exam, and now isn't the time to get our wires uncrossed. But when you come back, you and I are going to have a long talk. And we're going to get our shit sorted out, *cielo*. Got it?"

Sebastian was close enough that I could smell his heady scent and feel his breath in my hair. I was so confused.

Clasping my hands in front of me, I glanced over at him. "You can't keep doing this. One minute you're a mean jerk, the next you're joking around and calling me *cielo*. Then you tell me you don't want to be friends."

"What the fuck are you talking about?" he asked.

Staring at him, I wiped my hands on my skirt. "I have no idea what you want from me, but please don't play with me." I hadn't meant to sound desperate, but I didn't like games, and this man could hurt me.

He studied me intently, but I turned to stare straight ahead again, my breath coming fast and my heart pounding.

Then he gently took my chin and turned me to him, studying my eyes. "That's fair—I deserve *most* of that. But we're going to talk when you come back."

Martina got back from the bathroom but stopped short when she saw us. "I can give you more time."

"No!" I pulled my chin out of Sebastian's fingers. "Thank you for dinner. I owe you." I started standing up, silently indicating he needed to move so I could get out.

"Yeah, you do owe me, but not for dinner. This conversation isn't finished." He slid out and let me go. As I passed him, he leaned down and spoke softly in my ear. "And I'm not playing."

Martina looked between us and hesitated, but Sebastian shook his head slightly.

He walked us to Martina's car. "Good luck with your bar exam. I'll see you both later." He waited until we got in, gave me a long look, then took off.

Martina watched him, then turned to me and pointed a finger in my face. "Okay, what the hell's going on with you two?"

I took a deep breath then let it out and laid my head back on the headrest. "I swear to you I don't know. He gives me whiplash, and I'm so confused. But the bar exam is staring me in the face, and I can't get distracted by your hot, moody-as-shit cousin. I just can't."

Martina looked over at me. She started to say something, but in the end she just grabbed my hand and just squeezed it. "Okay."

Squeezing her hand back, I looked out the window so she wouldn't see the shine in my eyes.

I continued to avoid Sebastian for the next couple of days, and worked to put him out of my mind. I was still a little mad about his "what's up your ass" comment, and anxious about talking with him when I got back.

When I was in law school and found out Fern had cancer, I learned to compartmentalize so I could function. I needed to do that now. So, a couple of days later, I packed up my car and headed out.

For the next three weeks, I poured myself into preparing for the bar exam so I could move on with the rest of my life. I didn't know if that would include Martina's hot, grumpy, asshole cousin or not.

Chapter 17

The day after I finished taking the exam at the Pasadena Convention Center in Los Angeles, I drove to Las Vegas to see Luke and Joey. Luke didn't have National Guard that weekend, and Joey had traded shifts on Friday so we could hang out together.

Sebastian also sent me a text, and when I saw it, my stomach dropped.

Sebastian: I hope the exam went well. We're talking when you get home.

I sent him back the grimacing face emoji.

When I made it to Las Vegas, we went to my favorite Napoli pizza place for dinner. "How'd the exam go? What'd you think?" Joey asked as she shoved half a slice of meat lover's pizza into her mouth.

"It was nerve-wracking at first. But then I kind of found my grove and zoned everything out. The real kicker was studying for the two or three months beforehand."

Luke grunted. "That sounds shitty. How do you feel about your chance of passing?"

I scratched at my earlobe. "I feel good about it, but I don't want to jinx myself. The California bar is one of the hardest." I paused and took a sip of my drink. "I think the pass rate is around thirty-three percent."

"Damn, that's low," Luke commiserated.

Shrugging, I took another bite. "I studied my butt off, took the recommended bar prep course, and did the timed practice tests. All of it. So I'm going to try not to worry about it until November when the results get posted."

Joey groaned. "God, I wish I were in your shoes. I'm sick of being poor, sleep deprived, and stressed out."

"You did get a pretty sweet paid internship this summer. Not sure you have much to complain about," Luke reminded her.

She nodded. "That's true. I never thought I'd be working at the Gaming Commission. But I do like the pay, even for an intern."

I shook my head. "Only in Las Vegas. That's what you get when you decide to take a gaming law class on a whim."

I hung out with Luke on Saturday while Joey worked two shifts. We talked about my decision to stay in Palm Springs and work with Ramone and Jonathan.

"Those two are basically your uncles. They're good guys, and I think it'll be a great place to start. They can also help you with your psychotic father if he goes postal on you again."

When we'd first become roommates, Luke and I had been in the kitchen one day when Victor called, screaming at me. He'd told me I was a stupid fucking idiot for transferring to Las Vegas, among other things. It had been traumatizing and humiliating because I hadn't known Luke well back then. He'd watched me freeze and turn pale, and finally he'd walked over, gently pulled my cell phone out of my hand, and pressed the off button.

"You don't have to listen to that bullshit," he hissed. Then he hugged me while I cried. That incident had cemented our friendship.

I got back to Fern's house late Sunday evening. I hadn't been back for almost three weeks, and even though the temperature was still in the triple digits, it was nice to be back. Except the talk with Sebastian hanging over my head.

I'd texted Martina to let her know, and the porch lights were on when I drove up. Dragging my things inside, I went to find her. She was outside, floating on her back in the pool, looking up at the stars. She had her swimsuit on tonight, but some nights she liked to swim naked. I hadn't worked up the nerve yet.

The outside lights were off, and the only light came from the half-moon. Martina saw me and waded over to where I sat dangling my feet in the pool. "Hey stranger. So how was the exam?"

"It was a long, stressful two days that I wouldn't wish on my worst enemy. And now I get to wait for a couple months to find out if I passed. How have things been around here?"

She smiled. "Go get your suit on–or not–and get in. Then I'll tell you all about it. And while you're at it, grab that cheap bottle of wine in the fridge."

"Okay. I'll be right back." I came back with the wine and two plastic wine glasses a few minutes later.

I handed a glass to Martina and waded in. "What's been happening?"

"Well, as of last Thursday, Kenny signed the divorce stipulation, and we only have a few more weeks until the mandatory six-month waiting period is over. Then I'll be legally and officially divorced."

"Holy shit, Mar, you did it! Cheers." We clinked our glasses together. "The last time I talked to you, he refused to go to mediation, wouldn't agree to any temporary orders, and said he was going to drag it out for years."

"Yeah, it turns out his attorney isn't as big of a moron as I thought." Martina raised her glass. "So, thank you—for being there that day. And for not kicking me out and disowning me after he threatened you."

"Now who's being the dumbass? I wouldn't kick you out. Your tres leches cake is too good."

Martina laughed and flicked water at me. Then we drank our wine and floated in the pool side by side for a while, just gazing up at the stars.

Monday afternoon after getting back from Las Vegas, I finally sat down a second time with Jonathan and Ramone to learn about the details of Fern's estate. I walked into their law office with a gift basket for Grace and Sheila.

"Hi, Grace. How'd you do in your golf tournament?" I put the basket down on her desk. "This is a small thanks to you and Sheila for letting me use your wonderful cabin to study. Seriously, that was a godsend."

"You're very welcome, and thank you. I didn't do as well as I'd hoped, but it was still fun. So how did the exam go?"

"Well, it's over. That's the best thing I can say about it. My brain still hurts though."

"I bet it does. You can head back, I think Jonathan is already in the conference room."

A couple of hours later when I finally left their office, I felt shell-shocked. Again. I suddenly didn't have to worry about how to pay off my student loans or my credit card debt.

Fern had bequeathed money to the local animal shelter, and a few other nonprofit organizations. But she and Jackson had steadily invested in the stock market. And like their real estate investments, they did their homework and took their time. I almost wished I'd gotten a master's degree in business instead of a law degree as I looked over the spreadsheets.

Fern had hired a competent financial advisor, and Jonathan asked if I wanted to keep him on.

I stared at the documentation in front of me. "Yes, please. I definitely want to keep him on."

Ramone patted my shoulder. "I know it's a lot to take in. But you'll learn, and your advisor will be a big help. You'll have a reasonable amount of money to travel with, and your kids will have their schooling paid for like your mom and Fern did for you."

"About that," Jonathan cut in. "Laurel, did your father send you the rest of your education funds for your last two years of law school?"

I looked up sheepishly. "Kind of?"

He glared at me over his reading glasses. "There's no 'kind of' here. Either he did or didn't. I noticed Luke gave you a funny look when you talked about Josephine's student loans. You took out loans too, didn't you? What happened?"

I put the spreadsheets down and sighed. Jonathan was a sharp observer, and it was a trait that made him such a fantastic attorney.

"Victor went nuclear when he found out I'd transferred law schools to be closer to Fern."

"So what happened?" Ramone asked.

"His accountant had already sent funds for the first semester of my second year, but when Victor heard I'd transferred, he blocked the funds after that, and I ended up getting a student loan for the last three semesters." It made me sad and angry all over again, just thinking about my conversation with Victor that day.

Jonathan took off his glasses and rubbed his face. "Damn it, Laurel, why didn't you tell anyone?"

"I didn't want Fern to know and have something else to worry about. It was bad. He's called me names before—you know how he is. But I've never heard him like that. Luke finally took my phone and hung up on him."

"I knew I liked Luke," Ramone muttered.

Jonathan sat back. "Don't pay off your loans yet, all right? I want to look into it."

I nodded and glanced back down at the spreadsheets. "I'm so grateful, and shocked by this." I gestured at the itemized invest- ments laid out on the spreadsheets. "But now I'm worried I'll screw it all up."

Jonathan smiled. "Don't be reckless. And you'll need to learn a few things about stocks and taxes. But other than that, you keep an eye it and just live your life like you've been doing." He made it sound so easy.

"You'll have more freedom," Ramone added. "And fewer worries about money. But Jonathan's right. It probably won't change a lot."

During my last semester when Fern was so ill, I'd severely overextended my credit card and resorted to selling some jewelry, and a few other items I'd inherited from my mother, to pay for necessary expenses and groceries so I could be around for Fern. I looked at them with a lump in my throat, and vowed I'd take care of the wonderful gift Fern had given me.

Now, I needed to figure out what Sebastian had meant when he said we needed to get my "shit" sorted out.

Chapter 18

My reprieve was over. Martina told me Sebastian had been working out of town for a few days the night I got back. I'd breathed a sigh of relief. But I also missed him, which confused and worried me.

So I kept myself busy going through Fern's documents and accounts, trying to familiarize myself with her affairs. I also met with Lydia, her accountant, and reviewed spreadsheets and tax documents with her.

After our first meeting, I got home and walked into the kitchen, then slumped onto a barstool.

"Fern's accountant makes me feel dumb."

Martina stood at the counter prepping hors d'oeuvre trays. "You don't like spreadsheets and taxes? I'm shocked. Martini Monday starts in an hour, though, so you need to snap out of it."

"I'm not sure I can fix being dumb in an hour."

She smirked. "True. And you're not dumb."

I got up to wash my hands and help her. "What martini recipe did you pick for tonight?"

Ramone and Jonathan had taken over Martini Mondays for the past few weeks while I was gone, and I'd heard they'd served delicious fruity summer cocktails.

Martina held up a bottle with dark pink liquid in it. "Prickly pear martinis, in celebration of Sebastian's birthday on Friday. He's back in town."

My insides jumped, and adrenaline hit my system. "That flavor fits him perfectly. Is he coming tonight?" I tried to sound casual.

Martina slid me an exasperated look. "Yes. And since I'm the designated host this week, I also invited our new neighbor up the street. He introduced himself a couple of weeks ago out by the mailbox, and I think he's living alone there. I don't know if he's gay or not, but probably."

"Is he in the white house with the pink door?"

Martina nodded. She held up her hand and started ticking off fingers. "But he just moved to Palm Springs, he dresses well, he's in good shape, and good-looking. So there's an eighty-six percent chance he's gay."

I nodded because it was pretty much true. I had a sudden thought. "Hey, is Sebastian gay?"

She squinted her eyes. "You know he's not gay."

"You just said it yourself. He lives in Palm Springs, dresses well, he's in good shape, and he's good-looking. So there's a pretty good chance—"

She shook her head. "No, Dopey, he's not gay."

"Did you just call me Dopey?"

"Yeah. He finally told me why you used to call him G–for Grumpy." Martina glanced at me. "And today, you're D for Dopey. Or Dumbass. Take your pick."

"Rude! So, while we're on the subject, is Damien gay?" I asked.

Martina shook her head. "No. And don't let Sebastian hear you asking about Damien. You'll *think* Sebastian's grumpy then."

"Why would Sebastian care? Although, those two seem to have a strange relationship. I can't tell if they're friends or not."

"They're friends, unless it involves certain things." Martina looked down at the dark pink prickly pear syrup bottle. "Now quit fishing. You and Sebastian need to get your shit sorted out without my interference."

I remembered Sebastian saying we needed to get our wires "uncrossed" after I took the bar exam. It made me wonder if I'd misjudged our situation. I had an uncomfortable feeling in the pit of my stomach, but Sebastian had been a grumpy asshole when we first met.

That evening, we all sat around the large indoor dining table off Fern's kitchen. It was still blisteringly hot outside, even late at night.

The new neighbor with the pink front door was a nice guy. His name was Scott McCullough, and he'd recently bought an interest in a bar in downtown Palm Springs.

"What's the name of your bar?" I asked him.

"The Cockpit."

"Oh. Does it have an aviation theme?"

Ramone choked on his martini and started laughing.

"Hmmm, something like that," Scott answered, grinning.

Sebastian had been mostly silent since he got here, but he smiled for the first time.

Martina smirked and shook her head. "It's a *gay bar*. And it's called The Cockpit. As in cocks?"

"I'm sorry! I get it now, and it's a fantastic name for a gay bar."

"Thanks. I think so too. And I'm gay, so it's a good fit."

Martina wiggled her eyebrows at me. "See? Eighty-six percent chance." Then she turned to Sebastian. "How do you like your prickly pear martini?"

Sebastian shrugged. "It's fine. What're you two talking about?"

"Laurel asked me today if you're gay."

I choked and glared at Martina, then I slowly turned to Sebastian. He quirked his eyebrow at me.

Martina saved me from having to answer. "She knows you're not gay. I told her that if there's a handsome man who's in good shape in Palm Springs, he's likely gay."

Sebastian grinned. "Nice to know you think I'm handsome and in good shape."

Camila, Matías' wife, leaned forward. "Laurel, Sebastian's been flirting with you every time I've seen you guys together."

My eyes rounded in panic, and I took a gulp of my martini to give me a second to think.

Martina nodded. "He lets you call him Grumpy, for hell's sake."

I plunked my glass down. "Uh, guys. Let's not have this conversation. Camila, you've seen us together, what, twice now? He was just being nice. He feels obligated because of Martina, and maybe Fern."

I shifted uncomfortably and turned to Sebastian. "I know you were just being nice." I thought about it for a second. "Well, actually, you're not that nice. You barely talked to me, or if you did, you'd grunt, ask me what's up my ass, or roll your eyes."

Matías laughed long and loud. "She knows you well, man."

I kept talking. "I'm sorry I was teasing you. But in my defense, you were a jerk, and you kind of deserved it. I didn't realize I was irritating you. Okay, the first few times we talked, you made it pretty clear. But then you started being decent. And then you weren't. You give me whiplash sometimes."

Someone coughed, as if trying to cover a laugh. But nothing about this conversation was funny to me. "I thought we were becoming friends. I thought you liked hanging out with me. But now I know you don't want to be friends—"

"You said that before. Who the fuck told you that?"

I stared at him in confusion. "You did. You said exactly that."

"When did I tell you that?"

My head reared back. "A while ago in Fern's kitchen, when we were having Thai food. After the Kenny incident, Martina gave a toast to 'whatever you two are,' and then I said we were friends, and *you* said no, but I could think that if it made me feel better. I even asked you again if we weren't friends, to make sure I hadn't misunderstood." My voice got a little ragged, so I shut up.

Sebastian exhaled. "Ah, fuck."

Everyone else was dead silent.

"Hey, I understand. I'm fine just being... acquaintances." I looked down at my plate.

"Well, I'm not." Sebastian got up and walked over to my chair. "*Cielo*, we need to talk. But not in front of these nosy fuckers. Let's go for a drive." He squatted down, then put both hands on my cheeks and turned my head toward him. "I'm sorry I hurt your feelings. That wasn't what I meant."

I looked at him. "It's okay. Really. You didn't hurt my feelings. We're fine."

He stood up. "Liar. Do you really want to have this conversation in front of everyone?"

I sighed, giving in, because he was right. I didn't want everyone listening. "You're going to have to drive then. I've had two martinis. Wait, how many have you had?"

"One sip. And yeah, I'm driving. Come on, *mi cielito.*" Sebastian grabbed my hand and pulled me up, then started walking toward the patio door.

"You said you liked the martini," Martina called.

Sebastian didn't turn around. "I lied."

"*I* like the martini," I heard Camila say. "And I'm really liking these Martini Mondays. This is better than watching a telenovela."

Chapter 19

Sebastian kept hold of my hand as we walked to his truck. Without saying a word, he opened the passenger door, then helped me up.

I tried to bat his hands away. "I can get in myself."

"I know you can. I just didn't know if you would. Buckle up." Sebastian carefully grabbed my knees and twisted me sideways into the truck, then slammed the door.

"Where are we going? We can talk here at the house," I said when he climbed in.

"Not with them around. We're going to my house, where we'll have some privacy and can sort your shit out."

I turned to him. "*My* shit?"

"Yes, *your* shit. I know what I want."

I looked out the window. "Seriously, what's there to talk about? It's not a big deal." He didn't answer.

Sebastian lived less than five minutes away from Fern's house. He parked in his garage and led me inside, then switched on a lamp.

He folded his arms. "We can talk in here or out on the back patio."

I froze, thinking about his infamous hot tub. "Here is fine."

He gave me an assessing look, then inclined his head toward the couch. Instead, I walked over and sat in one of his navy chairs. He put his hands on his hips and bowed his head, but still didn't say anything. He walked over and sat on the couch across from me. I glanced around his clean, minimalist living room, then finally looked at Sebastian and raised my eyebrow, determined not to start the conversation.

Sebastian watched me. "What's this about me saying I don't want to be friends?"

My gaze slid away from him. "Exactly what I said." I paused and tried again. "I already told you. It's not a big deal, and I'm sorry if I've annoyed you. But, to be honest, everything and everybody seems to annoy or irritate you. Just never treat me like Mia, or Francesca, and we'll be fine."

Sebastian leaned forward, and looked at me for a few seconds as if choosing his words. "A lot of people annoy me. That's true. And I don't like getting hit on when I'm working, or with friends or family."

"But you could still be civil."

He shook his head. "For all Francesca knew, you were my pregnant fiancée, and she was asking me in front of you if she could come over to fuck in my hot tub."

I held up my hand. "Okay. I get it about Francesca. But the rest—when I first said hello, and also thank you at the Inglenook Inn, you were a jerk. For no good reason. And when I saw you outside the law offices, you were still a jerk. Then those first couple of times at Fern's house—a jerk. There was a definite pattern."

I rocked in the chair anxiously. "Then you started not being a jerk, and actually joked around a little. And you hung out with Martina and me. It was nice. We seemed to get along, so I thought we could be friends. But you've made it pretty clear you don't want that. So again, I'm fine, it's fine, it's all good." I stood up.

"Sit." Sebastian pointed at the chair. "You've had your turn. Now it's mine."

I hovered above the seat.

"Sit," he asked again softly.

I slowly sank back down.

He ran his hand through his hair. "It's true. I don't like most people. They're usually a pain in my ass and want something from me. I've dealt with rich assholes most of my life. While I worked in landscaping with my father, as a bartender, and now in security and property management."

I understood what he was saying. My father was one of those rich assholes.

Sebastian leaned back. "And I've had clients hit on me, sometimes with their husbands or wives in the other room. So I stopped doing house calls."

He stared at me intently. "Yeah, I've fucked women, and that's all I wanted from them. I also made it very clear I didn't want anything more. Most got it, others not so much. So I've had to be a dick occasionally to get my point across. It's efficient, and it usually works."

I stared at him for a long minute. I was shocked at all the words coming out of his mouth, but less shocked about what he was saying.

I pointed at him. "When you were mean to me, you thought I was going to what? Want something from you? Hit on you? What, exactly, did I say or do to make you think that?"

"Nothing. I didn't like you before I met you," he admitted bluntly. "I pictured an entitled, rich, spoiled law student from New York, who I'd have to deal with if Fern left her shit to you."

I glared at him.

He held his hands up. "But you aren't like that. You did annoy me at first. No offense, because everyone does. But your jabs and half-assed jokes were kind of funny."

"Half-assed jokes?" I huffed.

He grinned, then studied me. "And you offered to have Martina come live with you after I'd been listening to her cry herself to sleep because of that dumb fuck, Kenny. You stood up for her, and you were gutsy and smart about it. You're a good friend. And sweet, and goofy as fuck."

I sat up straight. "I'm not goofy."

"That's what you're going to focus on?" Sebastian shook his head. "Then you started freezing me out, and I had no idea why. Now I do. So yeah, we're going to get your shit sorted out. And be friends. For now." Sebastian spit the word "friends" out like he was chewing glass.

I thought about what he'd said a couple of months before. "Why did you say I could think we were friends if it made me feel better?"

Sebastian's eyelids lowered. His lips pressed together, and his arms flexed. He seemed to weigh his words. "I don't remember exactly what I said. I sure as fuck didn't mean to hurt you or scare you away. Let's start over. And quit avoiding me or running away every time I'm around."

I knew what he was talking about, but I didn't admit anything. "You've talked more tonight than all the other times I've been around you—combined." I paused, trying to find the right words. "I think you know Victor, my father, treated me poorly while I was growing up." I looked away for a second. "I lost my mom right before I turned twelve, and Victor vacillated between being cruel or ignoring me. I decided a long time ago I wouldn't let anyone else treat me that way. I'm old enough to have a choice now, and I refuse to live like that again."

Sebastian slowly nodded. "Understood. I hope I never meet your father, and I'm sorry about your mom. I'll try to take better care of your feelings."

"Thank you. I'll hold you to it. Victor is my sperm donor. Being a father is something that's earned, just like being a friend."

We stared at each other for a few seconds.

He finally broke the silence. "Tell me how the bar exam went. And about your trip to Las Vegas."

I smiled, happy that he was making an effort. "The bar exam was horrible, but I got through it. I've never been so nervous in my whole life."

I told him how it had gone, and then we talked about his work. He asked me how my little brothers were doing. Before I knew it, I was sitting on the couch next to him, and we'd been talking for almost two hours.

He took me home not long after that, and we didn't talk as he drove. But it was a comfortable silence. It made me wish we could've been friends from the start.

It wasn't until later, when I was almost asleep, that I realized he'd never answered my question about what he'd meant when he said we weren't friends.

Martina woke me up the next morning with a cup of coffee and a million questions.

I hissed when she opened the curtains to let the morning light in. "It's so early."

"Trust me, I know. I'm the one who has to go to work early this morning. The employee who's supposed to be working with me today took three days off to go camping with her boyfriend. She said it's too hot. Boohoo."

"And you couldn't have waited until tonight?"

Martina sat on the edge of my bed. "No way. So? What happened last night? I was kind of hoping you wouldn't be here this morning."

I opened my other eye and looked at Martina. "We barely started talking again. We're friends, and I'm not that kind of girl."

She grinned down at me. "Yeah, but he's that kind of guy. Are you two okay now? Did you get your shit sorted out?"

I rubbed my face. "He said basically the same thing to me. And it's *his* shit that needed to be sorted." I sat up and took the coffee cup. "Thanks for this, at least. Do you need help today? I don't have any plans and won't start work for a couple weeks."

Martina gave me a funny look.

"What?"

"Have you ever cleaned before?" she asked slowly.

"Not as a job. But I've cleaned my own place since I left home. And I used to follow Rosa around the house after my mom died, until she finally put me to work."

"Who's Rosa?" she asked.

"Our old housekeeper."

"You had a housekeeper growing up?" Martina shook her head.

I felt a little uncomfortable. "She was more than a housekeeper to me. After my mom died, Rosa made sure I had food, clean clothes, and got my schoolwork done. That kind of thing. I had to forge her paychecks for a few years. Victor was bad about taking care of me and making sure the household stuff got done."

"You forged his signature? You little felon." She smacked my shoulder. "How old were you?"

"Twelve."

Her eyes widened. "You were... twelve?"

"My mom died right before my twelfth birthday, and nothing got paid for a couple of months after she was gone." I reached up and scratched behind my ear. "It was Rosa who finally told me Victor hadn't paid her in almost three months. We figured out the household account my mom used. A direct deposit went into it every month, and we went through and paid everything that was overdue, and automated what we could."

She stared at me. "Wow. Your childhood was different than what I thought."

I set my coffee cup down. "Victor had no idea. As long as the house was clean, he got his morning coffee and his dry cleaning was picked up, he didn't want to be bothered."

"Did Fern know? Did you have any other family around?" Martina asked.

"Fern and Jackson contacted me frequently. She sent me a cell phone, which was a godsend. Victor was a complete prick when he finally found out about the phone. He was a jerk regarding anything to do with Fern."

She patted my hand. "It sounds like he's an asshole about most things."

"True. I told him my school counselor recommended I have a phone, which wasn't true, and I needed one for safety reasons since I was home alone so much. That made him back off."

"Why didn't you go live with Fern? She would've been happy to have you."

I sighed. "Victor wouldn't let me. He told Fern he'd never allow me to live with her, and if she pressed it, he wouldn't let me visit or even talk to her. This is depressing. I'm sorry for dumping all this on you."

"No, I'm glad you're telling me. God knows I've talked about Kenny and my divorce enough. I always thought you had this charmed, perfect life, and it was hard to like you." Martina grinned and lightly punched my arm. "At first."

I snorted. "Charmed? I've had a boring, mundane life, except for Fern and Jackson. Anyway, let's go clean houses."

"I don't know if I can afford you."

I thought she was only half joking. "I'm sure I'll be a lot slower than you, but I'm better than nothing. How about if you be in charge of dinner for the next few days, and we call it even?"

Martina looked surprised and relieved. Then she grinned evilly. "It's a sucker's deal. But thank you. And since I'm in charge of dinner for the next few days, I'm inviting Sebastian too. Just so you know."

Chapter 20

My stomach did a lazy somersault when I thought of seeing Sebastian over the next few nights. Then I shook myself out of it, threw on some cutoff shorts and a tank top, and ate a yogurt and a banana while Martina drove. The first house we cleaned was a large, sprawling Spanish-style home in Rancho Mirage, tucked between two sprawling golf courses.

Martina introduced me to the homeowners, Mitzy and Harold. "This is Laurel. She's helping me clean today." We walked into the front foyer and put our cleanings supplies down. "She just graduated from law school last spring. How do you like having a future attorney scrub your toilets?"

"I think it's one of the most worthwhile jobs she'll have as an attorney." Harold laughed at his own joke while Mitzy scolded him. "I'm just kidding. I'm sure you've heard worse attorney jokes, and you'll hear plenty more."

Mitzy slapped Harold's arm and turned to us. "Martina, we're dropping Hercules off at the groomer and running some errands after that, so we probably won't see you before you're done." Mitzy picked up the cute little white terrier next to her. "Thank you, ladies. Have a good day." They waved goodbye and walked out.

When Martina heard the garage door close, she let out a relieved sigh. "I love those two, but when they're here while I'm cleaning, one of them usually follows me around, talking, and it takes forever to clean."

We worked together to begin with, starting in the main bathroom and bedroom. When Martina realized I was a decent worker, we split up and had the house cleaned in just over two hours.

The second house we cleaned wasn't far from Mitzy and Harold's home. Martina told me on Tuesdays she cleaned homes in Rancho Mirage, then usually cleaned for Sebastian's property management company in the afternoons.

"I make more money per hour cleaning short-term rentals, but it's inconsistent and I never know exactly what I'll be walking into," Martina explained. "It's usually fine. But occasionally I find a big mess."

"How does Sebastian like property management?"

"He says it's good money, but I know he gets fed up sometimes. And he seems to get propositioned regularly."

"Really? Why do you think that is? I know Palm Springs is a vacation town, but that's pretty forward."

She shrugged. "He deals with rich, and sometimes famous people who think they can have or buy anything. Or anyone. A few months ago, he did an 'emergency' service call for a long-time client, who ended up propositioning him with her two naked drunk friends to see if he was interested in having a foursome."

My eyes went wide. "That's a lot of naked women."

She smirked. "One of them was a naked man."

"Oh. Well, that's a lot of naked people then."

At the second house, I shook my head at all the dirty dishes in the kitchen sink, and the fast-food wrappers on the coffee table in front of the large screen television. We decluttered the home first, then we cleaned. I found a condom under a bed and cringed while I picked it up, even with rubber gloves on.

"I charge John and his brother more," Martina explained when I told her about the condom. "I call it hazard pay. After lunch, we get to clean the mystery house."

"What's the mystery house?"

"It's a short-term rental in Palm Springs off La Verne Way. Sebastian's company manages the house for a couple who live in Seattle. Jane and Jolie come stay a few times a year when the rain in Seattle gets to be too much, then they rent it out the rest of the time."

We'd decided on lunch at a little vegetarian restaurant in the Smoke Tree shopping center, and Martina parked in front of the Ace Hardware store. The store reminded me of going there with Fern to pick out some stylish black-and-white lounger cushions.

A few of the older male employees had come out and admired Fern's convertible, then asked if they could sit in it and take a few photos. It had been a good day for her.

"You still haven't told me why you call it the mystery house," I reminded Martina.

We'd ordered and found a place to sit. Our small table by the front window looked out onto a cannabis dispensary across the atrium called Leafy Greens. I thought the store was a cafe specializing in salads the first time I read their sign.

"We call it the mystery house because we keep finding weird shit there. It's a beautiful mid-century modern home, and it has a bright red front door. The backyard is sweet, with a pool and spa similar to yours."

"Similar to Fern's?"

Martina looked exasperated. "You keep calling it Fern's house. And Fern's car, Fern's pool, Fern's furniture. You inherited those things, and she wanted you to have them. I don't think you've referred to any of it as yours since she died."

I started to deny it, but then thought back. "I didn't even realize it."

She patted my hand. "Hey, I think it's understandable to miss her, and still be grateful for her generosity. She'd get a kick out of knowing you were giving your dad—sorry, Victor—the middle finger and enjoying the house."

Martina took a sip of her lemonade and studied me. "Inviting your little brothers to come is icing on the cake."

The cashier called our number, and we got our food. We didn't talk for a few minutes as we inhaled lunch.

"This is so good. Here, try the basil lemonade." Martina handed her glass to me and took another big bite of her black bean burger.

I tried the lemonade. "That *is* good. Try this." I forked some stir fry onto her plate.

When we finished our meals, I brought up Fern again. "Maybe it would make her death too final for me. And I don't feel like I deserve any of it."

Martina pointed a finger at me. "That's Victor talking."

I sighed. "Probably. It's going to take some time to feel like the house is really mine."

"Lucky for you, Fern had great taste. She could have decorated in gold leaf and shag carpet."

"True. All right, let's go see if we lucked out and the mystery house doesn't actually have any 'weird shit' this time."

We weren't that lucky. The cul-de-sac where the rental was located had a nice, well-cared-for feel to it. Most of the homes had been remodeled and professionally landscaped. But the first indication that something was wrong was the potent smell of smoke pouring out the front door when Martina opened it.

She covered her nose with her t-shirt and looked back at me. "Oh God, I'm scared to look. I've found some strange stuff in this house, but no one's ever tried to burn it down before."

We hesitantly stepped inside, then stopped and listened. The house was silent, but it smelled horrible. I put my hand over my nose.

Martina looked around. "I don't see any smoke. Most house fires start in the kitchen, so let's start there."

I quickly noticed the home had a fun, bright vibe to it, with retro furniture and vintage art on the walls. But when we walked into the kitchen, there was flame retardant all over the oven and stove top. The oven door had been left open, and several severely burned pizza boxes were stacked on top of each other inside.

Martina growled as she stalked toward the oven. "Those fuckers."

"Mar, no wait." I touched her arm. "Before you move anything, we need to take pictures. If this was a crime scene, the first thing we'd do is take photos before we touch anything."

"Okay. You're right. How about if you take the photos, and I'll call Sebastian and let him know what we found. I swear I have a love-hate relationship with this house."

I looked around. "It's a neat house. I love the 1950s wallpaper."

She nodded and pulled her phone out. "The owners did a beautiful job, but it seems to attract a strange crowd. I found a brand-new wedding dress no one claimed one time. And another time, a box of used sex toys." Martina grimaced. "*And* an entire case of absinthe, minus one bottle. I had to google what it was, because, seriously, who drinks that stuff?" She shook her head.

I cringed, then chuckled. "Yeah, that's all pretty weird."

Martina called Sebastian while I grabbed my phone and took photos of the mess. I could hear her talking to him.

"It looks like they tried to cook three frozen pizzas at once, but they left the pizzas in boxes and probably the plastic wrappers. And they stacked them on top of each other." Martina paused and listened.

While they talked, I opened the kitchen trash can and looked inside. Sure enough, there were four empty THC gummy packets sitting close to the top. I grabbed some rubber gloves then sifted through the rest of the trash.

Besides the empty packets, there were alcohol bottles and candy wrappers, but that was about it. I snapped photos of everything I found.

"Yeah, Laurel already had the idea—she's taking photos right now. And she's searching through their trash." Martina paused again and listened to whatever Sebastian was saying. "Kayla went camping with her boyfriend last minute, so Laurel volunteered to help. She's been with me all day."

I motioned for her to look at the gummy wrappers. She walked over to see what I'd found and shook her head.

"She found empty THC gummy wrappers in the trash. It looks like the renters got totally baked, then had the munchies and cranked up the oven to cook all the pizzas at once."

While they talked, I walked over and opened the sliding glass door in the kitchen, then opened the window above the kitchen sink as well. It was hot outside, but we desperately needed fresh air.

Martina continued talking to Sebastian. "Okay. The smell of smoke was bad when we opened the front door, but I don't see any damage besides the oven. All right. I'll see you in an hour."

Martina hit the off button, then blew out a breath. "When you get done, text those photos to Sebastian, will you? Then let's clean the rest of the house like we've been doing, except leave the kitchen for now."

I sent the photos, and we got to work. I was finishing up the last bedroom and had just bent over to dust the nightstand when I saw Sebastian leaning against the doorjamb watching me. I'd had my earbuds in, but straightened and pulled one out when I saw him.

Instinctively, I hesitated before greeting him. "Hey." I lifted a hand awkwardly.

He saw my hesitation and his jaw tightened, but he walked into the room.

Then he looked me up and down and smiled. "This is a different look for you."

Clearing my throat, I fidgeted a little. "It's hot, and this is the coolest outfit I have."

I probably looked like a sweaty fifteen-year-old in my cutoff shorts and thin little tank top. All day, my mind kept circling back to our talk last night after leaving Fern's house—my house—together.

"Hmm." He stared at me.

"Well, my string bikini would have been a little cooler."

He slowly grinned. "I'm sure a few clients would have liked that."

I cringed inside. I had no idea why I'd said that. "What's happening with the charbroiled pizza mess in the kitchen?"

Sebastian's mouth turned down. "I got the burned boxes out. We'll have to replace the oven and deep clean the kitchen. I'll also get a couple of air purifiers and odor absorbers to deal with the smell."

"Sounds like a lot of work."

He rubbed the back of his neck. "I've seen worse. A crew will come in tomorrow and replace the oven. Those fuckers could've burned the house down, but I'm glad at least one of them wasn't too high to use the fire extinguisher."

I finished wiping down the nightstand, then gathered the cleaning supplies, and we walked back to the kitchen.

The mess had been partially cleaned up. The kitchen still smelled like smoke and fire-retardant chemicals, but it was already much better.

"Martina said you two are about done. What're you doing for dinner?"

I shrugged. "Not pizza, I hope. Our deal was I'd help Martina clean, and she'd take care of dinner. After this strange day, I think we'll probably hit a drive-thru on the way home."

Martina came into the kitchen and took off her rubber gloves. "I'd settle for drive-thru. I was telling Laurel about this crazy house earlier, and then we walked in on this mess."

Sebastian looked around. "I need to call the owners and let them know what happened. Why don't you two head home, and I'll grab some takeout and meet you at your house?" Sebastian looked directly at me.

I didn't reply. I figured Martina was the one in charge of dinner, so she could make the call.

She nodded enthusiastically. "Yes, please. Bring your swimsuit and let's sit in the spa afterward. No pizza though, okay?"

Sebastian and I grinned at each other.

"That's what Laurel said. I'll meet you two at the house in an hour." He brushed past me as he walked out. "You can wear your string bikini in the spa. That'll keep you nice and cool, *cielo*. See you later."

When we heard the front door close, Martina turned to me. "How does he know you have a string bikini?"

I blushed a little. "I, uh, may have mentioned it."

"Ah, that explains it. A typical conversation between friends, right?"

I shook my head. "Just shut up. Let's get out of here, I smell like a chain smoker." We finished up and headed home.

Sebastian walked into the house later that evening, carrying two bags from a local café and his swimsuit slung over his shoulder. Martina and I had both showered and were getting drinks and plates out.

Martina dug through the takeout bags. "Oh good, you went to Lula's. Did you get the berry mango salad?"

"Yeah. And a few panini sandwiches."

Martina smiled. "You know me well."

I helped pull food out. "That sounds delicious, and thanks for picking it up. I'll pay you back after I eat."

"That wasn't part of our sucker's deal. I'm paying for it," Martina reminded me.

Sebastian cut us off. "I already got it. You can pay me back with dinner tomorrow night." He looked over at me.

I smiled nervously. "Deal. Thank you, I'm starving."

We sat down at the bar and ate. When we finished up, Martina let out a long sigh then cried off going swimming.

"I've had it, I'm exhausted. Sebastian, Laurel will go swimming with you."

"But you have your suit on under your clothes already," I pointed out. I was panicking a little inside, thinking about being in the spa alone with Sebastian. "Why don't you at least sit with us for a bit? It'll help you sleep."

"I'm too tired, and I didn't sleep that well last night. I've been worried about Kenny and my divorce."

I couldn't argue without sounding insensitive, so I just nodded and looked over at Sebastian. "It looks like it's just you and me."

He grinned and stood up. "It looks like."

Chapter 21

Sebastian turned on the jets and was already in the spa when I walked out. The water didn't need to be heated during the summer months, but the jets still helped to massage sore muscles.

I hadn't even thought about wearing my string bikini, but wore my basic black one. Sebastian leaned back against a jet with both arms stretched out. He looked tired, but relaxed. His eyes followed me as I walked over to the edge of the spa.

Climbing in, I sat down and kept a little distance between us. I groaned as a jet hit my sore back. "I need to get in better shape. I cleaned for one day, and I'm tired and my back is achy."

"What's achy, your upper or lower back?"

"Both, but mostly lower. I think it's from bending over more than I'm used to." I leaned forward and put my hands on my knees, then raised myself up a little so the jet hit the small of my back.

Sebastian sat up. "My back would get sore sometimes after working a double tending bar. If you trust me, I'll massage the kinks out."

I looked up. "What do you mean, 'if I trust you'?"

Sebastian eyed me. "You look like that. And we're here." He pointed at me, then at the spa.

"I look like what? And what does being in the spa together have to do with trust?"

Sebastian sighed ,then chuckled. "Looks like I need to spell a few more things out after our last misunderstanding. You don't pick up on the usual clues, do you?"

"Okay, I'm a little lost—again. And I'd like to avoid any more misunderstandings, so just be blunt."

He nodded and grinned wickedly. "We're alone at night in a hot tub. But you have to trust me not to try anything until you're ready." He leaned closer. "Because you're sweet, hot as fuck, and I like you and want to fuck you. Is that blunt enough?"

I stared at Sebastian. "Hot as...? You like me?"

"*Cielo,* you can't be this clueless. You're funnier than shit. You've got a brain, a sweet body, and better yet—you aren't annoying to be around."

"I'm not clueless."

Sebastian pinched the bridge of his nose, but he was smiling. "Okay. Again, that's what you're getting out of this conversation? I want to be more than just your friend. Is that clear enough? Come here." He spread his legs and patted the bench in front of him. "Let me rub some knots out."

I looked at him, a little shocked. "I didn't think you even liked me twenty-four hours ago. I'm not going to touch the rest of what you just said. Honestly, I thought you didn't. Like me, that is. And I like you too." Putting my hand over my eyes, I sighed. "Oh God, I'm screwing this up."

Sebastian took my hand and pulled me to him. "You're not screwing anything up. Trust me." He brushed a wet strand of hair off my cheek.

I looked down at his defined chest and abs. "If we're being honest, I like the way you look too." Then, for some ungodly reason, I looked lower.

"Hey. My eyes are up here." He laughed in my face, and I blushed to my roots. Then he gently kissed my cheek, turned me around, and settled me between his legs.

God, I was blushing *and* sweating. And I could feel his hard length against my lower back. I needed to finish what I started.

"I like you too. Not just the way you look. You can be nice, and your friends and family love you." I thought about it for a second. "Did I just say you were nice? I didn't see that coming."

He laughed again and pushed my upper back forward a little, then started massaging me.

I continued. "Martina loves you, and you help take care of us. Even though you can be a grumpy jerk sometimes."

Sebastian squeezed my shoulders in mock retaliation, then started kneading my lower back with his fingers, digging in and working the muscles.

An involuntary moan slipped out, and Sebastian paused. Then he started massaging again.

I cleared my throat. "I don't think I'm ready to handle you trying to 'get in my pants' just yet. I'm kind of new at this."

He paused. "How new?"

It seemed surreal to be having this conversation with him. I shifted uncomfortably.

He gently squeezed my shoulders. "I'll need to know sooner or later. Talk to me."

I sighed and glance back at him. "I've had sex with exactly one guy, and we dated for almost six months before then."

He froze for a second. "He's a fucking moron if he waited six months."

I didn't think Marcus had been a moron. He'd been patient and decent, even though he wanted to have sex before I was ready. And he'd looked like a young Jon Hamm. I didn't tell Sebastian any of this.

"He wasn't a moron. He was sweet."

"Sweet, hmm? Where'd you meet him?"

"A college roommate. I lucked out and had great roommates. And one of them introduced us." I hummed with pleasure as he massaged my shoulder blades.

"Why'd you break up?" he asked absently.

"He left for graduate school. Neither one of us was ready for marriage. I was miserable for a little while, but looking back, it was for the best." I glanced over my shoulder at him. "I've heard a few things about you."

"Like what?"

Bumping his knee, I glanced back at him. "That you've gotten your money's worth out of your hot tub."

"Huh."

"Your one-word answer speaks volumes." Tingles spread through my body from where he touched me. I shifted a bit.

"Some people are fine seeing more than one person at a time. But it's not for me—I'm not built that way."

"Okay."

"No hard feelings if we aren't compatible." There *would* be hard feelings. "I don't want to be with someone I can't trust. I'd rather not be with anyone, and I have no problem taking care of myself when the urge hits."

Sebastian abruptly stopped massaging me. "Not a good thing to say when I have you sitting almost naked between my legs."

"What? That it's a deal breaker, or taking care of myself?"

"Yeah, that part. And you're going to show me one day."

Heat flooded me at the image.

He rested his chin on my shoulder. "Don't worry, *mi cielo*, I'm aware you're not built for casual sex. I don't want that with you either."

Then he abruptly lifted me by the waist and put me on the bench next to him. "I can't keep touching you without wanting more." Sebastian laid his head down on the edge of the spa. "Let's talk about something else."

He reached down and adjusted himself in his suit. "How come your brothers are so much younger than you?"

I could still feel where he'd been touching me, and my body tingled. But I had a lot to think about, so I settled back.

"I guess it's obvious they're my half-brothers. Victor and Chloe probably weren't planning to have kids, and the twins were born almost ten years after they married."

I laid my head back and looked up at the night sky. "I love those little guys. They're mischievous, and can be a handful, but I'm so glad they're in my life."

"They love you too. I hope Lennie keeps his clothes on long enough to make it through elementary school."

I smiled. "Do you have any siblings?"

"Two sisters. My oldest sister is Araceli, and her husband's in the army. My younger sister, Liliana, is finishing up nursing school."

"Do you have any nieces or nephews?" I asked.

"Two. My older sister has one boy and one girl. They're moody teenage shits, but basically good kids."

"Can I ask you something?"

"Yes, *mi cielo*."

"Okay, that's another question. But my first one is how come you're not in a relationship already, or married?"

Sebastian didn't answer for a moment, while he stared out at the backyard. "I've had two serious girlfriends. One in high school, and we were way too young. The other one was right after I moved to Palm Springs and started bartending at Cecilia's."

He paused and reached over to take a drink from his water bottle, then handed it to me. "It's just water. It'll help your sore muscles."

I grabbed it and took a big drink. "Thank you. So, the second girlfriend," I prompted.

"I was in my early twenties and making decent money as a bartender. I also did some landscaping on the side. But my girlfriend didn't think it was good enough. Charlotte was a bitch about it, but she was right."

I waited for him to continue and finally nudged him with my foot. "And? What happened?"

He grabbed my foot, put it in his lap, and started kneading my calf. Licks of heat shot up my leg. I hadn't known a calf could be an erogenous zone.

Then he started kneading my thigh. Tingles speared through me, and I sucked in a breath.

Sebastian grinned knowingly. "Her parents came to Palm Springs every winter, and her dad always complained about not being able to find a decent property manager for his house. He'd ask me sometimes to do things for him because he knew I was handy. He also asked me to install a few simple security cameras once. I researched a bit and suggested a better option. That led to me doing more things for him, then his friends and neighbors, which led to me start my business."

"What happened with Charlotte? Is she still around?"

He shook his head. "She didn't like how much time I spent working once I started a business, and she finally gave me an ultimatum. I wasn't ready to get married, and especially not to her."

I fidgeted with my earlobe. "What do you mean, especially not her? How long did you date her?"

Sebastian watched me. He let go of my foot and motioned for my other leg. I held it out to him. Little sparks of pleasure shot through me again when he started rubbing it.

"We dated for about two years. I think she would've been better off not being born with a silver spoon in her mouth. While I was building my business, and starting another one with Damien and Zeke, she'd spend her time shopping, tanning, and doing her nails."

He massaged my other leg for a few minutes while we sat in companionable silence. I finally pulled my leg back and motioned for him to give me his. He stared at me.

I reached down and grabbed his calf. "You were on your feet too. So hand it over."

His lip twitched, and he finally extended his leg. I started massaging. He felt so hard and muscular, and I ran my hands up and down his thigh a few times.

Laying his head back again, he hummed. "That does feel good. I like having your hands on me." My stomach did a lazy somersault.

"So? Keep going," I prodded.

He groaned low in his throat, but finally continued. "I ended it when she started hinting about rings. Charlotte didn't handle it well."

"Do you still take care of their house?"

"Yeah, but I try to send someone else over during the winter months when one of them might be around. Last I heard, she was dating some rich guy from San Francisco."

I glanced at him. "Where'd you learn to be so handy?"

"My dad owned a large commercial landscaping company. I learned how to fix things, and run a successful business, working with him."

"He doesn't own it anymore?"

Sebastian shook his head. "He finally sold it. My parents travel a lot now, but they come for Christmas and birthdays."

"He seems like a great dad." I sounded a little wistful. "You're lucky. What about your security and investigations business?"

"That was Damien and Zeke's brainchild. You've met Damien Andreasen. And the other partner is Zeke Deegan. They brought me on because I do low-tech installation and had connections. It's been better than we hoped."

"Give me your other leg." I held out my hand.

Sebastian stretched out his other leg. When I started massaging it, he let out such a low sensual groan, and goosebumps broke out on my body. His eyes drooped, and even leaning back on the edge, I could see the definition in his chiseled chest and arms.

I cleared my throat. "I have another question. Why do you call me *mi cielo* sometimes? I think it means sky."

He looked at me with hooded eyes. "The color of your eyes reminds me of a deep blue sky."

My heart stuttered. "Have you called anyone else *mi cielo*?" I felt like a masochist for asking, but I wanted to know.

"No. I haven't had a serious girlfriend since Charlotte, and I don't think she liked me speaking Spanish to her."

"She's dumb. I like it," I said softly.

He smiled lazily at me. "My dad calls my mom *mi gordita*. So it could be worse."

Chapter 22

Sebastian's family took him out to dinner for his birthday, but he stopped by our house late that evening. We were so still so new I didn't know what to get him.

So we made a *tres leches* birthday cake. Martina also gave him a nice poker set, and I found a hand-tooled leather belt at an art fair.

He apologized for being late as I cut the birthday cake. "My sister, Lilliana, told our parents she wants to move to Palm Springs when she finishes nursing school."

"So? What happened?" Martina asked as I set the cake in front of him. "If they're like my parents, they want to keep their kids close."

"It didn't start well. But I reminded them Lilly has more family here now."

Licking a few crumbs off my fingers, I nodded. "That makes sense."

He watched me intently. "I can lick those off for you."

I smiled. "I bet you can."

Martina made a face, then slid a glass of milk to him.

She gave him a hug and a kiss on the cheek. "I'm going to bed. Happy birthday, old man. Now stop looking at my sweet, innocent roommate like you want to do nasty things to her."

He stared at me over his glass. "I do want to do nasty things to her. And with her."

"Good night!" Martina plugged her ears and walked away.

When she was gone, Sebastian pushed his stool back and pulled me to him. He put his arms around my waist and nuzzled my neck. Then he smelled my hair and groaned a little.

Goosebumps skittered across my skin, and I shivered. "Happy birthday. Did you have a good day?"

"Um-hum. You smell good." He ran his lips down my neck and lightly nipped at my collarbone. Heat raced up my spine, and I leaned into him.

"You smell good too." I still vibrated from his nip on my collarbone.

He stood up and gave me a long, hard full-body hug. "And you feel even better. If I stay, I'll do more than just smell you and taste your neck."

He sighed and pulled away. "So, I'm going home. We good for tomorrow night?"

It took me a second to remember. "Yes. We're meeting Ramone and Jonathan at the club if that's all right. Do you want to take your cake home or leave it here? I'm warning you, Martina and I are like two starving teenagers when it comes to sweets."

Sebastian smiled. He grabbed his birthday gifts, and we walked to the foyer. "I trust you. Just save a little for tomorrow night. I want another piece and some heavy petting."

I laughed nervously. "Okay then. Tomorrow after the jazz club. Cake and... heavy petting."

He set his gifts on the table in the foyer, then grabbed the bottom of my shirt and tugged me slowly into him. "I want one more thing tonight before I leave."

I put my hands on his chest. "What's that?" I whispered.

"My birthday kiss." He held my chin, then leaned in and kissed me. Sebastian licked his tongue across my lips and nibbled on me, and I whimpered low in my throat.

"You taste like vanilla and sugar," he said against my mouth, then pulled back.

My lips tingled, and I swiped my tongue across my bottom lip. "It's the cake."

"Hmm. Not all of it." He gave me another slow, soft kiss, then prodded my lower lip with his tongue until I opened my mouth.

Moving in closer, he wrapped his arms around me, drawing me in tight. His tongue slipped inside my mouth, and he deepened the kiss. My arms wrapped around his neck, and I pressed my swollen breasts into his chest.

Turning around, he backed me into the door, slanting his mouth across mine. His tongue plundered, and I met his strokes. Instinctively, I pushed my hips into his, then stood on my tiptoes and cradled his long, thick length between my thighs.

By the time he pulled back, we were both panting heavily, and I sagged against him.

He leaned over and licked the shell of my ear. "If our first kiss is this hot, we're going to set the fucking sheets on fire when I finally get inside you."

I shuddered in his arms, and he grinned and kissed my cheek.

"You're so fucking sweet. Lock the door behind me, *cielo*. I'll see you tomorrow." He let go, steadied me a little, then stepped back.

"Okay," I murmured and ran my tongue across my lips again.

Sebastian looked at my mouth with hungry, hooded eyes. "Lock the door," he repeated. Then he picked up his gifts and walked out.

Sebastian took me to The Blue Room the next night. The iconic jazz and dinner club was a perfect first date, and I'd asked if we could invite Ramone and Jonathan since I knew they liked jazz and enjoyed going there. I also thought they'd be a buffer and help ease my nerves.

Ramone came over Saturday afternoon to critique my potential outfits and help me get ready. We went through my closet while Martina lounged across my bed and watched.

"That one will do if you're going for the schoolmarm look." Ramone eyed the simple black sheath I had on. "And it's Palm Springs in late summer. Just... no."

Martina snickered. "Okay, you've brutally shot down her last three outfits. How about you try?" She waved at my closet.

"I thought you'd never ask." He hustled forward and started swiping through the hangers.

"*I* didn't ask," I grumbled.

Ramone ignored me. "No. No. God, no, and why do you have this in your closet?" He turned to me, holding up a shapeless, long-sleeved gray dress. "It looks like a sack."

He hung it back and kept swiping through my closet until he got toward the end, and suddenly paused.

"Now this is just fabulous. Where'd you get this?" He held up a chic mini dress in burnt orange. He flipped the dress around, revealing two sheer chiffon ties across the back.

"Fern gave it to me for Christmas a couple of years ago. I forgot I had it."

"I should have guessed," Ramone murmured, looking at the dress. He turned and handed it to me. "Go. Try this on. I'll look through your shoes."

Martina sat up. "If I ever start dating again, will you be my fairy godmother too?"

Ramone grinned. "Oh course, darling. Did you think you had a choice?"

I went into the bathroom to try on the dress. When I looked in the mirror, I knew it was the one.

Ramone held up a pair of tan espadrilles with ankle straps when I walked out. "You look beautiful and very stylish. These shoes are from Fern, too, I presume?"

"Do you even need to ask?" I took the shoes and sat on the bed to try them on.

Ramone smiled. "Not really." His smile faltered a little. "I wish she could be here to see this. I suspect she encouraged Sebastian to find projects they could do together just so she could introduce you two."

I started to stand but stumbled a little when his words sunk in. "No way. She wouldn't have done that."

Both Martina and Ramone laughed.

He put his hands on his hips. "Darling, you know she absolutely would have. Now that we have the outfit, let's talk about hair and makeup."

I sighed, long and loud, but followed Ramone into the bathroom. He and Martina poked and prodded me until they were satisfied.

When Sebastian picked me up that evening, he wore expensive-looking dress pants, the belt I'd given him, and a light blue button-down shirt with the sleeves rolled up. His hair was still a little damp from his shower. He looked so good and smelled faintly of expensive aftershave.

Sebastian studied me, and his eyes grew heavy. "You look very delectable, *mi cielo*."

"Thank you. And you look good enough to eat too." I paused, then blinked. "That sounded way more suggestive than I intended."

Grinning, he took my hands, then ran his palms up my bare arms. "We'll definitely get there. But for now, let's go enjoy the evening." He walked me out to his truck with his hand splayed across the small of my back.

The Blue Room had just opened back up after a summer break, so the crowd was smaller. But the music was still fantastic.

Ramone leaned over during a break. "Have you talked Sebastian into going camping with you yet?"

"No. It's been too hot, unless I go back to Idyllwild."

Sebastian's eyebrows went up. "You like to camp?"

"Yes."

"Hiking, then sleeping in a tent on the ground?" he clarified.

"Is there another kind? And I prefer a pad under my sleeping bag. But, yes. You seem so surprised."

Sebastian turned to Jonathan and Ramone for confirmation. "She camps?"

Jonathan smirked. "Yes, and she used to drag our asses out there all the time. I tolerate it better than Ramone. She even got Jackson to go a few times, and Fern went. Once."

Sebastian stared at me incredulously. "Fern went camping with you?"

I shrugged and took a sip of my cosmopolitan. "It was my sixteenth birthday, so she felt obligated. And we stayed in a campground."

He studied me. "Just when I think I'm getting to know you."

Ramone smiled. "And has she shown you any of her photography yet? She could make a nice living as a professional photographer."

Sebastian shook his head. "She hasn't. Yet."

The singer came back after her break, and we quit talking to enjoy the music. After the show, the boys said goodnight, and Sebastian took me home. Martina had gone out for the night, and the house was dark.

"Did you save me a piece of birthday cake?" Sebastian asked as we walked into the foyer.

"Yes, but it was a close thing." I turned on the entryway lamp and took my sandals off.

We walked into the kitchen and Sebastian looked around. "Have you made any changes to the house? It looks the same."

"Not yet. At first, I was busy studying for the bar exam. Now, I'm just working up the courage."

He rooted around in the fridge. "Do you want anything? It looks like there's an open bottle of wine."

"I'm good. I had two cosmos, and I'm still feeling those a little bit."

Sebastian poured us both water and slid a glass over to me.

"Thank you." I took a long drink, then we walked over to the couch in the living room area and sat down.

He put his arm around me and pulled me to him. "Do you need help going through the house? When my *abuela* passed, it was emotional for my mom."

I shook my head. "It's been almost four months. Martina offered, and so has Ramone. I think I'll go through her office first by myself next week and see how that goes."

"If you change your mind, I can help in the evening." He drew me closer.

He smelled so good. I turned my face to his chest and sniffed.

He smiled down at me. "What are you doing?"

"You smell nice. Like expensive shaving cream, and just you. It's comforting."

Sebastian squeezed my shoulders, then ran his fingers up and down my bare arm. "Comforting?"

I looked up at him and smiled. He bent down and softly ran his lips across my cheek, then up to the hollow behind my ear. He kissed me there, then skimmed his tongue lightly across my skin. My breath caught, and my heart rate sped up. Sebastian shifted slightly and ran his lips down my jaw, then kissed my mouth. His lips were soft but firm.

Leaning into him, I brought my hand up to his neck, then angled myself closer, wanting more. I instinctively opened my mouth and ran my tongue along his lower lip. And the kiss seemed to explode.

Sebastian growled into my mouth, and his tongue met mine. Our mouths opened, and the kiss turned wet and carnal. His hands came up to my cheeks and slanted my head for better access, pulling me closer. I twisted my body toward him, and somehow ended up straddling him.

We kissed and kissed, angling our mouths to get closer to each other. Sebastian palmed my breast, and ran a thumb across my clavicle.

He slid his hands up my legs, drawing my skirt up. His touch felt like a lightning strike across my body.

I became incoherent, and heat swept through me. Lowering myself down on his lap, I felt his thick arousal and instinctively ground down on him.

Sebastian ripped his mouth away from mine, both of us panting heavily. His hands went back to my face, his beautiful eyes dilated and heavy.

"Fuck." He laid his forehead on mine. "I want to free my cock, pull your panties aside, and drive up inside you. And I know you're wet enough for me to do it."

I whimpered, unable to speak.

He pulled his head back and rested his hands on my upper arms, holding me up. "But not tonight. Not yet. You aren't ready, and once we go there, there's no going back."

My heart raced, and I shook slightly.

His hands tightened on my arms. "When we start fucking—and it's going to be sooner rather than later—we're going to be insatiable."

My hips involuntarily moved at his words, and I ground down on him again. He gave me one more long wet kiss, then picked me up by the waist and put me to the side.

I knelt there for a moment, gathering myself. "Okay." I breathed in and out, trying to rein in my lust. "All right." I put my hands on my knees and leaned forward, then slowly sat down and curled into his side.

He pulled me closer and smelled my hair. "You smell like lemon shampoo, perfume—" he sniffed me again, "—and unfinished sex."

I grabbed his knee and squeezed, but he kept talking. "You have to tell me when you're ready. 'Sebastian, please fuck me' will do. And you can say 'please' as many times as you want."

My pussy spasmed. "Oh God," I whispered.

"You say *my* name. I'll be the one fucking you, *corazón*." He ran his finger lightly across my chest, and I shivered violently. "I need to go, or I won't be leaving tonight. Walk me out."

He took my hand, and at the door he kissed me hard and quick. "I have a couple of things to do in the morning, but let's meet for lunch."

I had to clear my throat and focus before I answered him. "Martina and I planned to clean the house tomorrow. We can do lunch here and you can have your birthday cake. Does that work?" An aftershock of lust rolled through me, and I shivered again.

He gave me a slow, pleased smile. "Yeah, that works. Lock the door behind me. Sweet dreams." He gathered me in and kissed me again, then walked out.

I locked the door behind him and rested my head against the door frame. I was in way too deep, but I couldn't bring myself to care.

Chapter 23

We went swimming on Sunday afternoon after lunch, and Sebastian was in the pool before I walked out. I'd changed into my favorite red bikini, and Martina hadn't come out yet.

He watched me with hooded eyes as I waded into the pool. "You're playing with fire," he growled.

Goosebumps broke out at the sound of his low voice. Stopping on the bottom step, water lapping between my thighs.

He lifted his hand, palm up. "Come here."

"I think that's a bad idea."

His lip curled into a wicked smile. "Don't think. Come here."

I stepped further into the pool and met him halfway.

He leaned in and kissed my bare shoulder. "You have a beautiful body, *mi cielo*."

I swayed toward him, then heard Martina open the patio door and stepped away.

While we swam, we mostly behaved ourselves. But Sebastian brushed by me, then trailed his fingers across my stomach a few times. So I swept my hands over his pecs and later across his abdomen. Martina watched us with a little smirk.

That evening, Sebastian and I went to the movies and watched some comic book action film.

Martina cried off with a little smirk. "I need to get ready for the coming work week. You two have fun."

I barely saw the movie. Sebastian held my hand as we walked into the theater, and he stood behind me with his arm draped across my chest while we waited in line for popcorn and drinks.

We toward the back of the theater, and when the lights dimmed Sebastian leaned over and whispered a few of the things he wanted to do with me. Then he slowly covered my neck with wet, hot kisses.

During the second half of the movie, Sebastian slipped his hand under my skirt and ran his fingers up and down my thigh under my lavender sundress. The seats around us were empty, but I grabbed the lightweight hoodie I'd brought and threw it across my lap.

My stomach twisted with lust, and I throbbed between my legs. Toward the end of the movie, I tensed and came close to orgasming when he ran a finger under the elastic of my panties a few times and grazed my slit. I finally grabbed his hand.

Sebastian gave me a slow, wicked grin. "I can feel how wet you are. You ready for me yet?"

"Yes," I finally gasped out. "But not here. Please."

He studied me and realized how close to the edge I was. His face softened, and he slowly dragged his hand back. "Tomorrow, you sleep at my house."

I nodded. Then shook my head. "I can't. Tomorrow we're going to Scott's house for Martini Monday. Come with me."

"Who the fuck is Scott?"

"Our new neighbor? You met him. He owns part of that bar, the Cockpit."

Sebastian chuckled. "I remember."

I huffed out a quiet laugh.

He leaned over and ran his nose along my cheekbone. "Then you sleep at my house the next night."

I gazed at him, wanting to agree but worried I was making this too easy for him.

He sighed, mistaking my hesitation. "How about Friday night—and I get you for the entire weekend?" He leaned over and kissed my neck. "And in the meantime, we can do anything besides fuck. Say yes."

His fingers grazed my bare collarbone, then dipped below my bra and lightly skimmed my hard nipple, then skimmed it again. My body lit up like a firework, and I pressed closer to him.

He leaned in and whispered in my ear. "Say the words, *mi cielito.*"

I gasped softly and arched into his touch. "Yes, anything." I knew those weren't the exact words he wanted to hear.

"Good enough. For now."

After the movie, Sebastian came inside when he dropped me off at home. He had to work early the next morning, so he only stayed a few minutes. But he made those few minutes count.

Martina had already gone to bed, and when we walked inside the foyer, he turned around and backed me against the front door.

After kissing me breathless, he hoisted me up on the hall table and unbuttoned my dress down to my waist.

My breasts felt heavy and sensitive, and my pussy pulsed with need. He dragged my bra down and sucked and licked my breasts until I was mindless and filled with scorching heat.

Sebastian wrapped my legs around his waist and rubbed himself against my core. I cried out softly against him, almost coming from the friction alone. He finally pulled away and lowered me to the floor. I could barely stand.

"I need to go, or we're going to end up fucking here on the floor. Don't take care of yourself tonight. Can you do that for me?" He searched my eyes.

Hot lust still pulsed through my lower stomach. My eyes were heavy, and I just wanted his cock inside me.

"Only if you return the favor." I thought that was only fair. If I had to suffer, so did he.

He grinned slowly. "Deal."

He palmed my breasts and sucked each nipple one last time, then he pulled my bra back up.

Kissing me hard and quick, he steadied me. "Lock the door. Sweet dreams." Then he walked out.

When he shut the door, I automatically flipped the lock and set the alarm. I was wet, flushed, and restless, and I wondered again how we'd ended up here after our talk just last week.

Martina and I walked down to Scott's house that Monday evening with a plate of Parmesan artichoke pastries as our contribution to Martini Monday. I had on a periwinkle blue halter dress that crisscrossed in the back, leaving my shoulders and a portion of my lower back bare. The dress was a few years old, but I loved it. Martina wore a yellow jumper with a tight bodice.

Before leaving the house, I'd texted Sebastian and invited him, but I hadn't heard back. When we arrived, Scott showed us through his house.

"Sebastian and I are going to remodel a house soon. Your home is beautiful," I told Scott as I gazed at his living room. It looked like a photo shoot for an architectural magazine.

He smiled happily. "Thank you. Let me show you around." Scot walked us through his bedroom and bathroom. "The previous owners remodeled the kitchen and bathrooms. But I had it repainted, and mid-century wallpaper hung on a wall in the living room, and one in the kitchen."

The living room felt light and airy. There were a few tropical plants and two elegant sculptural lounge chairs, along with a teal velvet couch. The streamlined hardwood coffee table and hand-woven geometric rug rounded out the room.

I gazed around. "Your furniture is perfect too. It's retro but subtle and tasteful. You did a beautiful job."

Looking around, he nodded. "Thank you. I like how it turned out too."

Scott was good-looking, friendly, and had great taste. I doubted he'd be single for long.

Ramone and Jonathan arrived with Grace and Sheila. A few of Scott's friends and employees from the Cockpit came as well, so it turned into a lively party. Scott also served candy-flavored cocktails and savory Spanish tapas.

Grace eyed her martini glass rimmed with colored Pop Rocks and filled with a sweet electric blue concoction. "I've never had a Pop Rocks cocktail before."

Martina stared at the drink. "I didn't know there was such a thing."

Grace took a sip, then licked the rim. "I feel them crackling in my mouth. It takes me back to my childhood."

Sheila held up her glass with a bright pink liquid. "I have the cotton candy one."

Scott had shaken her cocktail, then poured the cold liquid over a large ball of cotton candy in a chilled glass. He'd edged the rim with purple sugar, and three large, colorful gumballs on a skewer garnished the drink. My teeth ached just looking at it.

Scott's business partner was there as well, and Scott introduced us.

"This is Isiah Nixon. We call him Iz. This is Martina and Laurel, my friends from up the street."

Iz stood well over six feet tall, and based on his crooked nose and muscular frame, he'd played sports at some point—probably football or hockey. He was striking and oozed testosterone. Way too much testosterone for me. He wore black pants and a black button-down shirt turned up at the sleeves.

Iz shook Martina's hand first. "I think I've met you. You're Sebastian's cousin, right? And married to Kenny. I forget his last name."

She smirked. "Hello, Iz. Yes, you know me. I've been to your bar a few times too."

Then Iz took ahold of my hand. "Laurel. Are you married too?"

I shook my head and smiled. His gaze got a little more intense, and he seemed to zone in on me. My dress had a built-in shelf bra, so I hadn't worn another one. Suddenly, I felt a little exposed.

"Where did Scott find you?" he asked in a deep, resonant voice.

He might have interested me if I wasn't already deeply infatuated with Sebastian, so I carefully pulled my hand out of his.

Scott stepped forward. "I didn't find her. She and Martina found me. They're from my neighborhood. And I'm not sure, but I think Laurel's seeing Sebastian."

I started nodding when I felt a muscular arm slip around my waist. I could tell by his feel and smell it was Sebastian. Looking over my shoulder, I smiled up at him, happy he'd made it. He pulled me more snugly into his side.

"She is seeing me. Hello, Iz, you degenerate fucker. Quit looking at her like you want to eat her for breakfast."

Iz threw back his head and laughed. "Goddamn it, Mendoza. I did want to eat her for breakfast, and tomorrow morning too. There are a handful of available women in this town, and you're either related to them," he glanced over at Martina, "or you've already fucked them."

"Shut up, Nixon. She's more than a fuck. But Martina finally scraped off that prick, Kenny, so she should be free any day. If you can handle her."

Iz's eyes narrowed, then he glanced at Martina again.

She raised an eyebrow and sipped her drink.

He mimicked her, and raised his eyebrow too. "Good to know. Well then, let's go get ourselves a candy-flavored cocktail and catch up." He winced and Scott laughed.

We stood at Scott's bar, and Sebastian put together the ingredients for the Sour Patch Kids martini I wanted to try.

He read the ingredients. "Sour apple vodka, watermelon pucker, and lemon juice. You sure you want to try this one, *cielito*?"

I shrugged. "The glass is rimmed with sugar, and it has cranberry juice in it. Besides, I like sour things. Like you, Grumpy."

Sebastian's lip quirked. He made the drink then put the lid on the drink shaker. While he rimmed my glass with sugar, I picked up the shaker and shook it. When I looked up, both Iz and Sebastian were watching my chest intently.

"Oy! Eyes up here."

Iz turned to Sebastian. "You lucky fucker."

Sebastian leaned over and punched Iz in the shoulder without taking his eyes off me. I shook my head at them both, then poured the cold drink into the martini glass and took a healthy sip.

A cold and intensely sour flavor rolled over my tongue. I gasped and choked. "Holy... mother! That's so sour, my nipples are puckering."

Iz ground his teeth. "You lucky bastard."

"Yep," Sebastian answered, still looking at my chest. "Quit staring."

"She's the one who pointed them out," Iz retorted.

Uncaring, I reached over and grabbed Sebastian's glowing green Jolly Rancher martini and downed half of it. "Whew. Okay, I wouldn't recommend the Sour Patch one."

Chapter 24

Early that week, I tackled Fern's office with a vengeance and tried to keep my mind off my raging hormones. Sebastian enjoyed winding me up with slow, drugging kisses and stolen touches. He kept me in a near constant state of arousal, and I'd promised not to "take care" of myself. In hindsight, it'd been an idiotic promise.

Not long after I started going through Fern's desk, I realized she'd already ruthlessly organized it. I should have guessed. Fern had been a successful businesswoman, and she knew she was dying. She'd meticulously labeled the few paper files she kept, and only basic office supplies remained in the desk and credenza.

I did find a folder labeled "Demuth House–See Sebastian" and set it aside. Sebastian and I had made plans to meet Matías at the house later in the week.

When I finished going through the office, I rearranged the furniture a little so I could look out the window while I sat at the desk.

I also added a few framed photos and put them on the credenza, then I looked around the room. It felt a little more like my home.

On Thursday morning, I met Sebastian and Matías at the house. It was located a couple of blocks from the park, and the neighborhood was an interesting patchwork. During the last housing boom, many of the homes had been remodeled.

Some of the other houses probably hadn't been updated since they were built fifty years ago as part of a veteran's housing program. But there were still a lot of nice properties, a sprawling golf course, and the large Demuth park within easy walking distance.

The house itself had three bedrooms, a two-car garage, and a pool. But it needed new paint, the pool resurfaced, and the landscaping overhauled. And that was just on the outside. Fern's notes helped me understand her vision.

I knocked on the door, then let myself in. Matías and Sebastian stood in the kitchen area discussing cabinets and kitchen fixtures.

"Hi, guys."

Matías lifted his chin. "Hey, Laurel."

Sebastian stared down at my legs, and his eyelids lowered. It was a hot day, and I'd worn red shorts and a sleeveless top.

My face heated, and I looked around the kitchen for a distraction. And winced. "We have our work cut out for us, don't we?"

The cabinets were a cheap, thin oak, and the linoleum flooring was peeling and cracking. The house needed to be remodeled—about twenty years ago.

I laid Fern's folder on the scarred countertop and pulled out my laptop. "I found Fern's remodeling notes when I went through her office earlier this week. Give me a minute, and I'll show you her digital file."

Flying through my computer, I pulled up several sub-folders, then pointed to a spreadsheet.

"This is the amount she estimated for the renovations—plus a contingency. We may want to tweak it a little, but I want your input." I looked up and noticed both men staring at me. "What?"

Matías spoke first. "You actually want to be involved in this?"

"Yes." They looked dubious. "Why do you think I'm here?" I pointed at Sebastian. "How did you think this was going to go?"

He leaned his hip on the counter and crossed his arms. "Honestly?"

I nodded. "Of course, Grumpy."

Sebastian narrowed his eyes, but his lip quirked. "Okay. I thought you'd see the house has cheap finishes, an ugly green exterior, and an overgrown yard with a stained pool. Then you'd pass it off to me."

I put my hands on my hips. "I think you just insulted me. Fern's my aunt, for God's sake. I've spent more time with her than anyone else, and watched her do several remodels and renovations. Besides, I want to learn."

Sebastian grinned, then walked over and wrapped his arm around my neck. "Okay, *cielo*, I understand. You want to be involved. Show us her ideas and tell us how you'd tweak them."

I gave them both the stink eye but nodded. "Fine. Let's start with the pool and yard, since Matías is here for that."

He let go, and we reviewed Fern's notes. I also showed them a few of my own. They both listened, then started giving me their thoughts and ideas.

I was pleased and surprised at how well the first work session went. When we wrapped up a little later, we'd decided on what to do about the pool and landscaping, and a few other outdoor issues. It had been a productive meeting.

It was lunchtime, and we were all hungry. We decided on a little Tex Mex place on Sunrise, and Matías' wife, Camila, met us there. The three of them knew each other well, and they joked and laughed together through the meal. Matías clearly adored his wife, and a wisp of longing curled through me as I watched them together.

"I'm so full." Camila groaned as we walked out of the restaurant.

Matías patted her stomach. "The chips, tacos, and the chocolate-covered churros probably did it. You have a food baby."

She swatted his hand away and sniffed. "I regret nothing. Their chocolate-covered churros are almost as good as an orgasm." Camila had a dreamy look in her eyes.

I choked, then started laughing.

"I'm glad you said 'almost' or I'd have to spank you." Matías reached over and swatted her ass.

She grinned over her shoulder. "You can still spank me."

He grabbed her, spun her around, and gave her a scorching kiss.

I choked on another laugh and turned away. Sebastian shook his head and pulled me toward his truck.

He called to Matías. "Nobody wants to see you maul your wife. We're leaving. I'll talk to you tomorrow."

Matías didn't stop kissing Camila, but he put his hand up in acknowledgment as we walked away.

Sebastian had an afternoon appointment with a new client, so he took me back to get my car. I'd left my computer and Fern's folder on the counter, and he went inside with me to get them.

When we walked into the kitchen, he came up behind me and put his arm around my waist, drawing me back against him. Then he brushed my hair off my neck and kissed and licked me there.

He put his lips next to my ear. "Your legs and ass are fucking hot in those shorts."

"It's too warm for pants," I whispered back.

He reached around and turned my head to him. "Give me your mouth."

I lifted my face up, and he nipped and sucked on my bottom lip, then thrust his tongue inside. He kissed me until I was wet and panting for him.

I pushed back into his crotch and felt his hard shaft. My insides churned with need, and I rubbed myself against him.

"I ache inside and I need to come," I admitted.

He slowly grinned, then ran his hands up my ribcage and cupped my breasts. I grabbed his thighs and ground back into his length even harder.

"I can help you with that, *cielo*. We agreed to anything but fucking, and I want to feel your pussy."

A broken moan escaped me. He squeezed my breasts hard, then pulled up my shirt. Unclasping my bra, Sebastian pinched and rolled my nipples. Heat and fire licked through me as I writhed in his hands. I couldn't get enough, and I whimpered with need.

Then Sebastian undid my shorts and slid them down, palming my center. Lightning sparked through me, and I felt moisture saturate my panties. I reached behind and grabbed his cock through his jeans. His hips jerked reflexively, and he groaned.

I rubbed his length as I pushed myself against his hand, and he unfastened his jeans to free his cock. When he touched me, my mind shut down and my body blazed like dry grass after a long drought. I'd never craved anything the way I craved his touch, and I understood now how addictions began.

Sliding my panties down, he fingered my clit. Then Sebastian put his shaft between my legs and rubbed himself back and forth there.

He bit down on my neck and whispered in my ear. "Tighten your thighs around me." I gasped and brought my legs closer around him.

He thrust his cock along my folds while he worked my clit. Then he continued pulling and rolling my nipple with his other hand.

My breathing sped up, and I closed my eyes and threw back my head as a climax built. I could see stars bursting behind my eyelids, and my hips worked even faster against his hand and cock.

"Oh, God. Oh, God," I chanted as I started to come. He thrust even faster between my legs, then came with a low, rumbling growl.

The feel of his hot semen soaking the front of my thighs made me shudder even harder against him, and he tightened his hold on me.

We stood there, panting and still for a few moments as we came down, and he eventually pulled back. My slit and thighs were a mess.

Heat flooded my face when I realized what we'd just done—everything but fuck. I tried to keep my back to him, and quickly used my panties to wipe myself up the best I could, then pulled my shorts back up. I struggled to re-hook my bra.

Sebastian took over and fastened it for me, then grabbed my shoulders and turned me around.

He studied my face. "You okay?"

My eyes darted past him. "I... yes." My face and neck felt hot.

He took hold of my chin. "Then look at me." He leaned in and kissed and sucked my lower lip. "You feel a little better now?" I grabbed his wrists and nodded. Then I melted into him for a second.

Sebastian gently took my panties from my hand, and used them to matter-of-factly wipe off his length. He watched me as I stared down at his still-hard cock, entranced. He tucked himself in and fastened his jeans. Then he pocketed my panties.

My eyes flew to his. "Hey! Those are mine."

He shook his head and smiled. "Not anymore. I'm already late. Walk out with me." He grabbed my laptop and the folder off the counter.

"I don't know if I can walk yet," I admitted.

He grinned and grabbed my hand, then kissed it. "Just wait until we actually fuck, *cielo*."

Chapter 25

Sebastian came over for dinner that night, and my cheeks and insides heated when I flashed back to what we'd done that afternoon. He grinned and pulled me to him so he could thoroughly kiss me.

After dinner, Martina pointed at me. "She doesn't know how to play poker. I think we need to teach her." She grabbed some cards and slid the deck over to Sebastian.

He raised his eyebrows. "What are we playing for?"

I raised my hand. "I'm new here, remember? Let's play for pennies." They were probably card sharks, and I didn't want to lose more than a few bucks.

"Pennies then. For now." His eyes swept over me while he expertly shuffled the cards.

I was awful at it, and they started teasing me after a few games. When they'd explained the rules and listed the different hands, I wrote it all down on a sticky note and stuck it on the table next to me.

Sebastian shook his head. "You keep pointing at your cheat sheet every time you get a new card. We know what's in your hand."

I shrugged. "I know, but I want to learn. We're playing for pennies, so I think I'm good."

"I win." Martina scooped up the little pile of pennies after laying down her cards. "Never play strip poker. You'd be naked after three or four hands."

Sebastian smiled. "I'll play strip poker with you."

Martina started fake gagging. It reminded me of Willie. She shuffled the cards absently and watched us.

The thought of playing strip poker with him intrigued me. "I've heard about it, but obviously never played it. Have you?"

Martina slid the cards to Sebastian. "I don't want to know if he's played strip poker. And you two just need to play 'hide the pickle' already. You're giving me indigestion."

"Sorry." I didn't take my eyes off Sebastian.

He stared at my mouth. "Maybe we can play it when you sleep over tomorrow."

Martina cut in. "Just so you know, she's going to karaoke night with me at the Cockpit before your 'sleepover' tomorrow night. I told Scott we'd come, and she promised me."

"Fuck no," Sebastian bit out.

"Laurel said she'd go, and I'm not going alone. She'll be fine, and you can have her afterward."

He glared at Martina. "Don't give me that bullshit, *prima*. Karaoke night is the biggest pickup night of the week there, gay or straight."

"Well then, come with us if you're so worried about it." Then she dropped her bomb. "And my divorce should be final tomorrow, so I want to celebrate shedding my fucking ball and chain. It'll be a party!"

Sebastian stared at her. "Congratulations. I'm happy for you. I still don't want Laurel going to karaoke night."

He glanced over and finally noticed me glaring at him. "What?"

"Ramone and Jonathan will be there, and I was going to ask you to come. But not if you're going to be a grumpy asshole about it."

"I don't want you at some bar with this newly single crazy woman. The two of you together are cock magnets."

"Hey!" Martina snapped.

"Shut up, Martina. You know it's true." He turned back to me. "You'll be up there, wearing one of your sweet little dresses, or God forbid a pair of shorts, singing karaoke to a drunk crowd."

"So what? So will everyone else—because it's summer, and we live in Palm Springs. And it's karaoke. People get up and sing." I held my palms up.

He leaned over to me. "I may be a grumpy asshole—and you need to change that in your phone—but I'm also a *possessive* grumpy asshole."

"I like that you're possessive. It makes me all hot and bothered and I want to—" I glanced at Martina, "—do very bad things to you. But there's a difference between being possessive and controlling."

He rubbed his face. "You're mine. I don't want other men to see your hot legs and perfect tits. It's not going to change. You have to work with me here."

Martina threw her cards down. "I don't need to be here for this conversation. I'm going to bed. Goodnight, grumpy asshole." She stomped down the hall to her bedroom and slammed the door.

Sitting frozen in my seat, I stared at Sebastian. I panted a little, not knowing if I was more turned on or angry.

I took a breath and let it out slowly. "I told her I'd go since she needs a friend and I've never been. Then I thought we could start our weekend afterward."

Sebastian gritted his jaw. "Okay. I'll go with you."

I could tell this was costing him. "She just told me about it today, or I would've talked to you earlier. I'm glad you're going. It'll be fun."

"Yeah. Fun." His voice was purposefully flat, but his lip quirked. He grabbed my face and pulled me in for a firm kiss. "Now, your question about strip poker. No, I've never played it. I never had the patience."

"That's not surprising." I grinned, happy he'd worked with me.

"But I'd play strip poker with you." He ran a hand down my arm. "We'll need to work out some of this heat first, though."

I knew what he meant. We couldn't seem to keep our hands off each other, and I wanted to touch him all the time. I stood up, then swung my leg over his lap to straddle him. Putting my arms around his shoulders, I dropped my forehead to his.

Then I leaned over and whispered in his ear. "Please, I need you to fuck me."

Sebastian wrapped his arms around my waist, squeezed me to him, and buried his face between my breasts.

Then he pulled his head back and stared at me. "There it is. Thank fuck. You finally ready, *mi corazón*?"

I nodded, and he moved my torso back and forth, sliding my breasts against his chest. He ground his hips up into my center and pulled my hair back to kiss my neck. Then he bit my collarbone.

"Holy Jesus," I shuddered.

"If you're not on birth control, I've got condoms."

"I'm on birth control."

"Good," he clipped. "I went in and got checked before you came back from taking the bar exam. I'm clean and I always wear a condom. But I want to fuck you bare."

I nodded frantically. His words send red hot lava through my system, and I clenched inside.

"Here or my place?" he asked.

I heard him talking, but I couldn't process exactly what he was saying. He arched up into me again, and I moaned, low and broken.

"Here." He answered his own question, then palmed my bottom and picked me up as he stood.

I wrapped my legs around his waist, and he walked us to my bedroom. He kissed my neck and whispered dirty words in my ear.

Tightening my legs around his waist, I rubbed myself against him. Sebastian kicked the door closed with his foot, then stalked over to my bed and laid me down.

"I'm not going slow this first time." He spread my legs and fit himself between them, then ran a hand up my stomach to the undersides of my breasts. "Say it again."

I looked up at him. "Please, don't tease me."

"Say it, Laurel," he growled.

I could feel heat move down my neck and chest, but I grabbed his forearm and met his eyes. "I want you to fuck me. Please, I need you."

He smiled darkly and leaned over me. "That's it, sweet girl."

He deftly slid my shirt up and off, then kissed his way down my chest. He ran his tongue above my right breast, and my nipples tightened painfully as I shifted restlessly beneath him.

He leaned back and looked down at me. I had on a sheer blush-colored lace bra, and Sebastian traced the swells of my breasts with the tips of his fingers, then rubbed his thumbs across my nipples through the fabric.

I thought he told me I had beautiful, perfect breasts in Spanish. He leaned down and licked his way up my stomach, then put his mouth over my left breast through the lace. When he spoke to me in Spanish, my panties always dampened. I loved the sound of it.

Sebastian pulled down my bra cup and sucked on my nipple, then rolled it with his tongue. I pushed further into his mouth and wrapped my legs around his waist again. My hands ran up his back underneath his shirt. I tugged at it, wanting to feel his skin on mine.

His biceps and abs flexed as he pulled his shirt over his head. His perfect V leading down to his groin drew my eyes. I traced it with my fingers, and his stomach tightened.

I'd heard he worked out early in the morning a few days a week with his business partners, and I could feel his muscles under my hands. I ran my fingers inside the waistband of his jeans and lightly skimmed his firm abs, then the head of his hard cock, feeling his precum. He reached down and undid his pants to give me better access.

Pulling my fingers out, I brought them to my lips, tasting him. He growled low, then leaned down and grabbed my panties and shorts, pulling them off. I wanted him so much my pussy quivered in anticipation. I'd never felt this hot and turned on before, and I hadn't realized lust could be a physical ache.

He leaned in and nuzzled my slit, then licked between my hip and thigh. I gasped and arched into his mouth. The feel of his tongue on me was so arousing, an orgasm started to build.

He leaned in and lightly licked over my clit, then blew on it. My hips bucked. He started lapping at me, and slid a finger into my tight sheath. Then added another.

I didn't last long. My hips moved restlessly, and when Sebastian reached up and pinched my nipple, a climax rolled through me, starting in my toes. I gasped and shook as he pumped his fingers inside me.

When I came down, he crawled up my body, nudging my slick opening with his rock-hard cock.

The security alarm went off, and it was *loud*.

"Fuuuck," he growled long and low. "Stay here. Someone's triggered the house alarm." He laid his forehead on my chest for a split second, then slid off me, fastened his pants, and was gone.

I caught my breath at his abrupt departure, then fumbled off the bed, almost falling on my head. I pulled my shorts back on, felt around for my shirt, but couldn't find it. So I opened my top drawer and pulled out the first shirt I touched, then followed him down the hall. Lust, and now adrenaline, pumped through me.

When he headed for the alarm control panel on the wall by the front door, I peeled off and ran to Martina's bedroom. Just as I got to her door, Martina opened it. Her nightstand lamp was on, and soft light spilled through the hallway.

She looked down at my shirt, and her head quirked. "What's going on?"

"Someone triggered the alarm. Sebastian's checking it. Are you okay?"

"Yeah. But I heard glass shatter, and then a loud thump by my bedroom window. I looked outside but couldn't see anything. It's too dark." Martina looked at my shirt again. "What happened to your other shirt? And where'd you get that one?"

"Huh?" I looked down at the stretchy red tank top and noticed I had grabbed the shirt I'd gotten as a gag gift a few years ago. I wore it to bed sometimes. The words "Licked It, So It's Mine" in big white, sexy letters ran across the front.

"It was a gag gift."

"Yeah right. You probably ordered it online," she teased me.

Sebastian walked in and Martina turned to him. "Where's *your* shirt? Have you two finally threaded the needle, played hide the—?"

I smacked Martina's arm. "Enough, you filthy-minded woman."

"You two think this is funny?" He sounded frustrated. Then he looked down at my red tank top and paused.

He shook his head and turned to Martina. "This was directed at you. Someone put a brick through the driver-side window of your car. I heard a vehicle drive off down the street before I could catch anyone, but we'll pull the feed from the cameras."

Martina stiffened. "Right before the house alarm went off, I heard glass shatter, and then maybe one or two seconds later a loud thud by my window."

Sebastian clasped my arm. "*Cielo*, go grab your phone and call the police so we can make a report. I'm pretty sure Kenny is long gone, but we need to call it in."

"Okay."

He turned and started walking out the door. "I'm going to get a flashlight and see what's outside the window. Put shoes on if either of you comes out."

I grabbed my phone and made the call. Martina put on sneakers and grabbed a broom and a trash can.

I shook my head. "Don't clean it up yet. We need the police to see exactly what happened."

Martina leaned her head on the broom handle. "God, I forgot. Cleaning up messes is just a knee-jerk reaction, I guess."

She looked so dejected, I walked over and wrapped my arms around her. "It's going to be okay. We'll make a report and get it sorted out."

Martina hugged me back. "I'm so tired."

I led her over to the couch and we sat down, then I grabbed a throw blanket and laid it over us.

"Talk to me. I know you're more than just tired."

Martina laid her head against mine. "I'm depressed and angry. And frustrated." Her voice broke, and she paused. "And worried my family and friends are going to get sick of all the drama. I don't know what happened. He used to be funny and sweet."

She started crying, and I wrapped my arms tighter around her. I was scared for the first time; I'd never seen her cry before.

Martina got ahold of herself and sat up a little. "Our divorce should be final tomorrow, and that's probably what pushed him over the edge."

I rubbed her arm. "That's not an excuse for trying to terrorize and intimidate you."

"I know."

"I think he figured out he lost the best thing he ever had."

She held up her shaking hands. "He's the *worst* thing that ever happened to me."

"We'll make sure he gets the message he can't fuck with you anymore," Sebastian said from the doorway, making us jump a little.

He put his hand up. "I didn't mean to scare you. He smashed your driver's side window, and I found another brick outside next to your bedroom window."

I felt a little sick. "A brick?"

Sebastian nodded. "There's a small dent in the stucco, but nothing I can't fix. Looks like he missed the bedroom window."

I couldn't help it. A snicker escaped me. I bit my lower lip, trying to keep the next one in.

Sebastian looked at me like I'd lost my mind. "Why are you laughing?"

"I'm sorry. It's just that he really is a moron, isn't he?" I turned to Martina. "He missed the window. And it's huge."

Then Martina snickered.

Sebastian scrutinized us. "You're both fucking crazy." He walked over and kissed Martina's forehead. "I need to go put my shirt back on."

When the police officers came a few minutes later, they pulled up with their overhead lights on. I sighed. At least they didn't have their sirens on too.

While Martina and Sebastian gave their statements to the older police officer, the younger one walked over to me.

"I'm Officer Bennett. Whose house is this?"

"It's mine, I guess."

His eyebrow quirked. "You guess?"

"I inherited it a few months ago. I'm still getting used to it," I explained.

Officer Bennett nodded. "How do you know Martina?"

"She's my roommate and one of my best friends. She lives here with me."

His eyes flicked down to the tank top. I crossed my arms over my chest, and Bennett looked back to my face.

"What's your name?" he asked.

"Laurel Payne."

He pulled out his clipboard. "Tell me what you saw and heard."

I quickly relayed what had happened, leaving out the part where Sebastian and I were in my room almost having sex. "Martina found out today that their divorce should be finalized tomorrow. It's probably what triggered him."

"I need you to write out a statement as well, Ms. Payne," he said, handing me a form.

I took it, then saw movement on the street. Scott, our neighbor, walked up.

"Laurel, are you guys okay?"

"I am, but Martina's ex threw a brick through her car window. He tried to throw one through her bedroom window too, but he missed."

Scott blinked. "The guy who came over to Sebastian's house and pushed her around?"

"Yes, the same one."

Scott's eyes narrowed, and he pulled his phone out of his back pocket. I watched him send a text and wondered who he was contacting this late at night.

A few minutes later, I looked over Scott's shoulder and noticed Ramone and Jonathan hurrying up the street. They looked like they'd been in bed asleep.

"What's going on? Are you all right?" Ramone scanned me up and down, then stopped dead. "And what in God's name are you wearing?"

I blushed, remembering the tank top I'd grabbed. "My shirt isn't important."

"Honey, your clothes are *always* important. Now tell me what happened."

Scott told them what he'd pieced together. I stood there, blankly staring at the form in my hand, when a car pulled up. A sleek gray, late-model Mercedes parked behind the police car, and I couldn't be sure, but I thought Iz was driving. And it looked like Damien was in the passenger seat. I hadn't even known those two knew each other.

Rubbing my forehead, I tried to dispel the tension headache coming on. "Let's go inside so we don't wake up the entire neighborhood."

Scott and Ramone helped round everyone up, and we went inside.

Sebastian used my laptop to pull up the security footage for the officers. It looked like Kenny had parked down the street and hadn't passed the house. The only shot of him was from the garage camera, and it was a brief glimpse of a man dressed in black with two bricks in his hands and a hoodie pulled up over his head, obscuring most of his face. He wasn't recognizable.

"That's probably why he missed Martina's window," Sebastian said, pointing to the screen. "He knew he couldn't get close enough to the house without the other camera picking him up."

"He tried to throw a brick through her window?" Iz looked pissed. He turned to Martina and scanned her as if assessing for any injuries. "No offense, but I always hated that fucker."

A ghost of a smile flitted across Martina's face. "None taken."

Jonathan and Ramone headed home and asked me to call them with any updates.

Scott stared at the computer screen thoughtfully. "I'll check my cameras when I get home tonight, then send over anything I find."

Sebastian turned to Officer Bailey. "I'll forward anything Scott sends us. Give me your contact information." A few minutes after we got done with our statements, I escorted the officers out.

When I walked back into the kitchen, Martina was handing Damien a beer. "I hope you don't mind, Lollipop," Damien said.

"Lollipop?" Sebastian growled, putting his hands on his hip.

Damien grinned. "Ramone calls her Lolly sometimes. I figured you probably call her Lollipop."

"Why would you think that?" I asked.

Sebastian turned to me. "You need to change your shirt."

"Why?"

Sebastian just looked down at my chest.

I re-read it upside down. "I'll go change."

He dipped his head. "Thank you."

Damien grinned. "Don't change on our account, Lollipop. Sebastian, did she lick—"

"Don't even fucking finish that sentence, asshole," Sebastian growled.

I threw up my hands. "Oh, for the love of God. The tank top was a gag gift."

Iz chuckled. "A gag gift?"

Then Damien, and even Martina, started laughing.

I shook my head tiredly. "I hate you guys."

When I got back to the kitchen after changing my shirt, everyone was discussing the incident and what to do about Kenny. So I made a big batch of chocolate chunk cookies using my mom's special recipe while they talked.

It was my go-to comfort food. Then we stood around the kitchen counter, talked some more, and ate warm cookies until well after midnight.

Chapter 26

Early the next morning, I got up to clean the glass out of Martina's car. I swept her seat off first, then pulled out the shop vac and tried to vacuum up the small glass pellets scattered all over.

As I finished, Sebastian pulled up. "What're you doing out here so early?" he asked as he got out.

I raised the shop vac hose and waved it at him. "Cleaning up the glass before Martina wakes up."

Sebastian walked over and gathered me in his arms, then kissed my forehead. "Thank you. She needs nice people around her right now."

"She needs you too. Not just nice people." I poked him, then dropped the shop vac and hugged him back. "What're you doing over here so early?"

He brushed a loose strand of hair out of my eyes. "Same thing. I didn't want her to see the mess."

"You're a good man. You just hide it well sometimes." I gave him another hug.

Then I ran my hands down to his butt and squeezed them both, smiling up at him a little sheepishly. "I've wanted to do that for a while. I hope it's okay."

Sebastian laughed and kissed my cheeks. "I've had my fingers in your pussy and my mouth on your breasts. It's more than fine."

My insides quivered when I thought about how close we'd come to having sex last night.

"Have you talked to Martina this morning?" he asked.

"No. She was asleep when I came out."

He turned to look up the road. "Scott went home and looked at his security cameras. He caught Kenny on camera walking past his house with bricks in his hands."

I tilted my head. "He had a hoodie on. How could you tell it was him?"

"Scott's camera also caught his car when he drove by and parked. The stupid fuck drove his own car." Sebastian's smile was mean.

My eyes widened. "This is serious. He'll get criminal charges this time. And if the prosecutor thinks he was trying to break into the house, maybe felony burglary charges."

The front door opened, and Martina walked out in her bare feet. "It's the ass-crack of dawn. What're you guys doing?"

"I came by to clean up the glass, but Laurel beat me to it," Sebastian told her.

Martina looked at us and her eyes got glassy. "I could have done it. But thank you."

Sebastian squeezed my hand. "Can I have a cup of coffee? I have an hour before I have to be anywhere, and I have some news."

I squeezed his hand back, then let go. "Of course. Come in."

He leaned over and finished wrapping up the cord to the shop vac. "I'll put this away and meet you inside."

When Sebastian walked into the kitchen, Martina and I were making breakfast. He washed his hands then came over and started cutting up the cantaloupe I'd left on the cutting board.

"Did Laurel tell you what Scott's camera picked up last night?" he asked Martina.

"Tell her what you saw," I urged.

Sebastian told Martina what Scott found on his cameras while he finished cutting the fruit. When the food was done, I put scrambled eggs and toast on three plates and poured him a cup of coffee. We sat down at the bar and ate.

Martina shook her head. "He drives a royal blue sports car with distinctive, after-market wheels. That slimy little asswipe."

I agreed. "He's going to have bigger legal problems than you divorcing him. If the prosecutor believes Kenny tried to break into the house, they could charge him with felony burglary." I glanced between Martina and Sebastian. "Has he made any threats against you lately?"

Martina didn't look at either of us as she picked up her coffee cup and took a sip.

Sebastian studied her. "I know you, *prima*. What aren't you telling me?"

I took a stab in the dark. "He's texted you lately."

Martina's head jerked. "How—?" Then she cringed. She knew she'd given herself away. "Damn it!"

Sebastian erupted into blistering Spanish.

"I *do* trust you. And I *know* you're trying to help," she yelled when he finally took a breath. "And I'm not being stupid!"

I put my hand on Sebastian's arm and squeezed. When he didn't stop, I squeezed harder. He finally looked at me.

"Yelling at her might make you feel better. Believe me, I understand. But it's not helping."

He clenched his jaw, then let out a breath.

I turned to Martina. "We need to see the texts. Will you get your phone?"

She sat there, breathing heavily through her nose. She put her palms to her face and scrubbed back and forth. "I did this by marrying him. I may have been young and naïve and stupid, but I brought this on myself. Now I just wanted to clean it up myself."

I understood why people sometimes felt guilty or ashamed if someone they loved broke their trust and physically or emotionally abused them. I'd also learned that, no matter what anyone says or does, those feelings are complicated and don't magically go away.

Martina was clawing her way out of an abusive relationship, which was something my mother never did. I loved my mother to the depths of my being, but I'd also been angry at her when she died. For leaving me, for not leaving Victor before she died, for bringing me into a damaged relationship. I didn't know what to say to Martina, so I told her the truth as I saw it.

"You are the strongest woman I know. And you *are* cleaning this up yourself. I wish my mother had been half as strong and determined as you are." My voice wobbled a little, and I cleared my throat. "Go get your damn phone so you can get him out of your life once and for all."

Martina's face was pale and her eyes were wet, but she sniffed and nodded. Then she walked into her room to retrieve her phone.

Sebastian wrapped an arm around me and curled me into him, but he didn't speak.

A little over an hour later, Ramone called Martina to let her know the judge had signed her divorce decree. She was legally a free woman.

The few texts on Martina's phone from Kenny had been crude, hateful, and full of vitriol. I didn't know why she hadn't blocked him, but it paid off. I noticed Kenny sent the texts late at night, probably when he'd been home alone drinking.

One, in particular, said if Martina went through with the divorce, he'd come after her, and she would be "one sorry bitch." Officer Bennett thought it'd be enough for the prosecutors to charge Kenny with felony burglary.

We debated whether to go to the Cockpit that night for karaoke, but Martina was adamant. She didn't want to change her plans because of Kenny. So late that afternoon, we shopped and primped.

When Martina came home from work, I took her to my favorite boutique in Palm Springs, and then a nail salon. I wanted to treat her to an outfit and a pedicure to celebrate her divorce and shake off the trauma from the night before.

At the boutique, Martina found a sophisticated, flirty green V-neck dress with an open back and a short, flared skirt.

I looked her up and down. "You are smoking hot in that dress. I vote for this one."

The shop clerk laughed. "I second that vote."

At the shop, I also found a sleeveless magenta silk top that lovingly hugged my breasts and left my back bare. It would go perfectly with my tailored black shorts.

Then we went to the nail salon and got pedicures to match our new outfits. The nail technician had long, acid yellow nails and matching disco ball earrings. "What are you two celebrating?" she asked Martina.

Martina's smile was brittle. "My divorce."

The older lady looked up. "I'll be right back." She went to the break room and brought back a cheap bottle of sparkling wine with three flutes. "Honey, life is complicated and messy, and divorce can definitely be something to celebrate." She deftly poured and handed us a drink, then lifted hers up. "My first marriage was an absolute shitshow. So here's to your new freedom and a fresh start."

We clinked our glasses together, and Martina's eyes grew a little damp. I tipped the woman well.

Until then, I'd only spent money from Fern's account on household and living expenses, and paying off my credit card debt. When I'd finally been able to pay off my credit card bill, I cried a little.

But I thought Fern would approve. I also liked to think it was something she would've done herself if she'd been alive. Now I just needed to make it through karaoke night.

Chapter 27

The Cockpit sat on the corner of Indian Canyon Drive and Arenas Road in downtown Palm Springs. It was a popular area for gay bars. I'd gone to a couple of other bars in the area for drag queen brunches with Ramone and Jonathan, but I'd never been to the Cockpit.

This was also my first karaoke night. Martina had already signed up to sing a melancholy Amy Winehouse song about love being a losing game. I didn't think it was very celebratory, but tonight was her night, so I kept my opinion to myself.

Martina had a gritty, sexy singing voice, and she also loved to dance. I could understand the draw of karaoke for her. But I was just an okay singer.

Scott had reserved a table for us, and Ramone and Jonathan were there when we walked in. When Ramone saw us, he got off his stool, looked us up and down, then gave us both cheek kisses.

He clutched his chest. "I'm so proud. My little girls have finally grown up into chic, stylish women."

"You're so funny." I lightly smacked his arm, but smiled happily. Maybe Fern had rubbed off on us after all.

Martina's hair was pulled up in a partial updo, and she'd applied smoky eye makeup.

I'd left my hair down and styled it in soft curls that floated around my face. My makeup was more subdued, but I'd put a little glitter on my eyelids and painted my lips the same shade as my magenta silk top.

Martina looked down at their table. "Have you ordered drinks yet?"

"Jonathan ordered a whiskey. He said he needed it to get through the evening."

Jonathan toasted us with his glass. "We all have our coping mechanisms."

I walked over and hugged him.

Ramone smiled. "I thought I'd wait until you ladies got here. What would you like?"

We looked over the drink menu. I ordered a vodka and cranberry, and Martina and Ramone ordered cosmopolitans and a few appetizers. Sebastian hadn't arrived yet.

An hour later, the karaoke was in full swing, and Sebastian still wasn't there. Martina sang "Love is a Losing Game," but she'd sung it with a little smirk and a pissed-off look. It was a bizarre but fascinating combination. And for half the song, she appeared to be having a staring contest with Iz.

The next karaoke singer, who wore an edgy drag costume with a black bustier and a soft pink chiffon skirt, sang Beth Hart's "Bad Woman Blues" while the crowd clapped along. Then the DJ announced that I'd be singing Dua Lipa's song, "Levitating."

Martina gave me a shit-eating grin and pointed at the stage.

I narrowed my eyes at her. "Fine. But you're coming up there with me and doing backup."

"No problem." She grabbed my arm and dragged me up to the stage.

Martina asked the DJ for another microphone, and I spoke into mine just before the music started.

"I'm a karaoke virgin up here." I pointed at myself.

"I'll take care of that for you!" someone shouted back, and the crowd laughed.

"You can," I drawled out, "by singing the chorus with me and clapping. And come up and dance with us if you're brave."

Then the DJ started the song, and I concentrated on coming in at the right time. The crowd picked up the clapping quickly, and a half dozen brave souls got up on stage with us and worked through a simple routine I'd seen on the video. I tried to remember some actions myself, and by the time we got to the chorus, Martina joined in, and the stage got more crowded.

I encouraged people to sing the chorus, and by the time it ended, I'd made a few mistakes, but overall it was a breathless, fun four minutes. We got a standing ovation and a few whistles and catcalls, and I turned around and clapped for our impromptu dancers.

When we made it back to our table, I noticed Sebastian standing next to Jonathan with his arms crossed.

I walked up to him, and he pulled me closer and put his arm around my waist. Then he ran his hands up my bare back before turning me around to face the stage.

He lowered his mouth to my ear. "I was a little surprised to walk in and see you up there with backup dancers." He kissed my neck. "Nice shorts, by the way."

I shivered, then smiled and leaned back into him, turning my head to give him a kiss.

We crowded around our table, and a little while later, Scott came over. "Martina, I didn't know you could sing like that. Have you thought about performing?"

"I used to play at a couple of restaurants in Los Angeles when I lived with my parents. It was fun, and I'd usually got a nice meal out of it. I used to DJ a little too."

Scott nodded. "I got a few requests from the crowd for you and Laurel to go up and sing another song together. You guys up for it?"

"Fuc,k no." Sebastian glared at Scott.

Scott grinned and slapped Sebastian on the back. "What, you don't like everyone in here enjoying the view? They're quite the pair."

Sebastian turned and stared at me. "Cock magnets," he muttered.

I grinned and shook my head. "I used up all my liquid courage already, but Martina signed up for another song." Scott gave her a thumbs up, then headed back to the bar.

Iz came by not long after that. He nodded at the men, then turned to us. "Ladies, we all enjoyed your song. Laurel, I'm glad we could pop your karaoke cherry tonight."

"Shut up, you horny fucker," Sebastian growled. "And they're not going up together again. Scott already asked."

Iz shrugged philosophically. "They're like hypnotic eye candy together." He turned to Martina. "And you have an amazing voice."

Martina lifted her eyebrow. "Thanks."

They stared at each other for a few seconds until a worker found Iz and asked him about cutting someone off at the bar. He gave Martina a last glance and took off.

"Okay, what's going on with you two?" I nudged her.

She fidgeted with her drink. "Nothing. You saw when I talked to him at Scott's house."

"I think there's more to it. So spill."

She looked over my shoulder. "Oh, there's someone I know. I'll be back." She took off like her hair was on fire. What a little liar.

We stayed until around midnight. Ramone and Jonathan left not long after Sebastian came, and Martina drank two more cosmopolitans and continued to circulate.

Sebastian leaned over and took both my hands when we were alone at the table together. "You do look like eye candy. Nice shorts."

"Kind of a legs man, aren't you?"

His eyes drifted down to my breasts then back up to my face. "Yeah. And also an ass, tits, and face man. Basically, the whole package. Which you have."

Heat coursed through my system, and my eyes felt heavy.

I leaned forward and gave him a slow kiss across the table. "I'm a whole package person myself."

He licked my bottom lip and leaned back. "I'd like one night alone with you. Hell, I'd take fifteen minutes right now."

"An entire night sounds better." My voice was breathy.

He reached under the table and caressed my thigh, sliding his hand up to my shorts and running his fingers under my hem. My gut clenched and another wave of lust shot through me.

He saw my face. "Let's get a little fresh air."

I followed him outside and around the corner of the bar. He steered me past some landscaping and a low fence, then behind a flowering bush where we stood partially hidden.

He took hold of my waist and pulled me into him, sliding his thigh between my legs to rub at my crease. Running his hands inside my top, he palmed me just under my ribs. Then Sebastian brushed his thumbs across my hard nipples over my bra, and I sucked in my breath. His mouth found mine, and he slid his tongue inside.

I became dizzy and lost in his kisses, and he pulled back and tugged my bra down under my breasts. He pushed my top up to my shoulders and suckled each breast thoroughly. My head fell back. My breasts were exposed to the night while Sebastian sucked and licked at them. The thought made my pussy wet and my heart race.

I moaned. "Oh, sweet Jesus."

He bit down on a nipple just hard enough to hurt. I involuntarily jerked my hips into him. He bit the other nipple, then sucked it deep into his mouth.

Lust shot through my stomach. He let go of my shirt but left my bra under my breasts. Then Sebastian slid both hands up under my shorts and cupped my ass cheeks. He fingered my thong, and pulled on the string, teasing my clit a little. I involuntarily rubbed against him again.

"If you had a skirt on right now, I'd be inside you, fucking you against the side of the building."

I shuddered at the image and slid my hand down the front of his pants to palm his swollen shaft. I partially fisted his thick, rigid cock with my damp hand and pumped and stroked it. He froze and groaned low in his throat.

Pulling my hand out, he lifted me. "Wrap your legs around my waist," he growled in my ear.

I did as I was told, and he walked us both over to the wall and leaned me against it. He pumped his hips into me, and I ground myself down on his erection. Sebastian rotated a little, and I cried out softly when he hit my clit just right. Then we heard voices close by, coming our way.

Sebastian slowly stepped back from the wall, and I slid my legs back down. I tried to stand on my own, but wobbled a little, so I clung to him and laid my head on his chest.

I rubbed my forehead against his sternum in frustration. "My insides ache from being horny all the time."

Sebastian chuckled, then sighed. "My ache is a little further down. But I know what you mean. Let's go find Martina and see if we can talk her into leaving."

We found her as she sang one last bluesy man-hating song about smelling a rat, and we were finally ready to go. Martina and I had taken an Uber to the bar, knowing Sebastian would drive us home.

We were all quiet. I was tired but also a wired, and I wondered if I needed to stay with Martina tonight. She sat staring out the window with her chin in her hand.

"How're you doing?" I asked her.

"Good. A little tipsy still. Happy. Relieved."

From her glazed eyes, I thought she was more than a little tipsy.

She hummed a little. "But I'm sad too. Why am I sad?"

I glanced at Sebastian, then looked back at her. "Maybe it's normal to feel some loss and grief when a big change happens. Even if it's a good change. What do you think?"

Martina shrugged. "That's probably true. I feel like I failed, though. And I miss sex. Although Kenny was a selfish bastard in bed."

Sebastian winced.

I tried to redirect Martina. I didn't want to hear about her having sex either. "I'm sure Kenny was selfish about a lot of things."

"He was, and especially toward the end." She leaned forward and patted my shoulder. "Thanks for taking me out today. And for my outfit—I love it. Karaoke was fun, wasn't it?"

"Sure. Fun."

Martina poked my shoulder, then sighed. "I need to get away from here for a few days. I think I'll go see my parents next weekend after I get done with work."

"I bet they'd love to see you. Do you need any help this coming week?" I asked her.

"I'm good. Seriously, thank you for everything."

I smiled. "I didn't do anything except get dragged to karaoke night. I love you, Mar. You'll get through this just fine. One question though, why were you and Iz staring at each other like you either wanted to kill each other or play hide the pickle?"

Martina choked in the back seat.

Sebastian rubbed his face. "Fuuuck."

When we got to the house, Martina said a quick goodnight and shot out of the truck.

"We're going to have to postpone our weekend, aren't we?" Sebastian asked, watching her run inside.

"Yes. I don't think we should leave her alone right now." I reached out and took his hand. "You can stay here, though."

He leaned over. "No more interruptions. The first time we fuck we're going to be alone, it's going to be dirty, and I want at least two days to get this inferno between us under control. Next weekend. No matter what, *mi cielo*."

My breathing sped up. "Yes," I breathed out.

He leaned over and undid my seatbelt, then slid his seat back and pulled me into his lap.

Then Sebastian fisted my hair in his hand and pulled my head back. He slowly licked up my neck and whispered in my ear. "But first I want to make sure you go inside frustrated and wet." A half hour later when he walked me to the door, my legs were shaky, my breasts were swollen and heavy, and I was definitely wet.

Chapter 28

The week crawled by, and Sebastian and I spent a lot of time making out in his truck. I also used the time to sort through the house. It was an emotional process, but Martina pitched in and we sorted through the rest of Fern's belongings.

I gave Ramone and Jonathan a set of exquisite vintage wine glasses, along with a few other items. I also put aside a couple of Fern's expensive heirloom scarves for Grace and Sheila, and a classic pair of pearl earrings for Lydia, her accountant.

After going through the rest of the home, I finally tackled Fern's bedroom. I packed up her clothes and some of her jewelry that I didn't think I'd wear, and planned to take them to my favorite consignment store to be sold.

"I don't feel right about keeping the proceeds," I told Martina, eyeing the beautiful vintage pink pillbox suit in the closet.

"How about if you donate the proceeds to the local women's shelter in Fern's name?" Martina asked quietly.

I fingered the suit. "That's perfect. Thank you."

I also donated her bedroom furniture, but I couldn't part with the ivory velvet lounge chair where I'd spent so many evenings sitting and talking with her over the past two years.

On Wednesday afternoon, Sebastian met me and we shopped for replacement furniture.

He pulled me into him and nuzzled my neck. "You're going to need a king-size bed."

"You think?" I poked him playfully.

"Yeah, I do. And I plan to spend a lot of time with you in it, so make sure it's sturdy."

My face heated and I glanced over at the salesperson, who pretended to be studying the tag on the bedroom set.

"Okay. I'll get a sturdy one."

He chuckled and kissed my hot cheeks.

Finally, I picked out a solid wood bedframe and two complementary modern nightstands. I also bought a sturdy, king-sized mattress set after Sebastian and I tested a few together. The store promised to have everything delivered the next day.

I stopped at my favorite home goods store and picked out some plush sheets and a comforter set. Then I went by the lingerie store and bought some matching panties and bra sets and a couple of nighties. I blushed and fidgeted as the clerk rang me up.

The anticipation was killing me, along with a healthy dose of anxiety. Sebastian had so much more experience than I did, and I knew I was in over my head.

Finally, Friday arrived. I went for an early-morning run, then worked at the law firm for a few hours.

Over the past month, I'd started working in the mornings so Grace could show me the system. I also assisted with the phones and drafted basic documents until I could start practicing.

Grace told me that a neighbor of hers worked as a public defender, and her neighbor mentioned there was a juvenile court contract coming available. I asked Jonathan about it, and we looked up the job description online together.

He pointed at the pay range. "The pay is shit. But it's a good way to get some courtroom experience. You seemed to enjoy working in the juvenile court at the law clinic in Las Vegas, didn't you?"

"Yeah. It was worthwhile work, and I enjoyed the kids."

He nodded. "You'd be a great juvenile court public defender. I'd recommend practicing in another area of law as well. Maybe do real estate and contract law with me."

That afternoon when I got home, Martina was packing for her trip to see her family.

"Are you excited to go home?" I asked her.

"Yes. It's been a while since I've been home without Kenny around to ruin it." She folded a couple of shirts and put them in her bag.

"Didn't your family like him?" From what I'd seen of Kenny, I doubted anyone liked him. But Martina had at some point.

"At first, they thought he was okay. But he got worse, and he was always critical of me spending time with them." She pulled out a pair of sandals from her closet and finished packing. "It'll be a relief not to worry about him being a jerk to them." She hugged me, promised to drive close to the speed limit, and took off.

When she left, I decided to go swimming, then sat in the spa to calm my nerves.

I changed into a bikini, put up the sunshades, and had just gotten into the pool when Sebastian walked through the patio door. He was still in his work clothes.

"Hey. I didn't expect you for a few hours."

He watched me with hooded eyes and squatted down by the side of the pool. "Martina texted me and told me she left. I decided to take the rest of the afternoon off."

My heart stuttered a little, and I stared up at him. "Okay."

"Do you want our first time to be out here or in your new bed?"

My nipples hardened, and my insides pulsed. "I don't care," I whispered.

He nodded, then stood up and stripped his shirt over his head. He was as sculpted as I remembered, and the V trailing down to his groin made my insides jump.

He toed off his shoes, then undid his belt.

"Take off your suit." He watched me as he dragged his jeans down, then laid his clothes on the table. Picking up my towel, he walked toward me.

His cock was hard, thick, and long. It jutted out in front of him, and he palmed it absently as he watched me. I stood frozen and swallowed hard. He stalked to the edge of the pool, and a little anxiety slide through me. He was bigger than I expected, and it had been a long time.

"Take off your suit, *mi cielo*. I want to see you." He put the towel down, then sat on the edge of the pool.

I slowly reached up and pulled the straps down then undid the hook in back, letting my bikini top slide off my shoulders as my eyes strayed to his hard, thick length again.

"Your breasts are fucking perfect. After we've fucked a few times, I want to rub my cock between them and come all over your chest." He leaned back on his hands, his erection jutting in front of him.

My stomach contracted at his words, and I fingered my bikini bottoms.

He nodded toward me. "Take them off."

I hooked my thumbs in the waistband and slowly inched them down, then stepped out.

"Come here."

I let my suit float away and walked toward him. He sat up and spread his legs. When I reached him, he gently took my arms and pulled me closer.

The sun had already heated his skin, and his chest felt so good against my wet breasts. I could feel his thick erection against my stomach as he gathered my wet hair strands behind me and palmed my cheek.

"I'm going to suck on your tits and then lay you down and eat you out. Then I'm going to fuck you, hard, without a condom. You still on birth control?"

I nodded slowly. My insides skittered at his words, and my breasts grew heavy and sensitive.

"I need to hear the words again."

"Yes." I cleared my throat, then leaned in and bit his lip. "Please. I ache inside, and I need you to fuck me. Is that clear enough?"

He grinned darkly. "Yeah, that's clear enough."

He dipped his head and sucked one of my breasts into his mouth. And holy shit, it felt so good. Waves of heat shot through my nipple. He cupped my other breast as if he were measuring its weight and swept his thumb across the it several times. I arched into him and dragged my fingers through his hair.

He traded sides and sucked my other breast. Then he bit down on my nipple and licked it when I whimpered. My breasts were so sensitive, and I felt the heat spear right to my core each time he pulled. Finally, he moved off the pool edge and stood in the water. He pulled me into him and wrapped my arms around his shoulders, then he ran his hands down my sides and grabbed my legs, hoisting them up around his waist.

I could feel his broad head rubbing against my center, and I started panting heavily.

He ran his cock across my slit again, and I moaned softly. "Yes. God, yes."

He laid me down on the towel at the edge of the pool, and my insides spasmed. The towel felt warm on my back, and the sun heated my front.

Sebastian spread my legs out and perched them on each side of the pool ledge so I was wide open to him. Then he licked the inside of my thigh down to my weeping slit. His fingers slid through me, and he put his mouth on my clit.

Then Sebastian slowly licked and sucked. I gripped the edge of the pool and thrust closer to his mouth. He worked a finger inside me, then two, pumping in and out, slowly at first. Then he pressed his fingers deep inside me and found a sensitive spot. My back arched up.

I let out a high-pitched moan. "Please. That feels so... " I couldn't finish my thought.

He used his other hand to part me and pushed his shoulders between my legs, widening my thighs even more. Then he nipped and sucked on me.

"Oh, God!" I cried out.

My mind was a red haze, and an orgasm hovered. When Sebastian sensed I was getting close, he eased off and blew on my slit.

"No! Don't go." I partially sat up and tried to grab at him.

"Lay back, *mi cielo*. A little anticipation will make you come even harder." Dark lust shimmered in his eyes.

He rubbed me with his thumb, and I reluctantly laid back down. Kissing my lower stomach, he repositioned my legs, spreading them wide again.

"Leave them there," he ordered.

I realized Sebastian liked to give orders during sex. As long as he kept licking my clit and making me feel this way, he could give me all the orders he wanted.

"Keep your pussy open for me. Wide open. I love how smooth you are, then I can see every quiver and contraction." He leaned over and licked slowly up and down again. "All that moisture seeping out getting you ready for my cock, and you're going to need it. You're tight as fuck."

He glided two fingers back inside me, then sucked and licked my slit a few more times. But he pulled his fingers out *again* and lifted his head when he felt me getting close.

I started begging. "Please. I need you inside me. Oh God, I need to come. Please." My head thrashed back and forth, and my stomach cramped.

"I fucking love it when you beg me," he growled, then leaned back in and gently bit the inside of my thigh. I let out a long whimper.

Then he sucked my clit deep into his mouth. He impaled two fingers in me, and then he shoved in a third, pumping them in and out.

The extra pressure and suction pulled me to the edge, and Sebastian didn't let up this time when he felt my orgasm build. I started climaxing around his fingers and mouth, long and hard. I let out a low keening sound and shuddered while his tongue lapped me.

He leaned over me and rubbed my wet slit with his thumb. "That's it, sweet girl. Now open your eyes so I can watch you come while I finger fuck you." I opened my heavy eyelids and watched him through my climax. He studied my face and murmured soothing words in a low tone as I came down.

I felt a few teardrops leak out. I didn't know where the tears came from, but I'd never orgasmed that hard in my life. He stood up in front of me, his hard cock glistening.

"I need you inside me," I partially sat up and stroked the head of his cock, rubbing through a drop of pre-cum that leaked out.

He stood still for a second, then came out of the water in one swift motion. He pulled me up and brought me to the recliner under the shade. Then he sat down in it and pulled me over him.

"Straddle me and put my cock inside you," he ordered.

Instead of lowering myself onto him, I leaned over and licked his shaft.

He threw his head back and gritted his teeth. "You don't listen very well, do you?"

"Not really." I smiled and leaned over again. He watched me as he threaded his fingers into my hair.

I wrapped my hand around the root of his shaft as far as I could reach and slid my mouth over his tip. Then I pulled back and licked him like a thick ice pop. After several slow licks, I sucked him deep into my mouth.

I hadn't given a lot of oral sex before, but one of my roommates my senior year in college learned how to deep throat, and then explained it to the rest of us one night over a couple of boxes of cheap wine and a jumbo bag of Oreos.

Remembering her instructions, I opened the back of my throat and slid Sebastian's cock down as far as I could make it go. His hips pumped, pushing his shaft further into my throat, and I gagged a bit on his length.

After I'd regained control, I tried the whole process again. The third time I went down on him, I removed my hand from the base of his cock and filled my throat with him. He groaned long and low, then finally pulled out of my mouth and gave me a deep, probing kiss.

"You'll do that again—many times. But I want to be deep inside you when I come."

He pulled me up, then took my hips and steered me over his lap. I straddled him, and he reached between us and positioned his blunt head under my wet pussy. He grabbed my waist and pulled me down on him.

"Sebastian! Yes, oh Jesus God," I wailed as I finally felt him thrust his thick, hot cock into me.

He worked himself inside me, but stopped a few times so I could adjust to his size, his shaft stretching my walls tight. I felt full and dominated, and out of my head, as he forcefully worked me down onto him.

"You feel like a fucking vice," he growled when he was completely sheathed inside me. I shivered and could feel his cock pulsing inside me.

Then he pumped into me until he could move in and out without having to stop. It was a tight fit. He swirled his thumb across my clit and leaned in to brush his mouth across my nipples.

He nipped my neck, and licked where he'd bitten me. "I can't get enough of you. Your tight little pussy feels so fucking good."

He rolled us over without pulling out, laying me on my back and leaning over me. Pushing my legs up and out, Sebastian thrust deep, and I felt him bottoming out inside me. My mind blanked and I could only feel. He hit my cervix, and I felt pressure and some pain, along with bone deep pleasure. I moaned and mindlessly scrapped my nails along his back.

My thoughts scattered when Sebastian started thrusting hard and fast, just like he'd promised. The recliner squeaked and moved below us, but he didn't pause. His narrow, intense gaze never left my face.

He brought his fingers to my core and stroked me there, circling and strumming relentlessly, until I arched up into him and came again, letting out a long, broken cry.

He pounded into me a few more times, then shoved himself in as far as he could go and orgasmed. Hot semen flooded me.

"Fuck," he groaned as his hands clamped down on my hips so hard I'd probably have bruises tomorrow.

After we came down, he lay over me on the recliner for several moments before either of us moved. He raised his head and softly kissed my collarbone. Then he absently stroked inside me a few times, and leaned in and gently kissed my breast.

"That took the edge off, but I'm not done." He pulled out and rolled off me, then went to fish my suit out of the water.

I lay there unmoving on the recliner, my heart finally slowing. He grabbed the towel by the edge of the pool and walked over and looked down at me. His eyes glittered. He used the towel to wipe me up a bit, and he hardened again as he stared down at me, open and sprawled across the recliner.

He dropped the towel and crawled over me. "I need more."

Then he sunk his length inside me again. "I'm going to be spending a lot of time inside you. Just. Like. This." He thrust his hips, punctuating his words.

My eyes widened as I felt him get harder with each pump. Semen trickled out of me and ran down the crack between my legs, but I didn't care. My body heated up again.

"Aw, God. You feel so good," I moaned.

"This is going to be a long slow fuck, *mi corazón*," he murmured in my hair.

He impaled me over and over again. Bending down, he bit and sucked on my breasts hard enough to leave marks, while he held my hands above my head. I couldn't get enough.

He shifted our position and pulled my ankles up to his shoulders while he rotated his hips around, circling the inside of my pussy with his thick, solid cock. He slowly thrust in and out of me for a good long time, changing our positions and holding my hands captive again.

Finally, Sebastian flipped me over on my hands and knees, pulled my hips back toward him, and drove back inside me from behind. I had to grab onto the cushion underneath me so I wouldn't get pushed over as he powered into me.

Sebastian reached around and tugged and rolled my clit. I closed my eyes and saw white dots dance behind my eyelids as my hips involuntarily thrust back on his steel shaft.

"That's it. Take all of me. Fuck yourself on me," he growled.

He laid over my back and rubbed my clit as he powered into me. I threw my head back, panting his name over and over as my climax built.

"Please, Sebastian. Oh, God! Please." I drove back on him one last time, clamped around his length, and orgasmed hard and long. Then he buried himself in me, tensed and shot his semen deep inside.

We collapsed together on the recliner and lay panting, with him on top of me. When he finally pulled out, I gasped and he laughed softly. My vagina was well-used and sore, and fluids ran down my thighs.

He kissed my shoulder and palmed my bottom. "That might take the edge off for a few minutes."

I groaned, then smiled. "Maybe."

We cleaned up a bit, then went in search of food before we started round two.

Chapter 29

Sebastian eyed me as we slid into Fern's convertible. "You need to stay hydrated and fed—to keep your strength up for the rest of the weekend."

We were both in a postcoital, celebratory mood. I'd suggested Eddy's, the little vintage diner just down the street that had been around since the late 1950s. They served breakfast all day and made the best German pancakes.

My vagina felt swollen and sensitive, and I was on a chemical high after three orgasms. My body didn't know what to do with all the endorphins. I'd left my hair down and thrown on a little wrap sundress.

At the restaurant, Sebastian stared at me from across the booth with a satisfied smirk while we ate. "You look like you've been thoroughly fucked. I like it."

I blushed but smiled back at him. "That's because I have, big man."

He raised his eyebrow. "Big man?"

"It just came out. And you are... *big*." I eyed his crotch.

He leaned forward and took my hand. "Are you okay?"

"Yes, why wouldn't I be?"

He didn't let me evade. "Because you haven't fucked in a long time, and your cunt felt like a vice grip on my cock. Are you sore?"

My face heated, and I looked around to see if anyone could hear us. Luckily, the people in the booth next to us had left a few minutes ago.

"I'm fine," I whispered.

He looked amused at my shyness. Then his gaze slid down to my breasts, and he gave me a lazy, slow blink. I hadn't worn a bra, and my nipples puckered under his gaze.

"If you're not sore, let's go back to the house and fuck some more, then."

My insides clenched, and I felt myself getting wet. I *was* sore, but not sore enough to want to stop.

"Okay." I set my fork down. Suddenly, I wasn't hungry for food anymore.

He grinned, then reached over and took my hand. "I'll give you a little breather first. But I love how thirsty you are for my cock." My insides clenched, as if in agreement.

We drove back to Fern's house and crashed in my king-size bed together for several hours until early evening. Sebastian woke up first and checked some emails, then made a light dinner. After we ate, he led me back to the pool area.

Walking over to the spa, he turned on the jets. The soft twilight sky started to darken.

Sebastian hooked his arm around my waist and pulled me into him. "Fucking you in broad daylight today was perfect. But this lighting works too."

He ran his hands up under my dress and stopped. Then looked down at me and cupped my center.

"Did you sit across from me at the diner with a bare pussy?"

I breathed heavily as he slid his finger across my slit. "I had my dress on."

He squeezed me and tsked, then slowly pulled the ties on my dress and peeled it off me. I was naked underneath.

"You're a fucking wet dream," he said, looking down at my body. "It's good I didn't know you were bare earlier today, or I wouldn't have waited."

I had a few marks on my breasts left over from his whiskers, teeth, and mouth. He grazed over them with his fingers.

I wanted him naked as well, so I reached for his shirt and pulled it over his head. Sebastian quickly shed the rest of his clothes. He was so beautiful, it was no wonder he had women wanting seconds, even when he was grumpy and short. Jealousy flared, but I pushed it aside.

He guided me into the spa and stood behind me, softly caressing my stomach and breasts. Then he bit on my shoulder. "I want to watch you come on a jet. Are you willing to try?"

A spike of pleasure and a little fear speared through me. "Yes," I said softly.

"That's it, sweet girl."

He guided me over to a jet, then spread my thighs. I reached behind and found his hard length as he positioned me in front of the swirling water. The pressure felt strange and erotic.

I wrapped my hand around him and started stroking. He put an arm just under my breasts and used his other hand to roll and pinch my nipples between his fingers as the water surged around my clit.

I worked my hand up and down his cock, making him even harder. My channel felt empty, and I wanted his length inside me, so I pushed my bottom into his groin and rubbed against him.

"Are you hungry for my cock?"

"Yes," I whispered.

He pulled me off the jet and laid me over the edge of the spa. Then he worked himself inside me. I was inflamed and tender, but I loved how he felt even with the pain, and I pushed back onto him.

Sebastian lifted me—still attached to him—and put me back on the jet. He rolled his hips and started plunging into me. The water swirled over my clit again and I could feel a climax building.

"I'm going to fuck your mouth next. And then your sweet, luscious tits before you come." He cupped my breasts and squeezed and kneaded them. Sebastian had a dirty mouth, and my core clenched around him.

He ran his fingers down my stomach to my slit. Then he pulled me open even further, and the water from the jet pulsed more intimately against me. The sensation was strange and startling, but it felt so good. I thrust back against him and could feel my orgasm building. He pulled out and moved me off the jet before I could climax.

"I was so close," I complained breathlessly.

"Shh, *mi cielo*. I'll let you come. Eventually."

I knew what was coming next. He turned me around, pushed me down so I was kneeling in front of him, then pressed his thumb against my chin, parting my lips.

He slid his cock into my mouth, and gently but firmly pushed inside. He slid over my tongue several times, then he waited for me to open my throat.

I relaxed and finally took him down. He moved his cock in and out, then put his hand around my neck as if he could feel himself moving inside.

He paused a few times when he was all the way in, briefly cutting off my air. I was so high on endorphins and lust, my mind just drifted.

Sebastian finally pulled himself out, bent his knees, and slid his wet cock between my breasts. He pushed my breasts together and started tunneling between them.

His grip was tight, and my breasts were swollen and sensitive. I liked the little bite of pain.

Then he pushed his leg between the junction of my thighs and rubbed me there. I was so sensitive and sore I flinched but reflexively rolled my hips into him.

Sebastian was physical, highly sexual, and dominant. He positioned my body and mouth where he wanted me, and he knew where and when to suck, lick, and pinch to give me pleasure. I felt ravaged and cherished, and my mind was hazy with need and desire.

He stopped before he came. "Fuck. You make me want to blow my load every time I touch you." Then he gave me a long, wet kiss and bent me over the edge of the pool again to work his way back inside.

Sebastian moved me back onto the jet, positioning me so the pulsing water hit my clit again. Less than a minute later, I came long and hard as he rammed into me from behind. I moaned high and loud. Sebastian finally wrapped his hand around my mouth, cutting off the sound and my breath, and heightening my climax.

He drove into me a few more times, then grabbed my hips tight, slammed deep inside, and came seconds later. I finally stopped pulsing and crested from my high as he slowly thrust into me a few more times.

He eventually pulled out and cradled me in his lap. I laid my head on his shoulder. We sat in the spa, wrapped around each other as dopamine and endorphins floated through us.

Sebastian finally set me on the bench, then got up and haphazardly dried off. He went inside and made drinks for us. We sat in the swirling water with me on his lap, enjoying the sound of crickets and the smell of jasmine in the peaceful evening air.

"How do you like working with Ramone and Jonathan so far?" he asked.

"I like it." My head lulled against his shoulder. "They're busy and spend a lot of time with clients or on the phone. I'll be useful when I figure out what I'm doing."

I absently trailed my fingers down his chest while I told him about the juvenile court contract.

He nodded. "If you like that type of law and think you'd be happy doing it, you should."

"Jonathan thinks so too."

We idly talked about Martina, then his work, and finally got out and dried off. Sebastian saw me wince and shook his head. "You're tender, *corazón*."

"A little," I conceded, but grinned. "As Camila would say, I regret nothing."

❋❀❋❀❋

Later that night, while I talked with Lennie and Boo on the phone, Sebastian went to his place and grabbed some essentials and clothes so he could spend the weekend with me. We decided to stay here instead of his house, since Martina was gone for the weekend. I thought it was probably the pool and the spa that had sold him.

The boys were in first grade this year, so they had to be in school all day.

Lennie didn't like school much. "It's sooo long, Lolly. And I can't even take my socks off."

Willie didn't seem to mind it. He was more active and extroverted than Lennie, and he had no problem keeping his clothes on all day long. "It's okay. I like having two recesses. And guess what?"

"Chicken butt?" I asked.

He snickered. "Yeah. But during kickball? I kicked the ball into Karl's face. His nose bled all over." I assumed Karl was one of Willie's classmates.

"Ouch. I've heard noses bleed a lot. Did you say you were sorry?"

"Yeah, 'cause the teacher made me." Well, at least he was honest. "But I didn't do it on purpose. And Karl pushed me and called me a stupid wiener butt."

I tried not to laugh. "Hmm. I'm not sure what a wiener butt is. Are you and Karl friends again?"

"Yeah."

We talked about their soccer team, their teachers, and a few of their new toys. Then they got bored and went to play the new version of *Mario Kart* they'd gotten. I'd heard all about it during our previous phone calls.

"Okay, you little booger butts. Have fun playing your video game. Love you."

"Love you too! Bye, Lolly," Willie yelled as they ran out of the room.

When the boys were gone, I asked Chloe how things were going. She sounded tired and down.

"Oh, they're going. I haven't seen Victor in three days. I think he's having an affair."

"What makes you think that?" I wasn't surprised or shocked, which said a lot about Victor's character.

"A few things, but also a friend saw him at a restaurant in Manhattan with a woman last weekend." Chloe sounded resigned.

I shifted, trying to alleviate my soreness. "Could it have been a business meeting or something for work?"

"Not late on a Friday night. I'm not sure what kind of business meeting he'd have at that time."

It seemed a little surreal that Chloe was confiding in me like a friend.

"Huh. What are you going to do?" I got up and poured a glass of wine, then got comfortable on the couch.

"I made an appointment with a divorce attorney a few days after we got back from Palm Springs. She's been drafting up a

Divorce Petition, and I think I'm going to have him served next week."

I'd been slouched on the couch, but when she told me the news I sat up straight.

I was silent for several seconds, and Chloe finally asked, "Are you still there?"

"Yeah. I'm just a little surprised." I thought for a moment. "And relieved. I don't think he cares about helping you raise the boys. And he's not a good father or husband, from what I can see."

I worried Victor emotionally abused the twins, and pushed them around and manhandled them. I didn't know much about his and Chloe's relationship, but it didn't sound good either. Whenever I thought he couldn't possibly be more of a selfish narcissist, he'd surprise me.

I took a sip of wine. "Do you know what you're going to do while the divorce is in process? Or afterward?"

Chloe sighed. "I've requested to stay in the house with the boys, at least temporarily. When the divorce is final, I'm not sure where we'll end up living."

Her older parents lived in Florida somewhere, but I wasn't aware of her being very close to them. She also didn't have any siblings.

"Do you think you'll stay in New York?"

She sighed. "I don't know. I wish Victor would take an interest in the boys' lives. But it's been almost five years, and he hasn't yet." She cleared her throat. "I've even thought about moving to California so they could be closer to you." Chloe got quiet, and I wondered if she was trying to gauge my reaction.

Having the boys live closer to me would be wonderful. I'd have to deal with Chloe, but she'd gotten better over time. The thought of Victor coming to Palm Springs, however, made me feel nauseous. This wasn't about me, though. It was about what was best for my brothers.

"Chloe, I would love that. If you lived close enough, I could help you with them, and even give you a break sometimes."

"I haven't decided anything," she cautioned.

"The elementary schools should be decent, but we can supplement their curriculum, and even look into private schools if you want."

Chloe laughed, sounding relieved and happy at my enthusiastic response. "There's a lot that has to happen between now and then. And that's *if* Victor agrees to let the boys move out of New York."

I didn't think Victor would care at all about the boys moving away. But he'd care about feeling like he lost somehow, and he'd hate that they were moving here to be closer to me.

"You've probably talked to your divorce attorney regarding the best way to convince a judge." I thought about how she could do that. "Chloe, did I ever tell you about Martina's ex-husband? I videoed him pushing Martina around and threatening her. It helped with her divorce."

"What?! No, you never told me. Is she okay?"

My heart warmed a little at her response. Maybe Chloe really was trying to be less selfish. "She's fine now, and her divorce is final."

"I could have been there, and with the boys too! That's so scary."

"Anyway, it might be worthwhile to video some of his interactions with the boys. Like when he gets upset or angry with them. Or calls them 'little shits' and pushes them around." I held my breath.

"Mmm, that's a good idea. God knows I don't want to drag this out and spend all our money on attorneys."

She didn't mention what a long, ugly custody battle might do to the boys. Baby steps, I reminded myself. And as long as Chloe's prenuptial agreement was reasonable, she and the boys should be financially secure.

I heard Willie shouting in the background over her phone.

She sighed. "They got into a fight over using battle mode. Whatever. I've got to go."

"Okay, let me know how I can help. Tell the boys I'm sending a package soon. It'll be something quiet."

When I hung up, I felt a little hopeful Victor might agree to the divorce just to get rid of the headache and annoyance of a divorce. That hope didn't last long.

Chapter 30

Late that evening, Sebastian and I sat down to watch an episode of one of my favorite British comedies. But I felt restless and needy, so I crawled into his lap and straddled him.

He turned off the television and held my waist. "Do you need something?" Dark humor edged his voice.

I didn't say anything, but leaned in and kissed and nuzzled his jaw. Then I slowly licked up his neck, and bit his earlobe. He reached up and undid my little wrap dress, then pulled it down off my shoulders, exposing my upper body to him.

I still hadn't bothered to put on a bra or panties when we'd cleaned up earlier. He trailed kisses down my shoulder and collarbone, then slowly swirled his tongue around each nipple and softly blew on them. My nipples instantly hardened and my pelvis clenched.

He traced his hand up my thigh and reached in to sweep a finger across my slit. "You're still not wearing panties. Or a bra." He slid a finger into my slick opening, then added another one. "And you went out in public that way. You need to be spanked."

My insides contracted.

He smirked. "I felt you spasm. I think you like the idea of me spanking you." Grazing his lips across my collarbone, Sebastian watched me squirm on top of him.

My bottom clenched. "I... don't know if I'd like it or not."

"We'll have to find out. But tonight I want to fuck you in your new bed. We need to break it in." He sucked and bit on my breasts, then added a third finger in my channel. "Just like I'm breaking you in."

I moaned softly and leaned into his mouth. He fingered me a moment longer, then lifted me off and pulled me to the bedroom. We stopped in front of the enormous bed and stared at each other. My dress hung at my waist and my nipples jutted out. He took both breasts in his hands and squeezed and weighed them.

My eyelids closed, and my head fell back. "Oh God, they're so sensitive."

I reached over and palmed his length through his pants, sliding my hand up and down his shaft. Then I tugged on his shirt, wanting to see and touch all of him. He let go of my breasts and peeled off his shirt. He finished untying my dress and watched it slip to the floor.

When we were both naked, he pulled me to him. He palmed the back of my head and brought my ear to his lips. Sebastian whispered dark promises, then slid his tongue around the shell of my ear. I melted into him, alarmed and excited.

He sat down on the bed with his legs sprawled, and positioned me so I knelt above his length. He brought me down on him and worked his cock inside me, then started moving me up and down on his long, thick shaft. Wrapping my legs around his waist, his hands gripped my hips hard as he thrust me down to meet his strokes.

He fixated on my breasts. "I love watching your tits bounce every time I fuck you." I involuntarily squeezed around him.

When I started to pant and grind down, he pulled me off and swung me around to my hands and knees.

"Spread your thighs and lower your elbows to the bed." He didn't wait for me to comply, but kneed my thighs wider apart then pushed my shoulders down.

He positioned himself behind me and held my hips while he forced his cock back inside. I could feel every inch of his hard length in this position, and I moaned as he worked himself inside me.

Sebastian reached around and stroked my clit while he hammered into me from behind. My elbows slid forward from the force of his thrusts. He pinched me, and I raised up from my elbows and started thrusting back at him. Sebastian grabbed my shoulders and forcefully pulled me back onto his engorged cock.

My vision blurred and white-hot lust surged through me when he slid his hand around my throat and squeezed softly. A climax built as he pistoned inside me, and after several hard thrusts I orgasmed on a long, soft wail.

My passage clamped down on him. He buried himself deep and came hard. My arms were shaking, and I finally collapsed onto the bed. Sebastian followed me down, covering my body with his, still embedded deep inside me.

I thought idly as we drifted down together that we smelled like sweat, sex, and sunshine.

Late Saturday morning, Sebastian woke me up to apply a cold compress and lidocaine ointment to my swollen center. Sunlight streamed through the windows, and he sat fully dressed. He looked so good sitting on the edge of my bed that my heart squeezed.

"Come here, *corazón*. Open your legs for me."

"Good morning to you too."

He grinned and leaned down to kiss the swell of my breast. I stretched, then groaned when I felt how sore and sticky I was down there. Even my stomach muscles hurt from clenching so much.

My voice was thick with sleep. "I got into this mess because I already opened my legs for you. Too many times."

He smiled. "There's no such thing as too many times. Now let me take a look."

I suddenly felt shy. "I can do it myself."

"I want to see how bad it is in the daylight. Now open." His voice was warm but firm.

I still hesitated. It was one thing to open myself to him when I was out of my mind with lust, but quite another to do it in broad daylight so he could play doctor.

He smirked. "Are you Bashful this morning then?"

I finally smiled and pulled the sheet off. I slowly opened my thighs, and he moved closer, easing my legs wider apart.

Sebastian shook his head when he saw how red and swollen I was. "I can be rough. You need to tell me when I'm hurting you."

"Sometimes you like causing a little pain. And I like it too."

A corner of his mouth tipped up, and he stared at me.

I touched his chest. "From now on, I'll tell you if you're rubbing me raw because we're having too much sex."

He palmed my breast. "We'll never have too much sex." I silently hoped he was right.

Sebastian cleaned me with a warm wet cloth, then he opened the lidocaine ointment and pulled out some first aid pads.

"I need to apply this inside and around your vagina, and the cold compresses will help with the swelling."

I nodded, a little embarrassed. I laid back and kept my legs spread while he gently administered the ointment inside and out. Then he put a cold compress on me and leaned down and kissed my stomach.

I squirmed a little. "Thanks, Doc."

He smiled and rubbed the inside of my thigh. "That's better than Grumpy."

Sebastian had an issue come up with one of his properties later that morning. When he went into work, I took a bath, ran some errands, and picked up a few groceries.

The temperature was finally dropping, and it was in the low seventies when I left the house that morning. It had cooled off enough to start hiking again.

I thought about all the hikes I'd done around the Coachella Valley, and those I still wanted to try. I wondered if Sebastian would go with me, maybe even late that afternoon or tomorrow morning. So I texted him.

Me: Thoughts on a hike this afternoon or tomorrow?

He texted back a few minutes later.

Sebastian: Sounds good. Shorter today, longer tomorrow?

I felt giddy when I read his text. Two hikes in two days sounded like heaven. None of my friends or family, besides Joey and Luke, really liked to hike. And we'd been so busy with school, we only went a few times.

Me: Palm Springs tram today, then Indian Canyons tomorrow?

Sebastian: Yes to both

I quickly got online and bought aerial tram tickets for late that afternoon. Then I packed us a light meal and plenty of water, and made my chocolate chunk cookies to celebrate the weekend. When he got home, we took off.

Sebastian's hiking shoes looked reasonably worn in, and he had on high-quality hiking clothes. His performance pullover molded to his muscles, and he seemed completely comfortable on the moderately easy trail. I was happy to see he really did seem to enjoy hiking.

It was fast and painless to get to the tram and up to the top from downtown Palm Springs. The weather was also much cooler at the summit, and I wondered why I hadn't been dragging Martina up here with me all summer long.

We gazed around when we got off. I took a deep breath and looked out across the mountain and desert vistas. A cool breeze blew across my face, and the air smelled clean.

I smiled at Sebastian. "That breeze feels wonderful, and I can smell the pines."

Sebastian came up behind me and wrapped an arm around my front. "This is nice, since you need a little recovery time from playing 'hide the pickle'."

I bumped his hip. "Pickle? It's more like a baseball bat."

He grunted. "A baseball bat? Huh. I did make it around all the bases—several times—didn't I?"

I rolled my eyes, then squeezed his arm. "Guys and their sports analogies. Your, uh, ministrations this morning helped, Doc. I feel a lot better."

"I'll be wrecking you again over the next couple of days. We'll work on your stamina."

My breath caught. "Okay."

He pulled me closer and kissed my neck. Then he whispered exactly what he wanted to do to me to help build my stamina. I finally reached up and covered his mouth when I started getting wet and needy.

We headed up the trail and stopped periodically at the lookout points, or notches, along the way. When the late afternoon light started fading, I pulled out my camera and took a few photographs. Sebastian watched me set up some shots.

I took a beautiful shot of him looking out over the vista when he wasn't watching. I would cherish it when we weren't together anymore, I thought idly as I looked at it in my viewfinder. Then I wondered where that idea had come from, and my heart squeezed.

We found a relatively flat rock to sit on at the last notch toward the end of the trail. I pulled out the food and water, and we ate in silence while we watched the sun slowly set. The sky had turned orange, then a deep purple and blue across the horizon. The sunsets in the Western Desert were some of the most haunting and spectacular I'd ever seen, and I never tired of watching them. I finally pulled out the chocolate chunk cookies.

"These are delicious. Where'd you learn to cook?" Sebastian asked as he finished his second one.

"Rosa, mostly. And also Ramone—he's a superb cook."

He smiled. "Probably not from Fern, though."

"No. Fern didn't like to cook, so she was happy to let me have free rein in her kitchen."

Fern once told me she didn't get any satisfaction or pleasure out of cleaning or cooking, so she hired other people to do it and paid them well.

"Who's Rosa?" he asked.

I told him a little about Rosa. "I still go see her when I'm in New York. She taught me some conversational Italian, and finally gave me her family's red sauce recipe. Do you cook?"

He shrugged. "I can cook. I don't love it, but sometimes it's healthier and more convenient."

We talked a little more. It was peaceful and soothing to be with him in the mountains as the gloaming hour approached. When the light faded, we finally packed up the remains of our picnic and walked back to the tram. We had one more night before Martina came back, and I was eager to get back to the house.

Chapter 31

We made it back to the house and changed out of our hiking clothes, then went back out to the patio to enjoy the mild temperatures. We sipped drinks and enjoyed the quiet evening.

Sebastian leaned over and gave me a long, slow kiss. "How're you feeling tonight?"

"I'm good. Only a little sore. This is our last night alone here, and I wanted to, uh, try out the spa and pool again."

He was silent, so I pressed on. "If you're up for it."

He smiled down at me. "When it comes to you, I'm always up for it."

I stood, then reached up and pulled my shirt off before I lost my nerve.

Sebastian watched with a little smirk, but when he saw the string bikini underneath, his smirk dropped away and he leaned back in his chair, eyes glittering.

"That little scrap is barely even a string bikini. Take off your shorts so I can see the rest."

When we changed out of our hiking clothes after getting home, I'd put on my little white string bikini under my t-shirt and shorts. The top consisted of two small triangles that barely covered my breasts.

The tie in the back also wrapped around my ribcage a few times, giving the suit a subtle bondage look. Joey had given it to me for my birthday, and I turned beet red when I'd pulled it out of the gift bag.

The bottoms had a high Brazilian cut in the back, and strings held the sides together. I slowly nudged my shorts down, then stood in front of him in the few scraps of fabric.

"Holy fuck, you look like a dirty little angel in it. Turn around." He made a twirling motion with his finger. I turned around so he could see the back.

He got up and stood behind me. "Has anyone else seen you wear this?" he asked softly in my ear.

I shook my head. "No."

"Good." He palmed my ass cheeks, then massaged and spread them a little. Sebastian leaned in and licked and sucked the side of my neck, then he positioned me to face the patio table.

"Lean over and spread your legs, *mi cielo*. I want to give you a few swats on your tight little ass for even owning this suit."

My heart sped up and lust slammed through me as I froze in place.

He fingered the stings across my stomach then nuzzled my cheek. "I want to spank you and see if you like it. Are you willing to try?"

My vagina clenched, and I shivered, then nodded. "I got wet when you brought it up yesterday."

"I know—I felt you spasm around my fingers." Dark satisfaction edged his voice. "Along with a little pain, it can also give you a lot of pleasure during sex."

He put his hand on my back and gently leaned me over the table. Then he positioned my legs further apart.

"You ready?" He massaged my thighs and ran his hands up my cheeks.

"Yes," I breathed out.

He started with a few light swats using his open palm. After warming me up a bit, he spanked me a little harder, leaving a bright sting across both buttocks.

I gasped and started to lift up, but he gently held me in place and rubbed where he'd just spanked me. Heat unfurled, and my slit moistened as the pain turned to pleasure.

"Let it settle, *cielo*," he murmured, stroking my back.

When I started panting and could feel the sting turn to a pleasurable burn, he gave me a few more swats along the crease between my thighs and bottom. I whined and shifted as the pleasure and pain combined, confusing and arousing me.

Then Sebastian tugged the bikini bottoms aside and stroked me. He rubbed my clit, and I rotated my hips to get more of him.

He leaned over and bit my left buttock, then he bit and nibbled my other, sliding a finger inside me.

"You're soaking wet, *cielito*. I think your body likes being spanked. And finger fucked."

I breathed heavily and moaned. His words sent another wave of heat surging through me. I felt confused and vulnerable, but my body craved his touch. I was becoming addicted to how he made me feel, and a little worry slid through me.

My thoughts scattered when he put another finger inside me and continued to pump in and out. My insides clenched against the invasion, and I pushed back reflexively against his hand.

He pulled out and gave me a few more smacks before rubbing my bottom again. Then he pulled me up by my shoulders and stood behind me.

"I know you don't have a lot of experience, but I love how sweet and uninhibited you are with me."

I gasped for air. Please," I begged.

He palmed my breasts. "You're hot as fuck, and you have an insatiable pussy."

"I don't have an insatiable pussy," I whispered. Then I pushed my sore bottom back into his hard cock.

He laughed and stepped away, shedding his clothes. He took my hand and led me over to the pool.

"I want to fuck you while you're wearing this little scrap, then tie you up with it and make you take me down your throat again."

Lust shot through my insides. I couldn't string two words together right then.

He had the dirtiest mouth, and he liked to tell me exactly what he wanted to do to me. It flustered and aroused me, and sometimes I wondered what had happened to that grumpy, tight-lipped man I'd first met.

He sat on the edge of the pool and pulled me into his lap with my back toward him. Then Sebastian reached around and tugged my breasts out of my swimsuit top, baring them to the night.

"Your breasts are magnificent, *mi cielo*. Touch them for me."

It took a second to process his command, then I brought my hands up and cupped my breasts.

"Pinch your nipples." He watched as I played with myself. "Now roll them between your fingers. That's it. Good girl."

I worked them harder, following his instructions.

"Keep one hand on your breasts and use the other to pull your bikini bottom aside so I can see your pussy."

I slowly slid my hand down and did as he asked.

"Fucking perfect. Now show me how you like to be touched."

He ran a hand down my stomach and held my suit to the side, then watched me pleasure myself. He studied me as if he were memorizing each stroke.

I could feel his hard cock against my lower back. His legs were between mine, and he spread my thighs out, pushing me further apart.

"I want you inside me." I panted and rubbed my tender bottom cheeks against his erection.

He bit my jaw, then licked where he'd nipped. "You want my cock? Then admit you have an insatiable pussy."

"Only for you," I gasped.

He growled in satisfaction, then reached around and pulled the bikini further aside. He worked his long, thick shaft inside me, and I groaned as he pushed into my channel.

When I'd adjusted to his size, he started driving into me, his hips slapping against mine. He reached around and firmly massaged a breast, then rolled my nipple between his fingers.

"Watch me fuck you. Look at my cock pounding into you."

I obediently looked down at his length plunging in and out of me.

"Oh God, you're so far inside me. You feel too big sometimes," I breathed as I worked my clit.

He nudged my hand away, then gave my clit a few light slaps. I clenched around him as my climax started to build. He stopped thrusting and held me still, not allowing me to come yet.

"Gah. Why do you do that?" I cried, struggling to move.

He smiled into my neck. "Because it makes you come harder when you finally orgasm. And I like you needy and frustrated."

Sebastian kissed my cheek, then pulled me off his shaft. He hadn't climaxed, and I knew he wanted to come deep in my throat.

Peeling off my bottoms and slid the bikini top down my arms, he unwrapped the ties from my torso. My pussy was engorged and overly sensitive, and my breasts tingled.

He turned me around and pulled my arms behind my back. Then he wrapped the ties around my wrists and arms, securing them behind me. When he cradled my core in his palm, I spasmed beneath his hand. My mind was hazy with lust and need, and I panted.

"Are you steady enough to take me down your throat?"

Saliva pooled in my mouth, and I ran my tongue over my lips. "I think so."

He looked me over as if admiring his handiwork, then sat back down on the pool edge, splaying his legs apart.

"Come here."

I waded to him and dropped to my knees. The warm water came to my rib cage, and I nuzzled his rigid length and settled my mouth over the head of his cock. Then I sucked on his wide tip. His hips bucked.

He pulled out and held my cheek. "Slowly, *mi corazón*. I'm close to the edge." He nudged his cock back into my mouth.

I delicately licked along his shaft, and he tangled his fingers through my hair, holding the sides of my head.

After a few licks, he started guiding my head up and down his length.

"Your mouth feels like fucking heaven," he groaned softly.

I hummed around his cock, and felt his erection swell even more. He pushed toward the back of my mouth, and I opened my throat, trying to take more of him. He slowly worked his way in, then pulled out to let me breathe.

He brushed a few strands of hair out of my eyes, and cupped my cheek as he worked himself in and out of my mouth.

"I wish you could see yourself, with your arms tied behind your back, my handprints marking your sweet ass, and your beautiful mouth full of my cock."

He worked further in and stilled for a few seconds deep in my throat. My slit throbbed, and I drifted, hazy and euphoric as he played with my mouth and throat.

He surged in and out of me for a few more minutes, teasing me and massaging my breasts. Finally, he pushed himself down my throat, tensed, then erupted with a long, deep groan. I frantically swallowed, working to take all his come.

When he was done, he stroked my face and pulled his cock out, then bent down to kiss my cheeks, his breath coming hard. "That was fucking mind-blowing."

Sebastian helped me stand and wrapped his arms around my waist, holding me to him. "Are your arms all right, or do I need to untie you?"

I felt a little dazed and lightheaded, but I took stock of my arms and wrists and tugged on the bindings a bit.

I couldn't pull myself loose, but they weren't hurting me. "I... I'm okay, I think. But I feel vulnerable."

"Is that a good or bad thing?" He studied me.

"I'm not sure. It seems to heighten my arousal."

He gazed at me intently, cradling my face. "Good. I'll leave them on then." He reached down and stroked my clit until I moved restlessly against his fingers. Then he cupped my breasts and plucked at my nipples.

When I started whimpering, Sebastian turned me on my stomach and laid me over the edge of the pool, then he gripped the backs of my thighs and pulled my legs apart, stepping between them.

"Your ass makes me want to bite, spank, and fuck it all at once. I don't know where to start," he murmured as he stroked me.

I clenched, pleasure and anxiety spearing through me. He ran a finger up through my clit, and I shivered and held still.

He flicked and circled me before sticking his tongue deep inside my pussy. Then he sucked, nipped, and bit for several minutes, before shoving two blunt fingers inside me. He drove deep and adjusted my hips up to give him better access.

"Ahh, God!" I panted.

Then I felt him circle my anal opening with his thumb, and I tensed.

"Shhh, *mi cielo*." He stroked my hip soothingly. "You'll like the stimulation. We'll just play tonight, and I won't fuck you there until you're ready. It'll take some preparation."

I'd never had anal sex before, and I didn't know if I'd ever be ready. But I slowly relaxed, and he nestled his thumb just inside my opening again, then pushed a little deeper while pumping his fingers in and out of me.

Sebastian pulled his fingers out of me, and bent down to circle my labia with his tongue. I instinctively pushed back on his mouth and thumb as I got closer to orgasm.

My mind rebelled at the thought, but my body strained toward him. "I don't... that feels..."

He chuckled and ran his tongue up the inside of my thigh, then bit me there. I gave a startled cry.

Latching onto my clit, he sucked it hard inside his mouth. I bucked, my orgasm building.

"Oh, shit!" I'd had more orgasms than I could count in the past forty-eight hours, and I felt tender and well-used. But I was addicted to his cock, fingers, and mouth. I didn't know how I was going to survive him.

He pulled my bud back into his mouth and sucked on it, then leaned in and penetrated me with his tongue again. Less than a minute later, I spiraled into a long, almost painful orgasm, pumping myself onto his thumb and tongue as he licked and sucked me through it.

When I came down and quit spasming around his fingers, he stood up and bent over me, stroking my back.

"You're so responsive, and you go off like a fucking rocket when I play with you."

He untied the bikini straps around my arms and wrists, then lifted me and settled me in his lap. He was hard again, but he just gathered me close and rubbed my arms and wrists absently.

A few minutes later, he looked down at me. "How're you feeling?"

"Blissed out. Sore. And thoroughly used. How about you?"

He grinned and stroked my leg. "Fucking fantastic. I'm never going to look at this backyard the same."

"So every time we eat or have drinks on the patio table, you'll be thinking about bending me over and spanking me on it?" I teased.

"And fucking you on it. And in the pool, the spa, on the recliner—"

I put my hand over his mouth. "Okay! I get it." I smiled up at him. "Naked private time back here has been... I have no words." I hugged his neck and leaned up and kissed his cheek.

My breasts felt tender, and I still throbbed inside. It would be good to see Martina tomorrow, but I was going to miss being alone with him back here.

"Naked private time? I like it." He must have been thinking the same thing. "We'll have to send Martina to Disneyland next month so we can have another fuckathon back here."

"Huh. I didn't know that was a word."

Sebastian grinned. "I think we made it one this weekend."

Chapter 32

We headed out early Sunday morning to hike the Murray Canyon Trail in Indian Canyon. The five-mile hike was in the Agua Caliente Indian Reservation, and a portion of the trail loosely followed the stream up to the waterfalls. There were groves of tall, shaggy California fan palms along the way.

I glanced back at Sebastian. "How often do you get out like this?"

He looked around. "Not much anymore. Work gets busier during the best hiking months. I need to make time, though. I've missed it."

"You put in long days. Do you like being so busy?"

He shrugged. "I don't mind it most the time. There hasn't been a good reason to slow down."

"Huh." I wanted to ask what a good reason would be, but thought I might not like his answer.

I stopped a few times along the way to take photographs while the lighting was still soft and diffused. Sebastian stood patiently while I lined up a few shots.

When we reached the Seven Sisters Waterfalls area, we sat down and pulled out the apples and granola bars we'd packed.

"So, if you don't hike much anymore, what do you do for fun and relaxation?"

He thought for a moment. "I used to play rec sports. I still help Matías coach his kid's soccer team." He paused but didn't say anything else.

"And hot tubbing?"

He glanced over at me. "I plead the fifth, counselor."

I smiled weakly at him, but I knew I was right. There had been a lot of women in his past, and I wondered if I could trust him to be monogamous, or if he even wanted to be. I was quiet as these thoughts ran through my head.

He finally stopped in one of the palm tree groves, took my hand, and walked off the trail a bit.

"I need to know what you're thinking. I don't want to waste two or three months on another misunderstanding."

Searching his face, I wondered if I could tell him without ruining everything. But I didn't want a relationship without fidelity and honesty.

"I was thinking maybe you aren't ready to be in a relationship, and don't want to give up seeing other women." It was more like banging, fucking, or screwing other women, but I didn't say that.

He studied my face carefully. "Go on."

I sighed. "Maybe I shouldn't be so honest, but I wouldn't have done what we did this weekend if I didn't like you so much. I don't want to get my heart broken if you decide you need more... variety."

The intensity in his gaze was too much, and I looked away. But he gently took hold of my chin and turned my face back to him.

"I need to see your eyes."

It was difficult to hold his gaze. "I'm not interested in a casual hookup, or not being exclusive. I want to build something worthwhile with you. But we should end this now if you aren't serious, or plan to keep using your hot tub... with other people."

He squeezed my hand. "Anything else you need to get off your chest?"

I thought about it, then nodded. "If this doesn't work out, will you please be civil if we run into each other? I won't chase or hit on you, but it would hurt me to be treated like that."

I wanted to fidget under his intense stare. But this was important, so I raised my chin and met his eyes.

He stepped closer and cupped my face. "Don't second-guess what we're building here. And that's what we're doing. You're kind and smart." He kissed my cheeks. "And loyal. And hot as fuck."

I puffed out a laugh.

His lips twitched, and he went on. "There aren't a lot of women who have all those traits. I know because I've been looking for fucking years."

Reaching up, I grabbed his wrist while he talked.

"So, believe me when I say I don't want to fuck this up. You're mine and I'm yours. We're exclusive, and I plan to keep it that way. Will you trust me?"

Tears gathered in my eyes, but I tried to hold them back as I nodded.

He continued. "And I'll be 'civil' if we ever break up. I can't promise I won't want to beat the shit out of whomever you're with, but I'll be civil."

I smiled, and a tear slipped down my cheek. He swiped it away with his thumb and kissed me again.

"Okay?" he asked.

"Okay." That word seemed to convey a thousand meanings.

That afternoon, we got back from our hike and showered together. I'd never had a shower quite like it, and my legs were wobbly when we finally dried off.

Then we ate lunch and discussed the remodel in Demuth Park with Fern's notes as our guide. We looked over her breakdown and tweaked a few things to bring some costs down.

Sebastian pointed to the bathroom budget. "I like the idea of stone or marble for the bathroom floors and showers, but it's too expensive. A nice porcelain hex tile will work."

Sebastian pointed to the estimated difference in the prices, and I had to agree with him. We made several more tweaks.

He'd been in a lot of homes in Palm Springs, and he seemed to have a good eye. Damien's brother owned a construction company, and we planned to use him for the remodel. Matías had also begun work on the pool and landscaping, so I felt good about our progress.

"Until I pass the bar and get sworn in, I'm only working part-time. So I can do some legwork, talk with suppliers, and look at finishes and samples."

Sebastian nodded. "Sounds good to me. It's a time-consuming process, but the sooner we decide on finishes, the sooner we can start ordering."

Martina came home in better spirits on Sunday evening. We threw some shrimp and vegetable kabobs on the grill, and ate together out in the backyard. I opened a bottle of wine from Fern's collection, and we enjoyed the beautiful evening. I could smell the rosemary bush by the side of the patio, and the crickets were out chirping again.

At first, I felt awkward eating on the same table we'd used for other things earlier that weekend. Then I remembered what we'd done and started getting breathless. I glanced over at Sebastian, who gave me a knowing little smirk. Smiling sheepishly, I squirmed a little.

Martina shoved a piece of shrimp in her mouth and spoke around it. "I love my parents. But after spending a weekend with them hovering and asking six thousand questions, I was ready to sneak out in the middle of the night and come home."

Sebastian looked at me with suppressed laughter. My eyes went wide thinking about her walking in on us. That could have been very awkward.

She waved her hand. "Oh, don't look at each other like that. I knew you two were here humping like rabbits on spring break."

I rubbed my forehead. "Oh, my God. I can't believe you just said that."

Sebastian pointed at her. "It sounds like you need to find a rabbit of your own."

Martina shuddered. "Ugh. No, thank you." She leaned back and toasted us. "Cheers. I'm finally getting my life back, and you two finally pulled your heads out."

I frowned. "I never needed to pull my head out."

Sebastian grinned and took a swig from his beer bottle.

Martina rolled her eyes. "Yes. You did." Then she turned to Sebastian. "And so did you, so you can stop grinning. I've never seen two people so far in denial before."

Sebastian shrugged. "I'm not in denial anymore. In fact, I spent most the weekend inside—" I gasped and slapped my hand over his mouth. Martina burst out laughing.

Chapter 33

I always thought public bathroom sex was urban folklore.

That Monday night, the Martini Monday crowd met at The Blue Room. Ramone had reserved three large tables, and we filled them all with our regular group.

A wonderful jazz trio played, and we ordered decadent drinks, and laughed and chatted between sessions. It reminded me of our first date here. I'd been so nervous and excited then.

During a break, Sebastian grabbed my hand. "I can't fucking wait anymore." He turned to Damien. "If anyone asks, we're getting some fresh air."

Damien grinned knowingly and nodded. "Lucky bastard," he muttered. A furious blush crept up my neck.

"Where are we really going?" I asked Sebastian as he pulled me toward a private "family" bathroom down one hall.

He shook his head. "You wore that fucking dress and you're asking me that? I bet you're wearing a thong too."

Martina and I had gone shopping late that afternoon, and I found a deep purple halter dress with a short, flirty skirt. Martina whistled when I'd walked out of the dressing room.

"Sebastian's gonna love it, and he's gonna hate it," she'd predicted. She hadn't been wrong.

"Oh, God," I whispered as he pulled me forward.

"No, baby. It's going to be me inside you in about thirty seconds." He slammed the bathroom door closed and locked it, then turned to me. "Are you wet?"

I couldn't talk, so I just nodded. The lush bathroom had soft lighting and vintage fixtures, but I didn't notice much else. And he hadn't been lying. He pinned me up against the wall and was buried deep inside me about thirty seconds later. Sebastian had to cover my mouth when I came to keep the noise down, and my hair looked like I'd taken an egg beater to it by the time we finished. But the memory never failed to make my panties damp and put a stupid little smile on my face.

Time seemed to go by quickly that week, and Sebastian came over almost every night after work. He slept over a few nights, and I stayed at his house sometimes.

We had to get creative to keep the noise down with Martina in the house sometimes. He finally gagged me with my nightie one night when I'd been too loud. He made sure I liked it.

The next week, Grace and Sheila hosted Martini Monday at their home in The Movie Colony area of Palm Springs, also known as TMC by the locals. Fall Modernism Week had kicked off, and both Sebastian and Martina were working long hours, so I went with Ramone and Jonathan.

"Wow," I said, as I studied their home when we pulled up.

Ramone smiled. "Yes, wow. The house is one of the old Spanish revival homes in the area. See that arched front doorway, and red tile roof? Those are dead giveaways."

Climbing rose bushes grew around their front wrought-iron gate. The place had a fairytale feel to it.

Jonathan nodded. "The style is also called 'Spanish eclectic.' I think either description fits. The homes have a distinctive old world, whimsical charm to them."

Grace and Sheila had just finished up a major renovation, and they wanted to show off the results.

Ramone eyed their home when we drove up. "I've heard Grace complain so much about this renovation, I'm a little nervous to see how it turned out."

When we got inside and walked through the home, we all agreed it had turned out beautifully. The living room area had refinished wood beams and polished wood floors. The renovated kitchen and bathrooms also still held their 1940s character with vintage looking finishes.

Sheila looked around and sighed. "It took three times as long to finish, and cost about twice as much as the original bid. I hope I look back on it someday and be glad we did it."

Grace's neighbor and occasional golf partner came with her daughter, Harley Emerson. Harley was the attorney who worked in the juvenile court, and I wanted to talk with her and get her thoughts.

"Laurel's going to be working at our law firm, and she's interested in juvenile law. I wanted to introduce you two," Grace told Harley.

Harley was lean and tall—only a couple of inches shy of six feet. Her beautiful blond hair flowed down her back in natural waves, and she seemed friendly and confident. She also had a nice, firm handshake.

Grace pointed to Sheila. "If you two will excuse me, I'm going to help with the martinis."

I turned to Harley. "I just took the bar exam in July, and I'll be getting my results back next month."

Harley made a face. "The wait is a killer, isn't it? You're going to work for Lewis and Clark, huh? I love those guys."

"They make it fun. I'm excited about working there, if I pass the bar. Every time I think about it, I get the jitters."

"I threw up the morning the results were posted," she chuckled.

We talked about work and the bar exam for a while, then walked over and got a drink. I ordered a dirty martini, and saw Harley grimace. Laughing, I remembering the first time I'd tried one.

"My aunt started the Martini Monday tradition way back. Traditional martinis are an acquired taste—that some people never acquire. You should try a martini with sweet vermouth, or orange bitters. Or just do what my friend does, and order a cosmopolitan."

Harley nodded her head. "Bingo." She turned to Sheila. "That's what I'll have."

Sheila shook up a cosmo for Harley and poured it into a beautiful martini glass with an orange peel twist. Harley thanked her, then picked it up gingerly, and we found a bench in the backyard.

The ladies had strung fairy lights between the palm trees, and a few flagstone paths wound around the yard to whimsical sitting areas. Their small pool looked like a tropical oasis, and orange tree blossoms scented the air.

"Do you play volleyball or golf?" Harley asked.

"No. I've golfed three times in my life and was horrible at it. I play volleyball, but just for fun. I do like to camp and hike, though."

"Oh, I love both. We need to go sometime."

We'd just swapped contact information when I noticed Damien and another man walk into Grace's backyard. I stood up and waved them over so I could introduce Harley. I heard her gasp beside me, then Harley started pulling on my arm.

"Laurel, stop waving!"

I looked down at her, confused, while Damien and his friend walked over.

"Hey." Damien gave me a hug. "Who's your beautiful friend, and why's she tugging on your arm?"

"Damien, this is Harley Emerson. I just met her tonight and I'd like to be friends, so be nice."

"I'm more than happy to be nice to her." He grinned at Harley, flashing his dimple.

I shook my head, then turned to his friend. He was probably Sebastian's other partner, since he was also good-looking and impressively ripped. He watched Damien with an expectant smile on his face.

Damien introduced him. "This is Zeke Deegan. He's our other partner, and the surveillance and security expert. Zeke, this is

Laurel Payne. She's the one who videoed Martina's ex being a dick and pushing Martina around."

Zeke grinned and pointed at me. "I've heard about you. You called Kenny a fat jackass and a fucking asshole in Spanish."

I glared at Damien. "That's not exactly what happened."

Damien chuckled and shrugged. "Pretty close."

Zeke shook my hand, then turned back to watch Damien and Harley.

"How do you know Grace and Sheila?" Damien asked Harley.

She gave him a flat look. "You don't recognize me, do you?"

Damien stilled, then cocked his head. "Should I recognize you?" I noticed his eyes sharpen.

"Yeah. Because I almost broke your nose last fall."

Then I saw recognition hit, and he lost the smile. He also stepped closer to her.

"I didn't recognize you without your Viking braids and war paint."

Zeke let out a full belly laugh. "Do you still think she's beautiful?"

"Shut it, Zeke." Damien said absently. He wasn't grinning anymore, and the dimple was gone. He was also completely fixated on Harley.

Harley folded her arms and stared up at him. Neither of them spoke.

I looked between them. "Okay. Someone needs to tell me this story."

Sparks were flying, but no one said anything. Zeke was still chuckling, though.

I tried again. "A broken nose? Viking braids? Come on, someone tell me."

Zeke finally took my arm and pulled me away. "I think they need to talk, and maybe clear the air. Let's get a drink and give them a minute. And I'll tell you what I know."

I let him lead me away, but I heard Harley finally start talking. "Oh, stop glaring at me. I already told you I didn't do it on purpose. Quit being such a baby. You kept playing—"

We walked far enough away that I couldn't hear the rest of their conversation.

I looked over at them. "Well, that was awkward."

Zeke grinned wide. "But funny as hell."

A smile tugged at my mouth. "Maybe a little. I can picture Harley in Viking braids. What's the war paint though?"

"We play in a coed volleyball league, and Valkyrie over there is on another team. She uses black eye to deflect the sun, and probably for the intimidation factor. It's that black strip football players sometimes put under their eyes to deflect the sun."

"Huh. It sounds fun. Does Sebastian play with you?"

Zeke shook his head. "He used to, and he's good. But he got too busy at work over the last couple of years."

That made me a little sad. Then I thought maybe Sebastian should have kept playing recreational sports, and given up using his hot tub instead.

"Harley's the best player in the league."

I eyed him. "The best female player or best overall player?"

He looked over at them. "The best overall player. And I'll deny that if you repeat it. We've been trying to recruit her, but we haven't had any luck so far."

"Did she play in college?"

"Yeah, I'm sure she did. Her team's pretty bad though—except her. I don't know where she found them. I've never seen such a strange group of mismatched people."

Damien and Harley stood facing off against each other. "They're still talking, but neither of them looks happy. I hope they don't kill each other."

Zeke shrugged. "Well, there aren't any volleyballs around, so they should be good." Then he turned his naughty grin to me. "So you're Sebastian's woman, huh? I bet that's interesting. Tell me all about it."

Chapter 34

Martina and I were fixing dinner the following week when Luke called to let me know he and Joey planned to come for a visit.

"Luke! Yes, *please* come. I've been trying to get you to visit since May. I miss you guys so much."

"We've missed you too. Fall break is next week, and we wanted to visit before the semester gets too busy. How've you been?"

I walked out and turned on the grill while we talked. "Better every day. I get my exam results back next month. What's going on with you? How's Joey?"

"Joey's been busy. She's taking another gaming law class, and she'll probably end up working there after law school."

I paused. "Joey working as a gaming law attorney? She always wanted to go into disability or elder law. What happened?"

"Money," Luke said succinctly.

I sighed. "Her student loans. She shouldn't have to worry about money all the time."

"Yep, very true. The fact that she got where she is, it's a fucking miracle."

I walked back inside and put the salmon I'd bought for dinner in tinfoil and sprinkled it with seasoning while we talked.

"Hey, your Martini Monday geriatric crowd here says hello. They miss you."

"I miss them too. Tell everyone hi."

I picked up my wine glass and took a sip. "When exactly are you coming?"

"We have Monday and Tuesday off next week, so we plan to come Friday afternoon if that works. Then we'll take off early Tuesday morning."

I was glad I'd finally moved into the primary bedroom. There hadn't been too much I'd wanted to change in the house, and it was nice to have Fern's touches along with mine mixed throughout the home now.

"Luke, hold on a second, will you?" I covered the speaker and turned to Martina, who was sitting at the kitchen bar prepping zucchini for the grill.

"Are you okay if my old roommates from Las Vegas come to stay this weekend for a few days?"

Martina nodded. "Of course. It's your house, and it sounds fun."

"And you're my roommate." I elbowed her. "They're great, you'll love them."

"Luke? I just wanted to double-check with my roommate here. She said it sounds fun. I'll introduce you and Joey to her when you come." Leaning back against the counter, I grabbed my wine glass. "I have to warn you, though. She's going to try and drag you to karaoke night."

He chuckled. "Can't promise about karaoke night, but it'll be nice to meet her. What have you been up to?"

"Not much, and it feels weird. I'm in this strange limbo, waiting to see if I pass the bar or not."

I felt uncomfortable bringing up Sebastian with Martina listening, so I decided to tell them in person.

"What happened with your girlfriend when she moved back to Las Vegas?"

Luke sighed. "*Old* girlfriend, and it's a long story. I'll tell you about it later. I have a class this afternoon, so I'm going to run. We'll see you this Friday."

"Okay, Mr. Avoidance. Have a productive week. Tell Joey hi."

I pushed the off button and looked up to see Martina staring at me.

"What?" I asked. "Do I have something on my face?"

"You've got a dumb look on it," she shot back.

"Rude. I was just thinking about them."

She looked amused. "Your roommates in Las Vegas are Joey and Luke? You lived with two guys? How did I not know this?"

I smiled. "You're half right. I lived with Luke and Josephine, who goes by Joey. Why?"

"Has Sebastian met them before?"

"No."

"Does Sebastian know about them?"

I thought for a second. "Maybe? I can't remember. Ramone and Jonathan know them. Why?"

"No reason." Martina's voice was bland. "Except one of them is a guy."

I rolled my eyes. "He won't care."

She shrugged. "Probably not."

Sebastian and Martina were still working long hours. I'd barely seen Sebastian since Sunday, so we'd planned a late dinner at his house on Thursday night.

I picked up tacos on my way over. When I got to his place, he wasn't home yet, but I had the code to his front door so I let myself in. I checked my phone to see if I'd missed a text from him, but there wasn't anything.

It was strange to be here without him, and the house felt empty and too quiet. I wanted to eat my tacos while they were still warm, so I grabbed an iced tea from his fridge and headed out to the back patio. Turning on his patio lights, I sat and made myself comfortable.

He had a comfortable outdoor dining set and a few large pots with century plants around the periphery of his small pool. The hot tub also had a nice deck and sleek solar lights.

We hadn't used his hot tub yet, and I wasn't sure how I felt about it. The backyard was cozy and private, and I could see why he'd like to come out here and relax after a long day at work. And bring women back here to enjoy the hot tub with him. Okay, I needed to stop thinking about it.

I'd just finished my tacos and was enjoying the quiet evening when I heard his backyard gate open.

"Sebastian, are you out here?" a soft female voice called out. "We're back for the winter. Are you around?"

My heart sped up and I felt sick to my stomach. A figure rounded the corner of the house. And I blinked, then squinted.

It wasn't who, or maybe *what*, I was expecting. An older lady in a bright purple and green housedress and bluish white hair appeared.

"Oh, hello. I'm looking for Sebastian. Is he home by chance? I saw his lights on back here, so I knew it was okay to come back."

The lady seemed friendly and obviously knew Sebastian. And she wasn't one of his hot tub hookups. I was so relieved, I sagged.

"Not yet, but he should be home soon. My name's Laurel. Are you a neighbor?"

"Yes. I'm Carol Crawford. Eleanor's my sister, and we own the pink house a few doors down."

I knew exactly which house. "Oh, I've seen your pink house. It really pops."

"Thank you! We go to Colorado every summer, then come here for the winter. We just got in today, and our water isn't working."

Carol was wringing her hands and shuffling her feet. I'd seen Lennie and Willie do the same thing when they needed to use the bathroom. I called it the pee pee dance.

"Carol, do you and Eleanor want to use Sebastian's bathroom? I don't think he'd mind."

She sagged in relief. "Oh, can I? We could run over to the nearest restaurant, but I'm a little embarrassed."

I got up to let her into the house. "Absolutely. Come in."

She followed me inside the back door and hustled right to the bathroom next to the guest bedroom. She came out not long afterward, looking relieved.

"I feel sooo much better. That extra-large diet soda in Las Vegas wasn't such a great idea in hindsight."

I winced in sympathy.

"Can I go get my sister?" she asked.

"Sure. Then, if you want, I can do a quick google search to see if we can figure out your water situation."

"I'm not sure how that would help, but it wouldn't hurt. I'll be right back." Carol let herself out.

I waited at the front door for them. When I saw Carol and Eleanor hustling down the street, I just opened the door wide and waved them in.

"Thank you, young lady." Eleanor hustled in and walked right past me to the bathroom. "I'll introduce myself in a minute."

Eleanor was a little shorter than Carol, and she wore a bright yellow and orange housedress.

After she finished in the bathroom, I led them to the back patio. We sat and I searched on my phone to troubleshoot their water issue.

I turned to the ladies. "Do you know if any work was done on the water lines over the summer? Could your water main be turned off?"

They looked at each other.

"I didn't get any emails. Did you?" Carol asked her sister.

"No. I mean, I could have missed it, but I didn't see anything."

I hesitated to ask my next question. "Did you maybe forget to pay your water bill?" As long as we were troubleshooting, it was a valid question.

The sisters looked at each other with wide eyes. "Eleanor, you *did* pay the water bill, right?"

Eleanor pursed her lips. "I may have forgotten."

Carol rolled her eyes. "Eleanor, how could you forget? I told you this would happen if you didn't keep it on autopay."

"You should be able to pay the bill online," I said, trying to head off an argument.

"And put it back on autopay," Carol added and gave Eleanor an exasperated look.

I put my phone down. "In the meantime, we can see about getting you some water for drinking and maybe flushing your toilet at least."

Just then I heard Sebastian calling my name.

"We're out here," I called back.

He walked out and saw the Crawford sisters sitting with me. He put his hand on the back of my neck and greeted the women. "Hello ladies." He turned to me. "I see you've met my favorite neighbors."

Eleanor waved, and I thought she might have blushed. "Hi, Sebastian. We just got in today. Our water isn't working, and we came over to see if you'd look at it for us."

Carol chimed in. "But Laurel already figured it out. Eleanor hasn't paid the bill for six months."

"Oops, sorry. I forgot." Eleanor smiled sheepishly.

Sebastian grunted, but smiled at them. "It happens. I can go pick up a few gallons of water for you."

"Laurel just offered," Eleanor said. "You know, she's different from the other women you usually have over." She eyed me. "I like her. Is she one of your cousins?"

He smirked. "No."

Carol chimed in. "She *is* different. You haven't gotten her into your hot tub yet, and you've been home for more than two minutes."

Both ladies cackled at Carol's joke.

I grabbed Sebastian's hand from my neck and squeezed it, then stood up. "I'll go pick up some water. You can eat dinner and catch up."

He studied me but didn't say anything.

"Do you ladies want me to pick anything else up?" They both declined, and Carol blinked at me.

I glanced over at Sebastian. "Your tacos are in the fridge. And I brought some beer. See you in a few." I waved at them and quickly walked out, my heart aching a little.

Chapter 35

At the grocery store, I picked up several gallons of water and a few simple groceries for the Crawford sisters, feeling despondent and a little heartsick about their comments.

I knew Sebastian had been with a lot of other women, and he liked to bring them home and use his lovely, private backyard, but to hear his neighbors talk about it so casually made it a little too real.

Sebastian watched me carefully when I got back from the store. We walked Carol and Eleanor over to their house with the water and groceries, and they thanked me profusely.

I looked around the inside of their home. "You're welcome, ladies. I'm happy to help."

Sebastian took my hand after we'd put the water and groceries on their counter. The ladies eyed us closely.

The exterior of their smaller home was painted a bright Pepto Bismol pink, with white trim around the windows and doors. The inside reminded me of a 1960s sitcom set with wood paneling on the walls, and gold linoleum flooring sporting a geometric pattern.

"Your place here is quite something." I didn't know how else to describe it.

Carol looked around proudly. "Thank you. We inherited it from our grandmother, and we haven't changed much over the years."

I believed her. Their house was like being in a time capsule.

We said goodnight and started walking back to Sebastian's house. He stopped on the sidewalk and turned me to face him. Then he leaned down and gave me a long, slow kiss.

He searched my eyes in the waning light. "Don't let them get to you. They haven't been around for almost six months, and before that they had a knack for coming over at the worst times."

"Well, I understand now what Carol meant when she said they don't go into your backyard anymore unless the lights are on." I turned and looked back at their house. "I just didn't see it coming."

"See what coming?" Sebastian asked.

"Confirmation from your neighbors about your 'extracurricular activities.' I was trying to work through their water issue one minute, and the next, they're debating if I'm one of your—anyway. I'm going to head home so you can get some sleep."

He sighed and wrapped his arms around me, then buried his nose in the crook of my neck.

"I want you to stay. You know you're not a casual hookup. Even they knew that."

My heart still hurt, but somehow I trusted him.

Slowly relaxing, I leaned into him. "All right. I'd like to stay, but you look tired. Are you okay?"

He nodded. "I'm not usually this busy, but I'm down two people—one for a funeral and the other for a baby."

"There's irony for you. The circle of life, and all that."

He chuckled. "Yeah, those are two events you can't get around."

"I can't do maintenance, but I can bring you food and remind your neighbors to pay their water bills. Let me know how else I can help."

He grinned down at me and cupped my cheek. "Thank you. Let's spend Sunday together. We can do another hike, or just go swimming and take it easy."

I remembered I hadn't told him about Joey and Luke coming.

"My old roommates from Las Vegas are coming for a few days this weekend. They're some of my best friends. We bonded through mutual suffering."

"Huh. Fellow law students?" he asked.

I smiled. "Yes. They'll be here tomorrow night and are going back Tuesday morning. Come over so I can introduce you."

He nodded. "Sounds good. Now come here so I can grope you."

I let out a surprised laugh as Sebastian ran his hands up my ribcage. I did spend the night. And he did grope me.

Luke and Joey arrived early Friday evening. I was so happy to see them, I ran outside and met them in the driveway when they pulled up.

After work that day, I'd gone grocery shopping, straightened up the house, and got their rooms ready. I also put together all the ingredients for a shrimp boil for dinner.

"You're really here!" I gushed and gave them both big hugs.

Then I tried to grab Luke's bag to help bring it inside. He held onto it and just grinned down at me. I rolled my eyes and turn to help Joey.

Joey eyed me up and down as she set her purse on the bed. "Well, look at you. You don't have bags under your eyes, you don't look stressed, and you're relaxed—" She stopped short and stared at me. "You've been getting yourself some, haven't you?"

"What? No!" I denied weakly.

"You're standing there lying. Right to my face."

"I don't know what you're talking about." My eyes shifted around, and I couldn't look at her.

She just hummed and gave me a look, then put her hands on her hips.

I caved like a soufflé just coming out of the oven. "Maybe?"

Her eyes got wide. "I actually didn't know for sure. Spill, woman!"

Luke came out of his bedroom that had been my room until recently.

"What are you two yelling about?"

Joey grinned. "I just tricked Laurel into admitting she's getting it on the regular."

Luke looked at me. "As in *sex*?" He put his hands over his ears.

She shoved his shoulder. "Oh, my God. You're like the older brother we never wanted. Yes, *sex*." She turned to me. "Out with it."

Joey was a tenacious, intimidating bloodhound when she wanted to know something. And I'd planned to tell them any-way—just not three minutes after they got here.

I pointed toward the kitchen. "Okay. Get situated, and I'll make mango margaritas and meet you in the kitchen in five minutes."

"And you'll tell us everything?" Joey persisted.

Luke shook his head. "Jo, it's fine if she doesn't tell us *every-thing*. There are things about you two I'd rather not know."

"You lived with us for two years, and you've known me since I was ten. You knew when we had guy problems, and when we had our periods, and even bought us tampons sometimes."

Luke winced. "Yeah. Like I said, things I don't want to know."

Joey sighed. "Okay, how about this? She gives us a general overview. Then later, I get all the juicy details."

"Fine." Luke turned to me. "But I want to meet him."

I blinked at him. "You do remember I'm twenty-six years old, right?"

Joey smirked. "So? You could be eighty-seven and we'd still want to meet him."

I couldn't argue with that. "Okay, fine. But Luke has to tell us what happened with his ex-girlfriend when she moved back."

Joey waved her hand. "I badgered that out of him weeks ago."

I pointed at Luke. "You've been holding out on me."

"Fine," Luke huffed. "But I'm gonna need a couple of mar-garitas first."

We met in the kitchen a few minutes later, and while I made mango margaritas, I gave them the edited version of how Sebast-ian and I got together. Then Luke told me about his ex-girlfriend.

"So she moved back into town after ten months, and just expected you to take her back?" I shook my head in disbelief.

Joey answered for him. "Yeah. And she wanted him to put a ring on it too. I dug through her social media and found out she was definitely seeing other guys in Florida."

Luke looked annoyed, but he didn't seem upset. "We broke up when she moved, so she wasn't cheating on me in Florida. Hell, I hooked up too."

"She wasn't the one, Luke," Joey said diplomatically.

He scratched the back of his neck. "I knew that after the first month."

I'd met Chelsie several times before she moved. She tried to hide it, but I could tell she didn't like me. And she *really* didn't like Joey.

People liked who they liked. So I was friendly, but it was a relief for all of us when she moved.

We talked for another hour over margaritas, chips, and guacamole. Martina came home while we were making dinner, and I introduced them.

"How long have you guys known Laurel?" Martina sat drinking her mango margarita and watching us prepare dinner together.

She'd glanced at Luke a few times, and I wondered what she was thinking. She also looked tired after her long work week.

Joey answered her. "Hmm. Over two years now? We've been roommates for most of that time. Luke and I grew up in the same neighborhood. Laurel told us you took care of Fern before she passed away. We loved her."

Martina nodded and sighed. "Yeah. I miss her. She was an easy person to love."

While the big pot boiled, we talked about Palm Springs and what Martina recommended they do. When the food was done cooking, I pulled out a large platter, and Luke drained the pot. Then we dumped the steaming shrimp boil out onto the platter.

"What's this called? It looks amazing." Martina examined the big pile of shrimp, potatoes, onions, corn on the cob, and a few lemon halves. It was all seasoned with Old Bay seasoning and butter.

Luke put his arm around my shoulder. "Laurel made it for us one night, and it became a favorite. It's a shrimp boil. I like it with sausage, but our pescatarian here won't eat it if it's boiled with sausage."

I wrinkled my nose. "Sausage is just nasty."

Luke had his arm around me and was grinning down at me when Sebastian walked in. He stopped short in the doorway, rocked back on his heels, and folded his arms across his chest.

I smiled. "Hey."

He didn't smile back, and Luke stiffened next to me but kept his arm around my shoulder.

The room suddenly went quiet, and I started to worry. "Sebastian, these are my good friends and old roommates I told you about. This Neanderthal here is Luke, and this is Joey." I patted Luke's chest and then pointed at Joey.

"You forgot to mention one of them is a man, *mi cielo*." Sebastian stared at Luke with flat, angry eyes.

Martina leaned back in her stool and swiveled around to face him. Then she reached back and picked up her margarita. "Yeah, a good-looking, tall military man with a great ass. Right around her age too." She wiggled her eyebrows and took a big sip.

Luke let go of me and started laughing. "Thanks. I think? You're a troublemaker, aren't you?" He pointed at Martina.

I nodded emphatically. "Yes, she is. A *huge* troublemaker, with a big mouth."

I walked over and wrapped my arms around Sebastian, then leaned in and nuzzled his neck. "Hello, Grumpy. I've missed you this week." He didn't unfold his arms, so I hugged him tighter, then pinched his butt.

He grunted, then finally bent down and kissed the top of my head. He let out a long, deep breath and unwrapped his arms. He hugged me back, then held my cheeks and gave me a deep, lazy kiss.

"I think she's got some explaining to do," Martina muttered.

"Oh shut up, troublemaker," I shot back, staring up at Sebastian.

He ignored her. "It's been a long, shitty week."

"That sucks. Come say hello and help us eat our shrimp boil while it's hot." I gave him another squeeze.

"It smells fucking delicious, and I'm starving." He finally let go of me and walked over to the kitchen bar.

We all stood around the heaping platter with our forks and plates and picked it clean while we talked. The meal was messy, communal, and it tasted as good as it smelled.

Sebastian pulled out a couple of bottles of beer from the fridge and opened one for Luke, then slid it over to him. Luke picked up the cold bottle and took big swig. Then he let out a long, happy sigh and tipped the bottle toward Sebastian.

Chapter 36

Sebastian stayed that night, and when we finally made it to bed, he took his time licking and marking me before finally thrusting into my soaking wet center. I fell asleep with him still inside me. In the dawn light, he curled around me and started all over again before rolling out of bed an hour later and heading to work.

When I looked in the mirror later that morning, I noticed a deliberate love bite right above my left breast. I narrowed my eyes and peeled off his t-shirt. Sure enough, he'd left several marks on me, in places where a swimsuit couldn't hide them. He was lucky he'd already left for work.

Luke and I went for a run before breakfast. Then Joey, Martina, and I did yoga on the back patio. The sky shone a dazzling blue, and the mild, warm weather made us all want to be outside.

Joey took pity on me, and picked an easy stretch routine.

"I hate you," I said to Martina as she executed a flowering lotus pose.

Joey kept her eyes closed. "Shh, you're oozing negative energy all over us."

Martina grinned. "I used to play soccer in high school. Our coach made us do yoga regularly."

I grunted as I attempted the pose. "That explains it."

"Let's concentrate on our breathing and finding our center," Joey intoned. Martina and I shut up.

After lunch, we went swimming and lounged around in the backyard for a few hours. And they all noticed the love bites.

Martina and Luke both grimaced, but Joey grinned. "Your grumpy asshole is a little possessive."

"A *little* possessive?" Martina smirked.

Joey sprawled on a recliner in the sun. "This feels so good. I didn't realize how much stress I've been carrying around."

Martina and I sat in the pool, and Luke lounged in the spa.

"You know what a good stress reliever is?" Luke said.

"Sex with Sebastian," I mumbled without thinking, then sat up quickly. "Oh God, I didn't mean to say that out loud!"

Joey and Martina laughed.

Luke groaned. "Damn it! Thanks for putting that image in my head. I was going to say a deep tissue massage, but sex might be a better answer."

Then Joey and I started discussing the merits of sex as a stress reliever, and Luke finally started swimming laps so he didn't have to listen to us.

That night, we went out to dinner at an outdoor farm-to-table restaurant called Harvest, and I invited Jonathan and Ramone to join us. The outdoor dining area reminded me of a charming

French countryside farm, and we ate, talked, and laughed for almost two hours.

When we got home that evening, it was late and we were tired, but I convinced Sebastian to stay over again. He'd been working so much lately, and I missed him.

Sebastian locked up, set the alarm, and met me in the bedroom. I'd gotten ready for bed and slipped on a little black silk nightie.

The hem barely skimmed my thighs, and the lace on the neckline played peekaboo with my nipples.

He stopped short when he walked into the bedroom and saw me standing there. The room was bathed in soft light from the bedside lamp.

He shut the door and leaned against it, watching me with hooded eyes. My insides clenched, and I tugged nervously at the short hem.

His lip quirked as he started toward me. "It's not going to be on long enough to worry about whether it covers your pussy, *cielito*."

I dropped my hands. He stopped in front of me and placed his palms on my thighs, then slowly slid the hem up above my center.

He looked down at his marks and his lips tipped up, then he bent down and took my nipple in his mouth, sucking it through the black lace. Sebastian squeezed my other nipple with his fingers and pulled on it as he licked me.

I reached down and tried to undo his pants, but my hands were shaky and I fumbled with his zipper. He stepped back and undid it himself, then shed his clothes.

He turned me around and pulled the nightie over my head, tossing it away. Then he slowly bent me over the edge of the bed and trailed his hand down to my center.

"You're soaked and your clit is rigid. I want inside."

"Yes," I gasped. I felt needy and jittery for his cock.

Neither of us seemed to have much patience tonight. Sebastian grabbed my hips and forcefully worked himself inside me. Then he slammed into me a few times before he stopped and stroked my back.

He guided me forward, and I crawled up onto the bed on my hands and knees with him still inside me. I pushed back onto his cock, impaling myself on him.

He'd become my addiction, and I couldn't get enough of his hard length inside me and his hands on my body. I craved his rough touch, and I loved everything we did together.

He groaned and plunged deep inside me, and I had to grab the comforter for leverage.

Sebastian wrapped his hand around my neck and pulled me up so my back was flush with his chest. Then he worked my clit with one hand and cupped my breast with his other, squeezing and kneading it.

"Open your eyes and watch me fuck you," he growled.

When I opened them, I realized Sebastian had positioned us so we were facing the mirrored doors on the closet. I could see his hips pistoning in and out of me from behind, and I watched as his hands worked my slit and breast.

The erotic sight stunned and enthralled me. His tan, muscular body dwarfed mine as he thrust into me. He invoked all my senses as his hips slapped loudly against mine, and our mingled scents permeated the bedroom.

"I can't get enough of your sweet, needy little pussy."

I reached up and wrapped my arms around Sebastian's neck. My breasts lifted and my body stretched out. This was the first time I'd seen myself having sex, and it was both unsettling and highly sensual.

The sight of us was so erotic, my climax rose. I clenched around his shaft, and whimpered at the pleasure mixed with a little pain.

Pulsing around his long, hard length, I shoved myself back on him, and started coming with a drawn-out moan. He put his hand over my mouth to stifle the sound, and the feel of him restraining me made me come even harder.

When I started closing my eyes, he shook me gently. "No. Watch."

So I watched, and saw myself convulse and orgasm as he continued to thrust inside me.

Seconds later, he let go of my mouth and crossed his arms over my rib cage, cupping my breasts tightly. Sebastian pounded into me, then tensed and shot his semen deep inside.

We eventually collapsed on the bed together, breathing hard. He wrapped his arms and legs around my body, fully surrounding me, and just held me to him.

Eventually, we stirred and got cleaned up, then crawled back under the covers. He pulled me on top of him, and I fell into a deep sleep.

Late Sunday morning, we took Joey and Luke to the drag queen brunch at the Cockpit. Martina, Joey, and I got ready together in the primary bedroom, and we laughed and made a mess as we debated clothes, accessories, and hair.

I picked royal blue high-waisted shorts with a cream silk halter top. Joey chose a purple dress with metallic threads and a short skirt, and Martina wore a V-neck, long-sleeved, teal romper.

Sebastian and Luke waited in the kitchen. When Sebastian saw us walk in, he straightened up. "Shit." He looked directly at Martina. "Promise me you'll behave yourself and keep everyone out of trouble."

Martina's chin jutted forward, and she put her hands on her hips.

Before they could start arguing, I chimed in. "I think what Sebastian *meant* to say is 'you ladies look lovely' or something a little nicer than 'shit.' Isn't that right?" I looked at him pointedly.

Luke grinned. "I think what he *actually* meant to say is you three look great, but you also look like trouble."

"Exactly." Sebastian didn't break eye contact.

I rolled my eyes. "Guys, people who go to drag queen shows are there for the performers. Have you seen the costumes and routines they come up with? And I think it shows appreciation and respect to dress up a little and not wear flip-flops and a t-shirt."

"Exactly," Martina mimicked Sebastian.

Sebastian finally sighed and took my hand. "Fuck. You'll make a brilliant lawyer. And you do look great," he said grudgingly. He didn't sound happy about it. "Come on, let's go."

The place was filling up fast when we got there, but Martina had reserved a table for us. Scott wasn't working at the bar, and he and Iz came over to greet us.

"You ladies look fabulous." Scott grinned and hugged us.

Martina gave Sebastian and Luke a pointed look, then hugged Scott back. "Thanks. These two said we look like trouble."

Iz pointed at her. "Because you are trouble."

She stopped smiling and glared at him. He leisurely looked her up and down, then slowly winked at her.

Luckily, a server came up just then to get our drink orders and change our larger bills into ones and fives. Then Iz and Scott took off to talk with the performers and other patrons.

Ramone had talked me through drag queen show etiquette the first time I'd gone with them to a show, so I passed on what he'd told me to Joey and Luke. One of my favorite performers, Bella De Balls, did a great number with big purple fans and an impossibly low-cut dress.

Another performer I didn't know had a fantastic orange sequin costume, and she was one of the best dancers I'd ever seen, especially in high heels. Luke and Sebastian got heckled a few times by the emcee, but they both took it well, and the afternoon sped by in a flurry of sequins, feathers, and 1980s pop music.

Right after the show wrapped up, I noticed Iz and Martina staring each other down again. Martina had a crazy look in her eye I didn't like.

"Are we ready to go?" I asked the group loudly.

Martina seemed to shake herself. "Yeah. I'm ready."

We gathered our things and waved goodbye.

"Great show! See you guys tomorrow night at my house!" I yelled over the music. Then I grabbed Martina's arm and dragged her out.

I pulled her ahead of the others, then turned to her. "Don't lie to me and don't change the subject. I want to know what is going on with you and Iz. He looks at you like he wants to rip your panties off, and you look like you want to claw his eyes out. Spill."

Martina didn't try to run or bullshit me. She just seemed to deflate, and her eyes got a little glassy. "It's not important. Seriously, I'm fine."

I gave her my best squinty eyes, channeling Joey and her bulldog tendencies. "You've got one week to tell me, and then I start digging."

Her eyebrow quirked, and she stared at me. "You stole that look from Joey, didn't you?"

"Yeah. Is it working?"

She nodded. "Kind of."

"Okay. I can work with that."

Chapter 37

I grabbed the skeleton by the pelvic bone and handed it up to Luke. For Martini Monday that week, I chose a Halloween theme and found a few interesting Halloween cocktail recipes to serve.

We were also putting up the Halloween decorations I'd purchased online now that I was a bona fide homeowner and could actually afford a few seasonal decorations.

"Raise his left femur a little," I told Luke as he installed the last of the three life-size skeletons. We'd positioned two of them so they looked like they were scaling the palm trees, and this one would be lurking on the side of the garage.

Joey came out and watched us for a few minutes. "You two are something else. I'm not sure what Fern would think about you desecrating her lovely front yard with those things."

My stomach dropped. "Do you think she would've hated them?"

Luke shook his head as he attached the skeleton. "Fuck, no. These are great, and Fern got a kick out of your weird obsession with Halloween. Remember her reaction to your costume last year when we FaceTimed her?"

I relaxed and let out a breath. Fern had been delighted at my Girl Scout costume when we'd called her before heading off to the annual university Halloween bash.

I smiled at Luke. "She especially loved your cute Boy Scout uniform, with your little khaki shorts and neckerchief."

He smirked. "Yeah, I do have nice knees, don't I?"

"That girl you hooked up with at the party seemed to think so. Who was she again?" Joey snapped her fingers.

Luke wiggled his eyebrows. "Erica. She had on the sexy nurse costume."

Joey shook her head. "How original."

We finished positioning the last skeleton, and Luke stepped down off the ladder. "There you go. Too bad Willie and Lennie won't be around for Halloween."

"I know. They'd love them. Thanks for helping me." I stepped back to gaze at them and rubbed my hands together. They did look fabulous, and now I just needed to pick up a few ingredients for the martinis. Then we'd be set.

I stood there for a moment, staring at this beautiful house with so many happy memories attached to it, standing next to two of my best friends. Sebastian was planning to spend the night again, and I'd soon have a house full of my favorite people.

I realized I was happy. Not just simply existing or getting by, but... happy. Looking back on that evening a couple of weeks later, I realized I should have savored that night even more.

After searching cocktail recipes online, I'd decided on blood orange martinis, bright green "flying monkey" cosmopolitans, and purple martinis with dry ice chips to make them bubble and fog.

Luke suggested the dry ice, and we'd picked up a few candy eyeballs and licorice spiders to use as garnishment. I had to freeze the glasses so the gel spiderwebs wouldn't dissolve, and work on the exact ratio of lime green coloring, but I thought the end results were worth it.

I'd also found a short black skirt with a spiderweb design and spider web earrings to wear.

Early that evening, I laid out the martini ingredients right before the party started as Sebastian read through the drink recipes.

"Huh," he grunted.

"What?"

He put his arm around my waist and rested his chin on my shoulder. "Did I just read lime green gelatin?"

"Yep."

"And dry ice?" he continued.

I grinned. "That's right."

He picked up a long skewer with three candy eyeballs impaled on it. "And this is your garnishment."

"Yes. They're perfect for Halloween."

He shook his head. "Well, they'll be interesting at least. I like your skeletons."

I beamed. "Thank you. Luke helped me put them up. Which means he did all the work, and I stood at the bottom of the ladder and bossed him around."

He chuckled and was nuzzling my neck when Harley walked in with Grace and Sheila. Sebastian nodded at them then started prepping the drink station.

"Hey guys. I have to warn you," I told Harley. "Damien's going to be here too."

"Who?"

I rolled my eyes. "The guy whose nose you broke last year? The one with the dimple?"

Harley sighed. "Ah, Dimples. I didn't actually break his nose. Did he whine about it to you?"

She complained a little more, and I couldn't help but laugh. It sounded like he'd gotten under her skin.

I shrugged. "He hasn't said anything about it. I just overheard you two discussing it. And I think it's fascinating you remember he stuck tissue up his nose, but you can't remember his name."

Harley stared at me. Then she shrugged. "Good point. What can I say? I thought it was kind of hot."

A throat cleared behind her, and she turned around to see Damien standing there. "Kind of hot?" he asked.

Harley glared at him, then she turned and pointed a finger at me. "You knew he was there."

"Maybe?" I turned to Damien. "You owe me."

He grinned and inclined his head.

We made our Halloween martinis and ate a light dinner. Sebastian added a classic black Manhattan to the menu, and that turned out to be the favorite.

Scott regaled us with stories from the Cockpit. Iz was working and hadn't come, and I thought that might be for the best until he and Martina got whatever it was worked out between them.

Later that evening, we finished straightening up the kitchen and said good night to everyone. Sebastian took my hand and walked me to my bedroom, then closed the door softly behind me. A little light filtered in through the gauzy curtains.

He slowly backed me up against the wall, then leaned down and whispered in my ear.

"Pull up your skirt, *mi corazón*."

I stared at him in the shadows, trying to read his expression. Then I slowly lifted my skirt.

He slipped his thigh between my legs, and firmly planted it at my apex so I was forced to straddle him. When we were together like this, and he whispered dirty commands and soft praise in my ear as he played with my body, I soaked it up like a desert during the first rain of the season.

"I've been wanting to fuck you all night." He bit and nibbled on my jaw while he tucked my skirt up in my waistband, then he took both my wrists and positioned them above my head.

"Leave them there," he ordered. He glided his hands up my ribcage, grazing my breasts, then ran his nose across my cheek and kissed the corner of my mouth.

I shivered at his soft caresses. Even his light touch heated my skin and made my toes curl in anticipation and lust.

He slid a hand up under my top and cupped my breast, then swept his thumb across my nipple over my bra. The touch zinged through my body, and I arched against him.

Reaching around, Sebastian deftly unhooked my bra, and I idly wondered how many times he'd done that to be so good at it. But the thought drifted away when he bit my ear.

He brought his index finger to my lips. "Open for me."

I opened my lips, and he slid his finger inside.

"Good. Now suck."

I didn't start sucking right away, but swirled my tongue around and licked it. Then I opened my mouth further and brought his finger all the way inside and sucked it deep. Sebastian rubbed his thigh more firmly between my legs and pushed up so I had to stand on my tiptoes.

"Ride me, *cielo*. That's it." He was breathing heavily in my ear. "Rub your clit against my thigh."

With his other hand, he pushed my top and bra above my heaving chest, and tugged my nipple. He pulled his wet finger out of my mouth and used it to swipe across my other nipple, then blew across it.

I panted. "That feels so good."

I rubbed myself against his thigh even harder, then brought my hands down to bury them in his hair.

"Your hands aren't above your head. Do you need another spanking?"

I held my breath. "Maybe?"

He chuckled darkly, then ran a hand up my thigh and pulled my leg up. He caressed my thigh until he reached my bottom and felt my bare cheek.

"Where the fuck are your panties?"

I smiled. "On me. And some are in my drawer, and a few in my hamper."

He pulled back. Then he cupped my pussy and felt my thong there. "These barely cover your clit, let alone your pussy."

"They're panties. They cover what they need to."

He pulled them aside and slid his finger through my wet slit a few times, then pushed into my channel. My knees buckled, and I grabbed his waist.

He pushed another finger inside and worked them in and out. "You still have your panties on, and I can do this to you."

"I know. That's why I wore them."

I wrapped my arms around his neck and hung on while he worked his fingers inside me for a few moments.

Then Sebastian pushed me back against the wall and yanked my thong down my legs, nudging me to step out of them. He unzipped his pants, and pulled himself out. Then he palmed the backs of my thighs and wrapped my legs around his back, lifting me up.

I squeezed him and held on. He rubbed his shaft against my slit and bent down to pull a nipple into his mouth, then he sucked hard. I bucked against him and moaned.

He pulled back and stared into my eyes. "I'm going to bury my bare cock inside your wet pussy and fuck you against the wall, and you're going to take it."

My insides clenched and pulsed at his words, and my hips involuntarily bucked. His rough demands and dirty promises always made my brain short circuit.

"Do you need my cock?"

"Good God, yes!"

He positioned me flush against the wall, bent his knees, and drove up deep inside me in one hard thrust.

I keened softly at the invasion. It hurt and yet felt so good. He was big, and I always resisted a little when he first pushed himself inside me.

He stopped and put his mouth on my neck, breathing heavily. "Did I hurt you?"

"Yes, and it felt so good." I panted a little. "Please don't stop. Take me hard tonight."

I felt him smile. "Whatever you want. I always love to hear you beg." He brought his hand between us and stroked me, then he held my body firmly against the wall and hammered inside me.

The pressure built as he hit my clit with each thrust. I tried to meet his strokes, but I was too out of my head. He suddenly stopped, and I cried out in protest.

"I'm not done with you yet." Swinging me around, he walked over to the bed and laid me down.

He quickly pulled off his clothes. My top and bra were still pushed up above my breasts. He left them there and brought my legs up straight and put my ankles against his shoulders.

Sebastian pulled my hips to the edge of the bed and surged into me again. My head pushed back against the bed and my hands clawed at the duvet. I could feel every long, thick inch of him at this new angle.

Watching me intently, he drove inside me. "Don't fucking close your eyes."

My breasts jostled with each hard thrust. He reached down and rubbed my clit, then pinched it between his fingers. I felt my orgasm building again and stopped breathing.

He continued staring down at me in the dark, and I worked to keep my eyes open and focused on him. He rubbed and pinched my clit again, and my orgasm washed over me. I came in a rush of contractions and pleasure.

Sebastian hammered into me a few more times, slammed as deep as he could go, then threw his head back and came.

"Fuuuck!" he growled, shuddering above me.

When he came down, he opened my legs and laid over me, propping up on his elbows. His cock still throbbed deep inside me. We lay there for several moments, catching our breath.

A tear slipped out, and I closed my eyes. I didn't want him to see it and think I was upset or hurt.

"Tell me why you're crying." He wiped the tear away.

I ran my hands up his back. "I'm happy." It was a simple statement, but I felt the truth of it to my bones. "Being here with you—with the people I love. I'm finally home."

He grinned teasingly. "I think you just said you love me."

His face was above mine, and I curled my palms around his shoulders. "I do love you." More tears escaped, but I smiled softly. "It might be too soon to say, but I don't care."

He leaned down and laid his forehead on mine. Then he kissed me, sweet and slow. "I love you too, *mi corazón*. I didn't stand a fucking chance with you."

We cuddled in the dark, talking and softly stroking each other until I started drifting off.

He finally prodded me. "Come on, Sleepy. Let's get ready for bed before you fall asleep with your bra and shirt still twisted around your neck."

I laughed at the nickname and shivered at the reminder of how my bra and shirt got there.

Chapter 38

On Tuesday morning, Sebastian and Luke walked out to the driveway alone before Luke and Joey drove back to Las Vegas. I looked out the window and wondered aloud what they were talking about.

"You, obviously." Martina didn't look up from filling her coffee mug.

Joey stood next to me. "Luke's probably telling Sebastian not to hurt you, and maybe a few other things."

Martina chimed in. "And Sebastian's probably telling Luke he's not happy about you having him as a roommate or friend, and if he ever tries to be more than that, he'll kick Luke's ass."

I shook my head and turned away. "Thanks, Martina, that makes me feel so much better. I love them both. They'll figure it out." I rubbed at my earlobe.

Martina smirked. "This is their way of figuring it out. They'll be fine—after a punch or two."

Joey pointed at Martina. "You're a provocateur. I can see why you get in so much trouble."

Martina smiled like Joey had given her a wonderful compliment.

Joey turned to me. "They're not going to fight. Now I want to circle back to your comment about loving them both."

Martina perked up. "You love Sebastian?"

"Maybe?"

She huffed. "It's a yes or no question."

I looked at Joey for help, but she just stared at me expectantly.

"Yes, okay? Yes! I didn't mean to. It's too soon. He's grumpy and rude sometimes. And bossy." I stopped and licked my lips. "I actually like it when he gets bossy."

Joey grinned, and Martina groaned.

❀☙❈☙❦

The days sped by, and Halloween came. I was a little disappointed we only got nine trick-or-treaters, but I still planned to put my skeletons up again next year.

I'd taken photos of the skeletons and sent them to Willie and Lennie. They called me back with a million questions.

"Are they real? Did you take off their skins?" Willie asked.

I cringed. "Icky! No, they're made out of rubbery plastic and bendable wires."

"Oh." He sounded disappointed.

"It rained here," Lennie said. "And my Batman costume got wet."

"Yeah, and Dad got mad 'cause we got mud inside," Willie added.

Lennie broke in. "He was mean, Lolly. I was scared."

Chloe changed the subject. "Tell her about your school party."

They told me about their school Halloween party, and promised to send me some pictures of their costumes.

After we hung up, I stared at my phone. I had a bad feeling in the pit of my stomach I couldn't shake. When Chloe called me early Saturday morning sounding shaky and upset, I wasn't that surprised.

"What's wrong? Did you finally get Victor served?" I asked.

"He was served yesterday. I did what you suggested and had someone install a few hidden cameras in the house. I'm so glad I did." Chloe started crying, and I could hear Lennie in the background trying to console her.

"Chloe, what happened? Are you guys okay?"

Chloe cried for another minute, then got herself under control. "I'm okay."

She must have put me on speakerphone because I could hear Lennie's voice. It sounded small.

"Lolly? Is that you?"

"Hi, Len. How're doing? What's going on?"

"Nothing."

"Where's Willie?" I prodded.

"He's in the bathroom. When are you coming to see us?"

I wished Boo were there. He talked more than Lennie did, and maybe he could give me more information.

"I can come any time if you need me. Are you okay?"

Then Lennie started crying too, and my heart sank. This wasn't his usual crying, where he was upset Willie had beaten him at Nintendo. He sounded heartbroken and scared.

Finally, I heard Willie's loud voice. "Did Dad come back?"

"No, William," Chloe answered. "Leonard's talking to Laurel on the phone, and he got upset."

"Lolly?" Willie asked.

"Hi, Willie. I hear it's been a bad day. Can you tell me what happened?" I tried to keep my voice normal, but I sounded hoarse.

"Dad came home and yelled at Mom. We were scared, and Mom told us to go in our room. But he said bad words, then he pushed her and hit her." Willie's voice got small and shaky. "I tried to stop him."

"Willie, when did this happen?" Anxiety rolled through me, and my palms started sweating, but I tried to keep it together.

He didn't say anything for a few seconds.

"Was it today, or last night, or a few days ago?" I asked.

"I think last night. Yeah, last night."

Lennie piped up. "And he broke stuff. He got the TV off the wall, and he threw glass things and broke them."

"I'm so sorry you guys had to see and hear that. I'll try and make sure you don't have to go through anything like that again, okay?" I didn't hear a response.

"Are you guys nodding your heads?" I finally asked them.

"Yeah," Willie said.

"Okay, hand the phone to your mom, will you? I need to talk to her."

When Chloe got back on the phone, I was scared and fuming, but I held it in.

"Chloe, take me off speakerphone, will you?"

"Alright. I don't know what to do." Chloe's voice shook.

"Can you send me the video? Did you call the police and make a report?" I tried to keep my voice calm, but I didn't feel calm.

"I'm not making a report. If this got out to the neighbors or our friends, I'd be mortified."

"I understand." I understood but I didn't agree. "Do you have the video saved? Send it to me, and your attorney, for safekeeping." My gorge rose, but I tamped it down. "It'll probably help you get a better settlement."

Chloe was a decent mother at times, but she was also self-centered. I needed her to send me that video so I could help protect the boys.

"I have it on my computer. Let me see."

It took a few minutes, but she emailed it to me. When the video finally came through I saved it, then breathed a sigh of relief.

"I have it. Send a copy to your attorney too," I urged again.

"Okay. I'll forward her the email right now. I need to go soon, I have a hair appointment in an hour."

I stood still, not sure I'd heard her correctly. "Chloe, you need to report this. You could get a criminal charge for failure to protect, or child neglect, if you don't."

Her voice rose. "What are you talking about? That's not going to happen! No one needs to—"

"Chloe, listen." My voice was firm. "I'll make a report too, okay? But you need to protect yourself, as well as the boys, and report it. Sometime today, a police officer should come by and take your statement and talk to the boys. You need to cancel your hair appointment."

"If I cancel this late, they'll still charge me—"

I cut in. "That doesn't matter. I'll reimburse you." I tried to get my temper under control. I didn't want to say anything I'd regret. "I'm going to make a report, Chloe. The boys need to be safe."

She sighed. "I don't want this to turn into a big mess."

"It's already a big mess. What Victor did is child abuse and domestic violence." I felt somehow liberated and heartbroken to say it out loud.

Her voice rose. "Will they come to the house? What if the neighbors see?"

"They won't know what's going on. And even if they do, you guys did *nothing* wrong. As a mother, you have a legal duty to protect your children. Chloe, you've raised some wonderful, awesome boys. And sometimes parents have to make excruciating choices to protect their kids. Don't bury your head in the sand." I wondered if I was talking to Chloe or the ghost of my mother.

I could hear her crying again, and I couldn't hear the boys in the background. She must have gone into another room and closed the door.

I sighed and rubbed my brow. "Chloe, you and the boys aren't safe. I can help you."

"How? He told me he'd leave me penniless and homeless if I tried to get child support and alimony." She was crying again.

"I'm sure your family law attorney told you that's complete nonsense. You have a prenuptial agreement. Review that with her."

Chloe probably knew all this, but was just scared.

I kept going. "You can blame me for the video cameras and calling the police. And you guys can stay here while you get your life situated and your divorce finalized."

She stopped crying and was silent for a few seconds, obviously thinking. "How would that look if I brought them to California?" she asked hesitantly.

Holy God, I wanted to strangle this woman. "It would look better than you getting your hair done and not getting them out of harm's way."

I was afraid to alienate her, but I wanted to yell at her so much my throat hurt from holding back. "How about this? You pack, and I'll get airline tickets and call in the report. How does that sound?"

She was silent for a moment, then sighed and finally agreed. "Okay. I can do that."

"Good. Now I need to talk to Willie and Lennie for a minute. Can you put them back on the phone?"

She hesitated. "What are you going to tell them?"

"That they're coming here for a little while, and we'll keep them safe while you work out your divorce with Victor. How does that sound?"

Chloe exhaled deeply. "That sounds good. All right, I'll get them packed."

I could hear her open a door. Then I heard her talking to the twins, and she put me back on speakerphone.

"Laurel? They're here."

I tried to sound calm and reassuring. "Hey, guys. I had a serious talk with your mom. You're going to come back to Palm Springs and hang out with me while she gets some things worked out. Are you guys alright with that?" I held my breath.

"Yes! We want to come," Willie shouted. "Can we bring our Nintendo Switch?"

"You'll have to talk with your mom about that. Good try though. Lennie, how do *you* feel about coming here?"

Lennie was quiet for a moment. "Dad scares me. He yells so loud, and sometimes he hurts us. I don't want to see him anymore." He started crying again.

"Oh, Len. We'll get this worked out." I prayed I could keep my promise.

Lennie kept crying. "He doesn't even like me. He's always so mean."

Listening to Lennie and not being able to hold or comfort him was torture. And I was deeply ashamed I hadn't done more to get them away from Victor before now.

"I'm so sorry, and I know how you feel. He used to scare me sometimes too." He still frightened me, but I didn't want to tell the boys that.

Lennie stopped crying a little. "He did?"

"Yeah, he did. He yelled at me and pushed me around too. I understand how you feel, and no one should treat people that way. Especially not their own kids."

Lennie's voice was so forlorn. "Why does he?"

And there was the million-dollar question. "I don't know, Len. That's the truth. I just don't know. I'm going to do everything I can to make sure he doesn't scare you anymore. I promise, okay?"

Lennie was quiet. I heard him take a few big sniffs, then let out a long, deep sigh. "Okay, Lolly. I'll wait for you."

My heart squeezed, and I thought of Fern. She'd also tried to comfort and protect me over the years. Now it was my turn to try and protect them.

Chapter 39

When I got off the phone, I watched the video Chloe emailed me. Seeing Victor screaming and shoving Willie as the little five-year-old tried to protect his mother made me heartsick and angry.

It brought back terrible memories, and feelings of helplessness and fear I'd suppressed over the years. I remembered his quick, explosive temper, his verbal and sometimes physical abuse, and then his long, drawn-out silences.

After looking at the video, I called Sebastian. He picked up, and when I heard his voice I started crying.

"*Mi corazón*, baby, what's wrong? Talk to me."

I heard him tell someone he had an emergency and had to go. When he got back on the line, I told him everything. He asked a few questions but mostly listened.

"How can I help?"

It was a simple statement, but I knew at that moment deep in my soul, I truly loved Sebastian and wanted a lifetime with him.

He could be grumpy and impatient sometimes, but he wasn't that way with me anymore. He loved deeply, and he took care of those he loved.

"You've already helped me, just by listening. Now I need to buy plane tickets and make phone calls. I love you. Thank you."

"I love you too. Let me know what's happening."

When we hung up, I felt more grounded and in control. I bought plane tickets, then made the police report. I also talked with Chloe's attorney, and she was not happy.

She sighed, long and loud. "Laurel, having Chloe take the boys out of state without informing anyone first doesn't help our position."

"We're more concerned about Victor terrorizing my little brothers, Elizabeth. You need to revise the divorce papers to request Chloe have full custody of the boys, with Victor having therapeutic, supervised visitations until he demonstrates he's changed."

Elizabeth hummed. "I'll check with Chloe to make sure she wants these changes. If she does, I'll revise the Petition."

"Chloe told me she does, but if for some reason Victor bullies her into changing her mind, *I'll* be filing for custody of the boys," I told her. "Someone needs to look out for their safety."

I could feel the tension ratchet up over the phone. I didn't want to alienate Chloe or her attorney, but thanks to Fern I now had the money for a long, protracted custody battle if necessary.

"Understood," she clipped.

We said goodbye, and I took a deep breath. I was willing to do whatever I needed to in order to keep my promise to Lennie and keep them both safe.

Less than twenty-four hours and three very expensive plane tickets later, I pulled up to the curb at the Palm Springs airport to pick up Chloe and the twins. The evening was mild, and the temperature felt cool enough to pick them up in Fern's convertible.

I'd wrestled the two child car seats into the back seat of the convertible, and put the top down so the twins could enjoy the ride home. They were all a little subdued.

Willie seemed disappointed the flight had been uneventful, and Lennie looked tired and despondent. I gave them both tight hugs, and for the first time in almost two days, I felt the knot in my gut unclench a little.

On the way home from the airport, I tried to cheer everyone up by detouring past a house in The Movie Colony area of Palm Springs with a yard that took up half a city block and had countless huge colorful robots and dinosaur sculptures in it. I'd seen the house in Grace and Sheila's neighborhood not long ago.

When Willie and Lennie saw all the big colorful metal sculptures of robots and dinosaurs peaking over the wall, they were in complete awe and made me pull over. One giant metal robot had been attached to the top of the wall.

Willie gasped when he saw it. "Wow! Lennie, look!" He bounced up and down in his car seat. "Can you see the huge pink dinosaur there? Where did they come from?"

I smiled at his enthusiasm. "The artist who lives here made them over the years."

Lennie stared at the sculptures, completely mesmerized. "How many are there? They're humongous."

I shrugged. "I don't know. This is only the second time I've seen them. Do you want to come back when we can walk around the block and check it out?" They both shouted yes, so we made plans to come back and get a closer look. Then I drove us home.

I'd made homemade cheese lasagna, garlic bread, and a big salad for dinner before I left for the airport, and Martina finished setting the table when we walked in.

"Hey, my favorite little dudes! How are you guys? Hi, Chloe, how was the trip?" Martina asked.

Willie was bursting with news. "Guess what? We saw the robot dinosaur place. There was a huge pink dinosaur, and a white robot on the wall. We're gonna go back."

Martina squatted down and opened her arms. Willie and Lennie ran over and gave her hugs and high fives. "I know that place. It's awesome. Hey, Lennie, you've got all your clothes on today."

"You guys hungry?" I asked.

Willie nodded enthusiastically. "I'm starving."

Chloe let out an exasperated breath. "William, you're always starving."

Martina stood up and put her hand to her chest. "I'm always starving too. Our friend, Harley, heard you guys were coming, and she brought over brownies and ice cream for dessert. If your mom says it's okay, we'll break them out afterward."

I'd never been so happy to have Martina as my roommate and Harley as my friend. We brought everyone's bags in and got them settled, then sat down and ate dinner. Willie and Lennie chattered away during most of the meal.

Chloe finally stirred and looked at me. "Laurel, I meant to tell you. I rented a house for a couple of weeks a few blocks away from here. But we can't get in until Friday."

My hand tightened on my fork, but I kept my expression calm. "You know you're welcome to stay here as long as you want."

"If we can stay until Friday, that would be nice. If we're going to be here for a while, then we need to have our own place. I'm sure you understand."

I wondered if Chloe was angry with me for making a police report or calling child protective services. It wouldn't have changed anything, so I decided not to worry about it.

"I get it. But come over whenever you want, okay? I love having you guys here."

She smiled faintly and seemed relieved. "Oh, I will. I'll need all the help I can get. These two are quite the handful."

"I'll get them ready for bed and tucked in. You look like you could use a good night's sleep," I told her.

"Thank you. I'm not good company right now. It's been a hellish week." Chloe stood up and gave the boys hugs and kisses, then dragged herself off to her room.

"You guys up for brownie sundaes, or do you want to go to bed too?" I asked.

Willie raised his hands. "Duh! Brownies."

Sebastian walked in while we were eating dessert.

I pointed my fork at him. "You made it in time for the best part of the meal."

He leaned down and kissed me on the lips, then licked his own. "Um, chocolate and vanilla ice cream. You taste delicious."

Willie made gagging sounds.

"Are you guys boyfriend and girlfriend?" Lennie asked.

Sebastian put his hand on my shoulder and squeezed. "Yes. Are you okay with that?"

I thought Lennie would just nod his head, but he paused a long time before answering. "I guess. If you're nice, and don't yell at her."

My heart cracked a little. "He's super nice to me, Lennie. He used to be a little grumpy and quiet, and he didn't talk a lot at first." What an understatement. "But that was before we got to know each other, and then started liking each other."

Lennie nodded. "That's okay. Just don't yell at her or hit her. 'Cause it's scary." His eyes were big.

Sebastian looked solemnly at Lennie. "I won't ever do that, Lennie, I promise. I'm glad you love her too."

Martina watched us, and she surreptitiously wiped at her eyes. I had to do the same. Willie sat still for once, looking between Lennie and Sebastian.

I cleared my throat. "Okay, you two. Let's set up your Nintendo Switch and play one game of *Dance Party*."

Willie groaned. "*Dance Party*? Why do you always want to play that game?"

Martina snickered. "Because that's the only game she can win sometimes. How about *Mario Kart*?"

"Yeah!" Willie pumped his fist.

I needed to take charge, or they'd be up half the night playing. "If Martina agrees, you can play one game of *Mario* with her since she's way better than I am." I looked directly at Martina. "One game."

"What?" she asked innocently and batted her eyes.

They quickly gathered their dishes, then ran off to set up the game console. I made a plate of food for Sebastian, and he sat and ate at the bar while I loaded the dishes.

"This is delicious, thank you. How are the boys doing?"

"I think Willie's bounced back okay, but Lennie seems to internalize things a little more."

We talked while he finished eating. He rinsed and loaded his plate, then turned to me.

He cupped my face. "How are you doing?"

"Honestly? I'm scared," I whispered.

"Of what exactly?" He slid his hands into my hair and brought my forehead to his lips.

I tried to verbalize my fears without giving too much away. "Of Victor taking Willie and Lennie, and me not being able to protect them. Of him ruining everything good in my life again. And of losing you in all this."

He shook his head. "You won't lose me." The knot in my stomach tightened again, and his words seem to mock me.

He kissed my forehead again. "You also have Jonathan and Ramone. And Martina. We'll get you through this. But be careful, *mi corazón*. He doesn't seem stable."

Nodding, I thought about my mother. I'd never told anyone, but on the afternoon before Victor's drunk driving incident that killed my mother, I heard her and Victor arguing loudly and violently.

I'd never know if Victor had purposefully driven drunk, or maybe wrecked the car to get back at her. But I thought he was capable of it. So I hadn't been completely honest with Sebastian.

I wasn't just scared—I was terrified.

Chapter 40

We quickly fell into a routine that week, with Willie and Lennie working on lessons in the morning while I went to work. Then we'd get together in the afternoons and hang out, and either swim or play games.

But I felt skittish and anxious, waiting for Victor to make a move. I also slept fitfully, and my dreams were dark and menacing.

When Chloe received a copy of the protective order from New York, Ramone advised us to register it with the court in Riverside County so there'd be an official record in case Victor showed up. I knew Victor, and I knew he wasn't done.

I'd heard enough about contested divorces and custody battles to know that Victor might be granted visitation and maybe partial custody if he could charm the judge. And then he would always be a threat.

So I started plotting, and I didn't include Sebastian or Ramone in my plans. Ramone would eventually forgive me, and I hoped to God Sebastian would too. But I knew if I told them, they'd try to stop me.

On Tuesday morning, I waited until Sebastian went to work and Ramone left for court, then I walked into Jonathan's office and shut the door.

"I need your help and you're not going to like it," I said bluntly.

He'd been working on his laptop, but he leaned back in his chair and looked up at me.

"What's going on?"

"I have an idea, but I don't want Sebastian or Ramone to know. I don't think they'll let me do it."

"Why?" He motioned to a seat in front of his desk.

I sank down and looked him in the eye. "Because it involves baiting Victor."

"With what?" he asked cautiously.

"Me."

He put his palms to his forehead. "I was afraid you'd say that."

I leaned forward. "You know he'll never let the twins go unless I *make* him. He'll always be a threat if he gets unsupervised visitation, or God help us—custody."

Jonathan exhaled. "I know. We watched what happened to you when your mother died. Fern and Jackson worried about you constantly." He studied the top of his desk for a minute.

I pressed him. "Please. I don't know if I can do this without your help."

He massaged his temples, then finally nodded. "Okay. I'm not sure what you have in mind, but promise me you'll be careful."

He sat back and studied me, then pointed a finger at me. "You'll help me smooth things over with Ramone when it's done. He's going to be livid."

"Believe me, I know. Ramone will forgive us—eventually. But Sebastian… " I swallowed.

Jonathan reached over and squeezed my hand, but he didn't try to placate me or alleviate my fears. He was a realist, and he knew Sebastian well.

He started drumming his fingers on his desk. "We need to hit Victor in his ball sack and make him careless and stupid."

I wrinkled my nose. "Nice imagery. Victor will probably try to drag the boys back to New York, where Chloe's more vulnerable and easier to manipulate. I need to push him into doing something stupid I can use against him."

Jonathan nodded. "Alright. Where is he vulnerable? What does he love the most?"

I didn't need to think about it. "Money. And the security and insulation it gives him. And prestige in his business and social circles. But mostly money."

"Okay. How does he make his money?"

"He's a securities analyst," I answered. Jonathan knew this, but we were thinking out loud.

"Let's turn up the heat there." He started typing furiously on his laptop and became engrossed in whatever he was doing. "Give me an hour or two and check back," he said absently. "I've got some ideas."

"All right. See you later." I had a few ideas of my own, and I needed to do some research and talk to Martina. So I texted her and we made plans to meet that afternoon.

When Jonathan surfaced a couple of hours later, Ramone was still in court. I thanked God for small favors.

Jonathan laid out what he'd found. "I think I have the hook. Your college fund was put into a custodial account, and once you reached the age of majority, that money legally became yours. I think Fern and your mother set it up that way on purpose, so Victor wouldn't be able to take it from you."

"So he stole it when he confiscated my college fund. Is that what you're saying?"

"Exactly."

"His accountant would send me tuition money every semester until I transferred. So wouldn't his accountant know that?" I asked.

Jonathan stared at me, thinking. "Yes. So we threaten his accountant as well. That will add pressure, and maybe it'll be what pushes Victor to act recklessly."

"So, how do we push him to act recklessly?"

Jonathan smiled devilishly. "We send nasty letters from your attorney, telling them we caught them red-handed, and we're not only going to sue them but report them to their respective boards."

I grinned. "Oh, he'll love that."

While Jonathan worked on antagonizing Victor, I tried to figure out a way to get what I needed, if and when he came here. Martina and her confrontation with Kenny gave me some ideas, and I met with her later that afternoon to lay it out.

We sat in my car in front of Brownie's Barbecue in north Palm Springs and ate greasy fried comfort food while we plotted. By the

time we had an actual plan, I'd binged my way through a plate of
fried seafood, and Martina had eaten an entire chicken platter.

"You're fucking crazy," she finally told me bluntly as she
wiped chicken grease off her face and fingers with a wad of
napkins. "Sebastian is not only going to beat your ass, but mine
as well."

I winced. If only she knew how true that was. "I know."

She stared at me. "In all seriousness, I hope like hell he still
talks to us after this is over."

The fried food had been delicious while I shoveled it in my
mouth, but now it roiled in my full and bloated stomach. I lay
my head against the car window.

"Me too," I sighed.

The week seemed to crawl by, and I jumped at every little sound.
I was scared and jittery.

Victor rang the doorbell early Saturday morning. He hadn't
wasted any time. When I got to the door, I watched him
through the peephole and held my breath.

He waited impatiently for a few seconds, then started
pounding on the door. "Laurel, I know you're here. Answer
the door."

His voice had an impatient, entitled edge that I hated. He
pounded again. When he finally started kicking the door, I took
a deep breath and swung it open.

Before he could blink, I stepped outside and partially closed
the door behind me. He took a step back.

I started talking before he could. "You're not supposed to be here. I have a copy of the protective order from New York, and you shouldn't be within 300 feet of Chloe or the boys."

Victor glared at me with disdain, and pinched his nose between his well-manicured fingers. I noticed he had more gray hair and a few more wrinkles, but he was still thin and handsome. His clothes were also immaculate and expensive.

"Let me in, or go get Chloe and the boys," he said dismissively.

"No. They don't want to talk to you, and you shouldn't be here. I sent both you and your attorneys copies of the order."

He put his hands on his hips and looked me up and down. "You've been nothing but a nuisance and an irritation since the day you were born. Why are you involved in my business?"

"So you came here looking for them? How do you know they're here?" I clarified.

"Because I know you, you stupid little shit. Get them out here. Now."

Tilting my head, I looked up at him. "I wonder how many times you've called me that. I don't even have a memory of the first time. And now you call Lennie the same thing. You're nothing but a drunk and an abuser. And a thief."

His hand sliced through the air, barely missing my face. "You think you're going to sue me, you idiotic bitch? And did you think my accountant wouldn't tell me your attorney threatened him over your fucking college fund?"

He jabbed a finger into my chest.

"You're on my doorstep, so you're both obviously worried," I retorted. "You're also trespassing and violating the protective order. Leave. My attorney will be in touch."

"You threatened to go after my securities license, you stupid shit. You back off or you'll regret it."

He shoved his hand against my shoulder.

I needed to keep him talking, and I needed him to do more than just poke or shove me.

"How will I regret it? Are you going to steal from me again? Are you going to bully and torment me again like you do Chloe and the boys now? Like you did my mother? Or maybe drive drunk again and kill them too."

He rolled his eyes. "Are you still blaming me for that? Get over it," he spat.

Somewhere in the last few seconds, my anger overrode my fear. "Willie and Lennie are nothing like you, and I plan to keep it that way. They'll grow up safe and happy. And far away from you."

"Those boys are *mine*, you insignificant little cunt. I have no idea how I ended up with such a disappointment of a child. I wish you'd been in the car instead of her. That it had been *you*."

My ears started ringing, and my arms went numb. I wanted to hurt this man who'd killed my sweet, defenseless mother and had already caused Lennie and Willie so much misery.

"You let her bleed out in the passenger seat next to you, while you whined about a split lip," I whispered hoarsely.

He gave me a mean little smile, but I could tell he was starting to lose it. "It was a long time ago, and it was an accident. You need to call your fucking shark of an attorney off, or I'll ruin your miserable little life."

"You are a nasty, pathetic, abusive man, and my shark of an attorney has just gotten started. Now get off my property." I stepped even closer and raised my head to look him straight in the eyes.

His face twisted in rage and contempt, and he finally lunged at me, his hands going around my neck. I didn't try to evade or fight back.

When he started tightening his grip, I brought my hand out from behind my back. I had Martina's stun gun, and the safety was off.

His groin was my target, because I wanted it to fucking *hurt*. He shook me and tightened his grip even more, but I carefully positioned the prongs and pushed the button. Then I pushed it again.

The pressure around my neck eased as I heard the crackle, and I watched his face morph from rage to agony. Complete and utter agony.

He froze in place, and his eyes glazed over. After several seconds, I dropped the stun gun and peeled his hands off my neck.

His fingernails scratched me as I pushed him away. He fell over, hitting his chin on the concrete. I didn't try to stop his fall.

Martina opened the front door all the way and stepped out onto the porch. She walked over and put her arm around my shoulders, then gazed at my neck. She looked pale and her hands were shaking.

"Never ask me to do something like that again. Those were the longest two minutes of my life." Her voice sounded raw. Then she glanced up at the outside camera.

My ears were ringing, and my neck felt bruised and sore. I was numb inside, and my brain seemed foggy.

Victor moaned, and we both turned. I looked down at him, crumpled and bleeding on the ground. It looked like he'd split his chin open.

I felt sick that it had come to this, but then I remembered my beautiful mother and my two little brothers. He'd done this to himself.

Martina bent down and picked up the stun gun. "I guess we should call the police. I wish I could have been the one to tase him."

I let out a huge breath. "I feel a little sick." I was shaking from adrenaline.

"Are you all right?" She hugged me again.

I started to say no, but remembered this wasn't finished yet. So I nodded.

Martina squeezed my shoulders. "When you told me what he was like, I thought you were exaggerating. You weren't, not even a little bit."

Just then, I heard a siren, and it was getting closer. I looked at her. "Did you call the police already?"

Victor groaned and turned onto his side, still clutching his groin. His chin was definitely split open, and he had blood all over his cheek. We backed up another step.

Martina shook her head. "No. But I think I know who did." She looked at the camera again. "Sebastian was here messing with the cameras while you were at work the other day. I think they set up live surveillance on the house."

I didn't know why Sebastian hadn't told me. But then again, there were a few things I hadn't told him.

About two minutes later, a police car pulled up. Sebastian and Damien pulled up a few seconds later in Damien's truck.

Sebastian opened the door and got out before the truck had fully stopped. He beat the police officers to the front porch. His jaw was clenched, and he looked like he wanted to kill someone when he took in the scene.

Damien walked over to look at us. "You guys okay? Did he hurt you?" He saw the scratches and bruises on my neck. "Holly fuck, Laurel. Did he do that to your neck?" He pointed to Victor.

"Yes." My voice wobbled, so I cleared my throat.

Sebastian's fists clenched, and he looked like he was thinking about kicking Victor.

Then he glared furiously at me. "You've got scratches and bruises on your throat, and you're shaking," he said in a low, enraged voice.

I nodded and wondered what he'd already pieced together.

"You fucking knew he was coming," he said softly. "You baited him."

I nodded again.

His jaw ticked and he looked down at Victor again. "And you didn't tell me."

My heart felt like it was being squeezed. He glared at me with frustration and rage.

Victor looked up. "You fucking bitch! You tasered me in the groin." Blood and saliva dribbled from his mouth and chin. "I'm going to sue you and see you rot in jail." He turned his head and spat.

"Is this him?" an officer asked Damien when they walked up.

"Yeah," Damien answered.

The officer bent down next to Victor and checked to see if he was in any immediate danger, then he stood up and looked around. "I'm Officer Sorrell. Someone tell me what happened."

When no one answered right away, I stirred and started to step forward.

But Damien started talking again. "His name is Victor Payne. He's got a protective order against him in New York regarding his estranged wife and two little boys. The order's been registered here in California."

Officer Sorrell looked at me. "How do you fit in?"

"Laurel is his estranged daughter," Damien answered again.

Martina raised her hand. "I live here too. He came here looking for his wife and two little boys. They've been staying with us after he assaulted them in New York. This man pounded on the door, then when Laurel didn't answer, he started kicking it. When she opened the door, he demanded to see his wife and kids."

Victor started objecting, but Officer Sorrell put his hand up. "Sir, you'll get your turn."

Martina went on. "When she told him to get off her property and reminded him she'd sent him *and* his lawyer a copy of the protective order, he pushed her and grabbed her around the throat and shook her." Martina's voice quivered a little. "That's when she tasered him."

The other officer shifted and looked down at Victor. "There's a definite pattern with this guy, isn't there? Everyone's estranged from him."

"Yeah, there is, Johansen. No one can stand the fucker." Damien put his hands on his hips and glanced at Sebastian, who still looked enraged.

I wanted Sebastian to walk over and hold me so I could fall apart in his arms. I wanted everyone else to leave so I could talk to him and explain. But he stared at me with hot, angry eyes. I lowered my gaze.

Damien gestured to me. "Laurel's been trying to keep her little brothers safe and out of the middle of his shitstorm of a divorce. We just found out Victor is going to be charged with domestic violence in the presence of children in New York."

That was news to me. Sebastian's phone buzzed in his pocket. He ignored it. It buzzed again.

He finally pulled it out and checked the screen. "It's Zeke. He's monitoring the surveillance cameras." He stepped away and took the call.

Officer Sorrell leaned down and spoke to Victor. "I called an ambulance when I drove up and saw you on the ground. They'll be here shortly. An EMT will look you over, and then we'll arrest you and take you in. Do you want to make a statement here or later at the police station?"

Victor rolled over onto his knees. He still held a hand over his groin. "You can't arrest me. You don't have jurisdiction. That hyped-up protective order isn't valid in California. I'll sue all of you." Blood still dripped from his chin, but he seemed to be rallying.

"The protective order's been registered in this state, making it valid and enforceable here. So we *do* have jurisdiction," Officer Johansen countered. "I'm going to Mirandize you, and then you can tell us your side."

Martina took my arm. "You don't need to watch this. Let's go inside."

I nodded numbly. After Martina spoke briefly with Damien and Officer Johansen, she pulled me toward the front door.

Sebastian glanced over at me, his ear to his phone, then turned away.

Martina took my hand and led me inside. She walked me over to the couch, sat me down, and draped the throw blanket over us.

"Do you remember when Kenny broke my car window right before my divorce was final?" She asked.

"Yes."

"And do you remember what you told me?"

"Maybe?"

She shook her head. "Victor is an arrogant, abusive, toxic asshole, and his actions are not your fault. You shouldn't have to live your life being afraid of him or feeling somehow ashamed. You did what you had to do."

I reached out and took her hand in mine. "Thank you. I don't know if I could have stood up to him without you. And your stun gun."

Martina smiled. "You stunned him in the freaking nuts. That wasn't part of our plan, but I'm going to laugh about it for years."

We sat in silence for a few minutes.

"You need to tell Sebastian exactly what you did," she finally said.

"I think he already knows," I whispered.

"He's going to be furious with you."

"He already is." Then I turned my face into Martina's shoulder and cried.

In making sure Lennie and Willie were safe and had a chance at a happy life, I'd probably thrown away my own chance.

Chapter 41

Officer Sorrell came inside for a few minutes to take photographs of my neck and collect our official statements. Then Damien checked on us, let me know Victor had been taken to jail, and that he and Sebastian were leaving.

"You have balls of steel." He held my shoulders and studied me. "He wanted me to check on you, but he's fucking furious right now. He'll calm down eventually."

I wasn't so sure, but I didn't want to argue with him. "Okay. Tell him I'm fine. Thank you for talking to the officers."

"You're welcome. Why in God's name didn't you tell Sebastian what you had planned?"

A few tears escaped, but I held it together. "People need to know what Victor's really like, and I thought Sebastian would try to stop me. I want my brothers to be safe."

Damien nodded. "You're right. He would've stopped you."

I looked him in the eye. "I'd do it again."

He shook his head, then hugged me and kissed the top of my head. "You're something else, sweetheart. Give him a little time. I'll tell him what you said, but probably not that you'd do it again." He waved at Martina and walked out.

I stood in the open front door and watched them drive away. Sebastian didn't glance my way, and his jaw was clenched tight. I closed the door softly and laid my head against it.

A few hours later, Ramone stormed over to the house, furious. Martina and I were making lunch when he rang the doorbell.

We didn't answer fast enough, so he rang three more times. When I opened the door, Ramone blew inside and turned to me with his finger in the air.

Then he saw my neck. The bruises had gotten more pronounced over the last few hours and stood out against the scratches. He slowly lowered his finger and just gazed at me.

"You let Victor do that to you," he said softly. "And Jonathan helped you."

"How did you know?"

"Damien called and wanted to know what in the hell I was thinking to prod that viper with threats of getting his securities license suspended. He told me exactly what Victor said. I didn't know what he was talking about until Jonathan confessed."

I looked at him with pleading eyes. "I'm sorry about getting Jonathan involved. And I'm sorry I couldn't tell you. I knew you'd be beside yourself with worry."

He nodded vigorously. "Yes, I would have. And I wouldn't have agreed to help you."

"I begged Jonathan. I reminded him of what it was like growing up with Victor, and I don't want that for my brothers. Please don't be mad at him."

He threw his hands up dramatically. "I *am* mad at him. He's going to have to do a lot more groveling before we're simpatico again."

My voice got thick. "Please. I don't want you to be mad at me too."

He looked at me with my bruised neck, red eyes, and sad face. I saw some of the anger drain out of him, and he let out a big sigh.

"Damn it. Come here, darling." He drew me in for a hug. "I can't stay mad at you." He held me tight, then pulled back. "I assume Sebastian is the other person who's mad at you."

I sighed. "Yeah."

"Hmm. That man can hold a mean grudge." He rubbed my arms. "Victor could have really hurt you."

"I just want him to go away and leave us all alone."

He nodded. "Me, too, sweetheart. Come over this evening and tell us exactly what happened. I'll open a bottle of wine, or three, and we can fuss over you."

"Okay. And for what it's worth, Jonathan and I just planned to bait Victor into violating the protective order. He didn't know this was going to happen." I pointed at my neck.

Ramone looked at me for a long moment. "But he knew it was a possibility. You aren't expendable, Laurel. A lot of people love you, so please take care of yourself."

He left shortly afterward, and left me with a lot to think about.

I called Chloe not long after Ramone left, and gave her a sanitized version of what happened.

"Oh God. Laurel, what if he gets out and finds us?" she asked in a panicky voice.

"He doesn't know where you are, Chloe. The jail should contact you when he gets out because of the protective order, and I assume he'll head back to New York as quickly as possible."

Chloe settled down a little after that. Then I talked with the boys, and they told me about their vacation rental.

"Mom cries a lot here. Can we come back to your house?" Lennie asked.

"It's not up to me, Lennie. But let's plan a sleepover if your mom says it's okay. And we'll go see the robot house this week too. How does that sound?"

"That sounds good," he answered glumly.

Two days later, Sebastian still hadn't contacted me. I lay awake at night, unable to sleep, craving his body and warmth.

When I closed my eyes, my mind replayed the confrontation with Victor like a movie reel, and I saw the fury and rage in Sebastian's eyes all over again.

And when I gazed at myself in the mirror on the second morning, I knew I couldn't live in suspense and dread anymore. My eyes were sunken, and my face looked blanched and haggard. So I texted Sebastian to see if we could talk.

Me: I'd like to come over and explain.

Anxiously, I checked my texts countless times over the next few hours. When I noticed Sebastian had read my text, but he still hadn't responded, I knew it was over. Anguish flooded me, and I put my head down on my desk and tried to stem the pain.

When the California bar exam results were posted the next day, I felt only mild nerves as I pulled up my results. I'd stressed and worried for days before Victor came to Palm Springs, and now I lived with the ache of losing Sebastian.

My mind couldn't process any more stress or loss. When I looked at my bar exam scores and saw that I had passed, I felt only mild elation before the grief rolled back in.

The next day, I texted Sebastian again. It was early in the evening, and I'd just gotten home from work. I hadn't run into him in the hallway at the office complex yet, but it was inevitable. We needed to talk before that happened.

Me: You promised you'd be civil when we broke up. I need to explain. Then I'll leave you alone.

I changed out of my work clothes and had just walked back into the kitchen when I heard a sharp knock on the front door. When I glanced through the peephole, Sebastian was standing there with his hands on his hips. Adrenaline raced through me and I started shaking.

I opened the door and drank him in, my heart pounding. He looked me up and down, then his eyes jumped to my neck.

The bruises had turned dark purple over the last few days, but the scratches were fading. He grabbed my hand and pulled me into the kitchen.

"You look like shit, *mi cielo.*" His eyes strayed back to the bruises.

One small sob escaped me, but I sucked it in and breathed deeply through my nose. "Please don't call me that anymore."

"Why?"

My eyes dropped to his chest. "Because it hurts."

"Look at me," he commanded.

I shook my head. The anguish and stress from the past week seemed to catch up with me. I closed my eyes for a moment and tried to keep my tears contained.

Finally, I met his gaze. I started to reach out and stroke his arm, but remembered I didn't have that right anymore.

So I clasped my hands in front of me. "I just want to explain why I didn't tell you. And maybe clear the air between us, so it won't be as awkward when we see each other at the office... or somewhere else."

His eyes narrowed, and he looked furious all over again. "First, we are *not* broken up. So get that through your thick head. Second, I needed time to cool off. And third, I don't think you're ready for a good, hard anger fuck yet."

He stepped closer and carefully took hold of my wrist. I gawked up at him, my mind trying to process what he'd just said. Then he pulled me closer and brought his fingers up to touch my neck.

Sebastian trailed them down my throat. "I've never been that fucking furious or scared in my whole goddamned life. Promise me you won't ever do something like that again."

I gulped, then let out a small exhale as his fingers continued down. "Okay."

"Promise me," he pressed.

I leaned in and tucked my forehead into his chest and just breathed him in. Tears leaked out, and I let them fall. "I'm so sorry. I promise—never again."

He gathered me in and held me tight for a few minutes while I cried in his arms. Then Sebastian called Martina and told her not to come home for a while.

"I'm still fucking pissed at you for helping her," I could hear him say. "But I'm over at the house now. We need a few hours to reach an understanding. So don't come home." He stared at me with naked lust and residual anger shimmering in his eyes.

I could hear Martina's laughter. Without saying goodbye, Sebastian ended the call. Then he stalked over to me and rubbed his hands up and down my arms. He stared at my healing bruises and scratches. I couldn't wait until they were completely gone.

"I'm still pissed at you too," he growled. "And I *would* have stopped you. But I understand why you did it."

"I couldn't tell you. The twins..."

He laid his forehead against mine. "I watched the surveillance video—several times. You let him grab your neck. You practically served it up on a platter."

I didn't say anything because it was true. Sebastian wrapped his arms around me, and I felt my anguish slide away.

He sighed into my hair. "Zeke finally told me he'd kick my ass if I watched it one more time."

"Good," I mumbled against his chest.

"I need to fuck you, *mi corazón,* and spank you. It's not going to be gentle or easy."

I shifted restlessly. "Good," I mumbled again.

He took my face in his hands and kissed me deep and hard. Sucking on my lower lip, he bit down and pulled on it. Then he backed me against the kitchen bar and ground his hard length into my stomach.

Sebastian stepped back and yanked my shirt over my head, then unhooked my bra, pulling it off me. He pushed me back so I bowed over the counter, then splayed his hands behind my back to keep me in place and sucked hard on each breast before licking and biting my nipples. I knew he wanted to mark me.

I gasped and bucked a little at the pleasure and pain as he rubbed against me while he ate at my breasts. My body sizzled with lust and needy anticipation.

"I've missed these," he growled between nips and bites. My hands twisted in his hair, pulling him closer.

He stood and pulled my leggings and underwear down. "Step out," he ordered. I obeyed, and he pushed them aside. Sebastian spun me around so I faced the counter. Then he pushed me over it, my feet dangling above the floor.

Planting one hand on the small of my back to keep me in place, he swatted my bottom and the backs of my thighs.

I yelped and writhed on the counter. But my feet couldn't reach the floor, and he held me firmly in place. He continued to spank me, and my bottom and thighs stung and felt hot and tender.

Then he ran his hands over where he'd spanked me. Leaning down, he bit one cheek hard enough for me to cry out and almost rear up.

"No. You're going to take it," he ordered. Sebastian spanked me several more times, then bit my other cheek. Pushing my thighs open, he worked two fingers inside me and pumped a few times. My soaked pussy welcomed his fingers, and I could hear moisture as he thrust in and out.

"You're dripping wet," he growled, curling his fingers inside me.

He stroked a sensitive spot deep inside, and I started panting and crying as I tried to push myself back on his fingers. My mind and body were confused with the mix of pleasure and pain, and I was so aroused I could feel my own juices dripping down my leg.

He leaned over me. "You're getting off lightly, *mi corazón*."

I heard him unzip his pants, then Sebastian drove his thick, hot length inside me in one deep thrust. I cried out and my arms flailed, trying to find something to grab onto.

He gripped my biceps, then positioned my arms behind me and used them to pull me back onto his hard cock as he plunged forcefully inside me from behind. My breasts rubbed back and forth against the hard, cold countertop. My bottom throbbed and my pussy clenched around his hard shaft.

He finally let go of my arms and reached between my legs to stroke my swollen clit. When he pulled his hand away, I moaned in protest. He rubbed my sore bottom with his other hand, then bent over and bit the back of my neck.

Pulling my head back by my hair, he whispered in my ear. "By the time I'm done fucking and spanking you tonight, you won't be able to move, and you'll be soaked in my cum."

Then he drove deep again, and I spasmed around his cock.

I felt my climax build. "Please. Oh God, please. I want to come."

He chuckled cruelly. "I know." Then he slowed down.

I tried to shove my hips back at him and started sobbing and begging. He partially withdrew and swatted me again.

I was in no mood for his long, tortured teasing tonight. So when he plunged back in, I squeezed my vagina around his length and raised my shoulders up. Then I planted my palms on the countertop and shoved myself back onto his cock a few times.

"Fuck," he snarled. He started thrusting in earnest, and reached around again to stoke my clit. His other hand came up, and he held my shoulder in place while he pounded into me.

My orgasm surged, and I screamed his name long and loud while I came. My walls spasmed around him, and he drove himself deep. Then he groaned in my neck, and I felt hot semen pulse inside me.

He leaned over me on the kitchen bar while we caught our breath. Then he slowly pulled out and helped me off the counter. He was still fully dressed, except his jeans were unzipped, and I was naked with his semen and my own juices leaking down my thighs.

When he tried to set me on my feet, my knees gave way.

He smiled wickedly and scooped me up. "That was a good start. Now let's try the kitchen table."

I whimpered, and my center spasmed.

By the end of the evening when he finally carried me to bed, I couldn't move, my clit and breasts were sore and throbbing, and I was soaked in his cum—just like he'd promised.

Chapter 42

That weekend I picked up the twins, then we grabbed pizza and soda and met Sebastian at his house to try out his pool and hot tub together. It was the way I'd chosen to celebrate passing the bar exam.

Willie's eyes went wide when he saw the big pizza box. "Wow, that pizza is huge!"

B.O.B.'s Pizza specialized in New York-style pizzas, and it was a point of pride that their triple extra larges were at least twenty-four inches in diameter. They weren't the cheapest pizzas in town, but in my humble opinion, they were the best.

"We can knock it out. What do you guys think?"

Lennie nodded enthusiastically. "Yeah, 'cause I'm starving."

We ate pizza on Sebastian's back patio, then swam in his pool. Sebastian had a few pool toys, and the twins loved the floating volleyball net.

We split up into teams, with Lennie and I facing off against Willie and Sebastian. It wasn't much of a contest, so Sebastian started playing with one arm behind his back.

"No spiking!" I shouted as I ducked one of his harder hits.

"You're supposed to hit it back, not duck," Lennie complained.

"You hit it back, Len! I like my face just the way it is."

Sebastian grinned. "I like your face too."

Willie made gagging noises.

When we finally got into his hot tub, Sebastian leaned over and whispered, "This isn't how I pictured our first time in my hot tub together."

The boys clambered in and sat down beside us with their floaties on.

I patted Sebastian's chest. "Think of it as an exorcism of sorts before our first time alone in it."

He smirked and put his arm around my shoulder, pulling me closer. "Fair enough, *mi cielo*."

Lennie pushed my thigh to get my attention. "Lolly, I heard Mom talking on her phone, and she said Dad came to your house. Is he still at your house?"

He looked worried, and I mentally cursed Chloe for being so careless.

I took his hand and squeezed it. "Lennie, he showed up last weekend, but just for a minute. I didn't let him inside, though, and the police came and arrested him."

Lennie's eyes got big. "He got arrested?"

"Yes. He knows he's not supposed to come to my house—or your house. I don't think he'll ever come here again. He didn't like being in jail."

I felt guilty for not telling them. But I didn't want him to worry like he was doing now.

"Did he do that to your neck?" Lennie pointed to the fading bruises there.

I hated seeing the anxiety in his eyes. "He's the reason I have the bruises. But Martina was with me, and Sebastian and his friend came over too."

"What happened?" Lennie asked.

"The police took him away because he didn't follow the rules. If it makes you feel any better, he got hurt way worse than I did."

Willie spoke up for the first time. "It makes *me* feel better. I heard Mom say you got him in his balls."

"Thanks, Boo. It's probably not good to hurt people, especially in their, uh, balls. Unless you're protecting yourself or someone you love."

Lennie snuggled into me. "I'd hurt someone in their balls for you too."

Sebastian laughed. "I like the way you think, Len."

Lennie leaned over and smiled innocently at him. "Thanks, Sebastian."

I looked at Lennie suspiciously. "Have you known his real name all along?"

"Uh-huh."

Sebastian rolled his eyes and smirked at me. "Definitely your brother."

Epilogue

T he whistle blew, signaling the end of the game. The kids had just played their last soccer match of the season, and players on both teams were jumping up and down, cheering.

Then they ran around the field, hugging and high-fiving each other. They did the same thing after every game, whether they won or lost.

"I don't know where they get their energy after running around the entire game too." Camila sat next to me on the sidelines, watching the mayhem.

Willie had turned out to be a good forward, and Lennie was a decent defender. But the star of the team was Sophie, Matías and Camila's five-year-old daughter. Sophie and the twins were also best pals now—when they weren't bickering like siblings.

Sebastian and Matías coached the team together, and we'd signed the twins up less than a week after Chloe announced she planned to stay in Palm Springs. It was now May, and the weather was getting hot.

Matías whistled for the players to huddle up. "Okay, my little *fútbol* ninjas. This was your last game of the season, and you all did great."

He looked around at their faces. "Tyler, you really stepped it up this week. Just remember, don't stop playing, even if an opposing player falls down and pretends to get hurt. They're usually faking it."

He pointed to Elodie. "You should braid your hair before or after the game, not during, so you aren't too distracted. Your braids look nice, though—not too crooked at all."

One braid was a good four inches higher than the other one.

Elodie patted her hair and smiled sweetly. "Thanks, Coach."

"And Sophie, you might want to pass to Miles or Willie sometimes instead of taking every shot."

"Why?" Sophie stared at her dad like he'd grown two heads.

"Because I officially have to say that."

Sebastian gave Matías an exasperated look, and Matías just shrugged.

"Now bring your hands in on three. One, two, three!"

"Go, Purple Pandas!" everyone yelled.

I watched the kids tell Sebastian goodbye and give him high fives or hugs around his legs. It had been enchanting to see him interact so naturally with them. They all adored their coaches.

He eventually walked over and curled his arm around my neck, kissing my temple. "Are you ready to go?"

I squeezed him around his waist. "Yes. I never thought I'd say this, but I'm going to miss these Saturday morning games."

He leaned in. "I can think of a few other things to do on Saturday mornings now."

My insides tightened in anticipation. "You'll have to show me. In explicit detail."

Our life together had been so good over the last six months. The twins settled into a nice, safe routine, and I'd been working with Jonathan and Ramone. I also worked as a juvenile court public defender now with Riverside County.

But I worried sometimes it was all too good to be true. After my altercation with Victor, I started having nightmares again. I'd wake up gasping and in a cold sweat sometimes.

Late one night after a nightmare, Sebastian gathered me in his arms and stroked my hair. We were both naked, and his soft touches, his smell, and the feel of his skin soothed me.

He'd pushed a strand of hair off my cheek and nuzzled my neck. "Your nightmares aren't going away, *mi corazón*. What can we do to help you?"

So I'd finally started therapy. I also convinced Chloe to get a therapist for Lennie and Willie. It had taken several months, but we were all slowly opening up and working through our trauma.

It was a process, and sometimes I still had dreams. But we were healing and happy.

No one had heard from Victor. Jonathan got a statement and a check in the mail with the rest of my college funds a few weeks after Victor left Palm Springs.

I was sure Victor's accountant had been behind it, but I didn't care. I finally paid off my student loans, and put the remainder into college savings funds for Lennie and Willie. Then I worked to build a beautiful life, like Fern had wished for me.

That Sunday was the anniversary of Fern's death. She'd passed away early in the morning exactly one year ago.

I woke up a little before five that morning and quietly slipped out of bed to make coffee. Then I walked out to the backyard and sat in her favorite spot. A couple of doves started cooing, and the early morning dawn sat quiet and pleasant.

I missed her so much, and I thought of her every day. She'd built her own beautiful life, even with her losses and heartaches, and then Fern helped me build one for myself.

The patio door opened, and Sebastian walk out in his sleep shorts. He didn't have a shirt on, and his hair was rumpled. It was a nice look on him.

"What're you doing up so early?" He leaned down and put my coffee cup on the side table, then scooped me up and sat down on the recliner with me in his lap.

I snuggled in and laid my head on his shoulder. We looked out at the soft daybreak together.

"I'm thinking about Fern. She died a year ago today."

"Ah. I knew it was coming up. I miss her too."

I turned to look at Sebastian. "Do you think she meant for us to meet?"

"Nope."

His quick, unexpected answer startled me. "Why are you so sure?"

"I don't *think* she meant for us to meet—I know she did. She'd been trying to introduce us for a while. That's probably why she asked me to be the bartender at her life celebration."

I sat up in his lap. "You're just telling me this *now*?"

"Yep."

"Why?"

"Because I was an idiot. I hate setups, so I put her off."

I gaped at him. He'd stopped talking, so I prodded. "And?"

"After a while, she stopped bringing it up. I was also sick of hearing how 'wonderful' and 'kind' and 'smart' you were. And then I met you, and you were all those things. And fucking hot—she left that part out." He grinned.

"Why were you so grumpy when we first met then?"

"It annoyed me she was right. And I thought I'd probably lost my chance, so I took it out on you. I'm sorry." He gave me a hard, quick kiss.

"Huh." I stared at him. "She never said a word about you to me. I wonder why?"

He smirked. "She probably didn't want to get your hopes up."

I rolled my eyes and pinched his side, then grabbed my coffee cup and settled back in his arms. I looked down at the beautiful, thick, gold engagement ring on my finger for the millionth time. He'd slipped it on during sex one night a couple of months ago.

He'd whispered in my ear as he drove into me, "You're my heart. I want everyone who sees you to know it."

I'd climaxed not long after that, then cried happy tears in his arms. I wasn't sure what we'd tell our kids about our engagement story, but we'd think of something.

Now, I looked at his beautiful face in the soft dawn light. "Fern has given me a lot of strange and amazing gifts over the years. But you're my favorite—by far."

He chuckled and rested his head against mine. "I'm glad you think so, *mi corazón*."

Aferword

If you'd like a bonus Epilogue of *Martini Mondays* from Sebastian's viewpoint, go to my website at http://jlbrannick.com and sign up for my newsletter! You'll also be notified of upcoming events, new releases, and progress on books and audiobooks.

Thank you for reading *Martini Mondays*. If you liked this novel (and even if you didn't) please leave a review on Amazon and Goodreads. Check out the next two books in the Palm Springs Poolside series, *Tequila Tuesdays* and *Whiskey Wednesdays*, available now.

To my beautiful family and tribe for your support—thank you from the bottom of my frosty, little heart. We make a great team! Thanks to my editors, Anna Bierhaus and Shannon Cave, and to my cover designer at Smart Mouth Publishing LLC.

Subscribe to my newsletter for the latest news, free giveaways, exclusive bonuses, and new releases!

https://jlbrannick.com/

https://linkfly.to/JLBrannick

Tequila Tuesdays

The second book in the series, *Tequila Tuesdays*, follows Harley and Damien. It's now available on Amazon in KU, as an ebook, in paperback, and where ebooks are sold.

When Damien compares her teammates to a Walmart parking lot crew, Harley goes for blood—and finds out Damien holds a mean grudge and has a dirty mouth.

Harley already knows the dominant, gorgeous man her friend introduces her to because she made him bleed the last time they met.

She tries to keep her distance and stay under his radar, but Harley needs his help when her youngest, most vulnerable client goes missing. And Damien owns the best investigation agency in Palm Springs.

As they work together on her case, Harley discovers Damien has a dirty mouth and an inventive mind behind that handsome face and damned dimple. She struggles and chafes at their explosive chemistry, but when old ghosts and new enemies threaten, will Harley run? Or will she stay and fight for the kind of life she gave up on years ago? And for the man who likes to tie her in knots, using silk ropes?

www.ingramcontent.com/pod-product-compliance
Lightning Source LLC
Chambersburg PA
CBHW030113310726
48970CB00004B/1264